I0670033

GOOD PRESS

The First Anna Harris Novel

A V IAIN

Chapter One

MOST PEOPLE CANNOT COMPREHEND what I
do. And, to be honest, I don't really blame them.
There's only so much empathy you can scrape together for
someone who kills people for a living. But, hey, that's the truth—a
girl's got to make a living somehow. Luckily the nature of my
work generally means I don't have to tell people what my real
job is.

I'm running late for a meeting with Brian Mathewson, a
publicist. I know what you're thinking. What am I doing going to
see a publicist? Am I looking to break out in the media, sell my
story to some tabloid newspaper about how I *was* a freelance
killer? Nope, not by a long shot. I'm sure the police would be
interested in having a word with me first if that was the case.

Truth be told, Brian is one of my most lucrative employers. It
turns out that his clients: politicians, high-ranking executives,
upper class scoundrels, would rather find a more permanent solu-

tion to their problems, something a little meatier than a super-injunction. And that's where I come in.

As I pass through the reception area of Mathewson's building —which he really does own, and has several hundred employees —I check myself in the mirror. Noticing that the collar of my blouse has got tucked under itself, I flick it out and stride on.

When I reach a turnstile, which blocks entry to anyone without the right credentials—especially journalists—I jab my finger onto the scanner. Its little light flashes red and the lock mechanism clunks off. And I'm in.

I take the lift up to the thirteenth floor—that's right Brian has a thing for numbers—I emerge into his corridor which is adorned with various marble statues while the roof is held at bay by a series of Greco-Roman pillars. Like the old saying goes: taste certainly isn't something that's bought.

A faint scent of mint pervades the entire building, as if Brian has it piped through the air conditioning, and knowing him he probably does. It sharpens my mind, makes me feel more awake, or perhaps it was that third espresso I knocked back a couple of minutes ago.

Large oak doors mark the entrance to Brian's office. A blonde secretary perches at a desk stabbing her computer keyboard with her index fingers, squinting at the monitor as if the computer's at fault for whatever she's just typed in.

She's new. Brian certainly doesn't pick them for their typing ability, or intellect. He should really overhaul his recruitment process.

The secretary cocks her cute head at me and smiles with teeth so far bleached that they're almost light blue. "Good morning, madam. You must be Mrs Harris, Mr Mathewson's eleven o'clock?"

"Miss Harris," I say.

She dials up her giddy smile a couple of notches.

That probably works with all the guys round here. Not with me, though. "Can I go in?"

"Mr Mathewson's out at the moment. He just left, said he'd be back in a few minutes."

"I'll just take a seat then, shall I?"

She shoots me the smile again.

I let out a long sigh then take a seat on the beige-coloured sofa. It's kind of springy, impossible to sink into, to get too comfortable. Just how Brian wants it.

The secretary twirls her hair round her finger. "You know, he's in a horrid mood today."

"Is that so?" I say, wishing I'd brought a magazine with me, or been allowed to hold onto my mobile phone—but, alas, security relieves you of almost anything electronic on entry.

"Yeah, this morning when Michelle brought him coffee, he said it was cold and fired her on the spot."

I think over Michelle. If I'm not mistaken she was Brian's personal assistant, although I have to stretch my mind on that one, considering Brian changes assistants almost as often as he changes secretaries—whenever they get the idea that because they're sleeping together they can exercise some kind of control over him.

I put on my brightest voice, dumbing myself down for the secretary. "What's your name?"

The secretary sinks her teeth into her lower lip.

I bet Brian loves those girlish foibles, the old perv.

"Candy," she says.

I resist the urge to double over with laughter there and then, unable to believe that anyone is seriously called Candy. Not in the twenty-first century. Not in England. In any case Candy will be dispensed with, just as soon as Brian sees her getting her foot in the door. They always try it, no matter who they are, how unintelligent they seem. If there's one thing I've learnt in this trade it's that, deep down, everyone is ambitious.

"What's your name?" Candy says.

I think about having some more fun with her, but decide that I'm not in a malevolent mood. "Anna. My name's Anna Harris."

Candy glances back at her screen, then lowers her voice, as if we were in the Brownies camped out in our sleeping bags and she were confiding a secret. "To be honest I'm not really sure what I'm doing. The only reason I got this job was because one of my friends gave me Mr Mathewson's number."

Goodness me. It's hard to believe that there are really city girls as naive as Candy. I consider telling her what she's in for, letting her out of her misery, but decide against it. It would serve no reason whatsoever.

I force a smile. "I'm sure you'll get to grips with it eventually."

The sound of determined footfalls hammer up the corridor.

I turn my head to see Brian, jacket open and flapping wildly, bee-lining for his office, for us. Without a word to me, he pads up to Candy, leans over the desk. "Hold all calls."

I get to my feet, flash Candy a final smile then accompany him into his office.

If the rest of the building is Rome then Brian's office is his Caesars' Palace. The office occupies the corner of the building and looks down on the city for miles around. Three quarters of the walls are ceiling-to-floor with windows, looking out on the London skyline. A little way in the distance you can make out Parliament Square. I have no idea how Brian gets any work done

4

at all with this kind of view. But, then again, Brian's not like most people.

He engages the electronic lock on the doors, then he shrugs off his jacket and hangs it on the coat stand. He rolls up his shirt-sleeves as he approaches me, a smile crossing his lips. "So I see you've met the new secretary."

"She seems up to the job."

"Yes," he says, "I believe so."

I take a seat on one of the squidgy chairs which looks down onto the street below. A tingle of vertigo passes up my spine, but I don't move away, determined to beat the fear. I haven't got into this position, in my life, from being afraid.

Brian struts up to his drinks cabinet. "Fancy something?"

"You know I don't drink."

He arches an eyebrow. "Always seem to forget."

Despite our professional relationship, and the fact that, if I wanted to, I could snap Brian's spine like the proverbial twig, Brian always maintains a sexual tension with our meetings. After our first few encounters I thought about doing something about it. However, as time passed, and I saw his interactions with other members of my gender, I came to realise that it's just how he acts —as natural as I breathe air.

"Right," Brian says, pouring himself a large whisky. "This job. It's a tight one and I want you to feel free to say no to it if you don't feel you're up to it."

I boil inside. "Just tell me what the job is."

Brian smirks. "I know just the buttons to push, don't I?"

"Yes."

He takes a swig of whisky, then smacks his lips. "A little thing, really. Love nest. Pretty standard."

"It's never 'standard' killing someone."

"Quite right," he says, setting his glass down, half-finished. "Chose exactly the wrong words." He covers his mouth with his hand, clears his throat then produces an envelope from his inside pocket, which he hands to me.

I take it from him.

"All the information's in there, as always: target, photograph, maps of the house."

I weigh the envelope in my hand, feeling the various piece of paper shuffle about inside. I've been working up to this moment for a long time, turning over the phrasing in my mind, perfecting it, getting it just right. "This time I want double."

He shoots me a side-on glance, then half-closes one eye. "All right."

That was much easier than I expected. I exhale then look down into the street, relaxing my taut muscles and watching the mid-morning traffic weave in and out.

Brian approaches me, lays a hand on the back of my chair and looks down into the street too. "Thing is, this isn't quite a standard job."

"You're saying that I should ask for triple the going rate?"

"If I were you, I'd ask me to add a nought to the end of it."

Brian moves away from the window, back over to the table. He finishes his glass of whisky then corks the bottle.

My attention drifts away from the scene outside, back into the office. "I think I'd like to know what I'm getting into before I go any further."

He rests an arm against the drinks cabinet, as if considering whether or not to snatch out the bottle again. For the first time in our relationship I've seen him display something approximating stress. It really is a big deal. "This is just like all the others, you understand? Client remains confidential. No questions asked."

"Of course," I say. "But you've piqued my interest now. And if you're going to make me a rich woman I'd like to at least know the risks I'm taking."

"Quite right," he says, then rolls his shoulders, grins. "Quite right."

I scratch at a chocolate stain on my trousers.

Brian finally takes a seat, in the chair opposite me. None of his childish charm remains, he's all business, hard and serious, like he always is when one of our meeting's is drawing to a close. "The client's in a very sensitive position. This . . . sweetheart of his has been threatening to go public. Expose the client's whole family. Blow everything out the water—his entire flawless media image gone."

"I'm sure the flawlessness of his image is courtesy of Mathewson Media."

Brian shifts in his seat, then glowers at me. He holds his finger out as if he were a headmaster, giving me a telling off. "It'd be better for you if you don't forget who you're working for. I made you, and I can just as easily destroy you."

My heart hangs in my throat and I realise he's serious. There's ruthlessness in his eyes, no one, *no one*, will get in his way. And, no matter how I approach this, I know that I need him far more than he needs me—I'm sure he could find himself another hired killer at the drop of a hat. I tell myself that I just need a few more contracts, then I can retire, especially if Brian's going to be paying me what he will for this hit. All this will be done with. When I speak again my voice is raspy. "I understand."

Brian lurches to his feet once more. "Good." He reaches a window on the other side of his office. "Good."

Only one thing could make Brian this twitchy, as nervous as this. I know that the client must be some kind of politician, and no backbencher, either. Whoever's behind this hit is in the Cabinet, it might even be the Prime Minister.

Still looking out the window, over the skyline, Brian says, "Needs to be done tonight. She'll be alone." He puffs out his cheeks. "Thing with this job is that it's got to look like suicide. The girl is the only one who can be implicated in this." He turns to face me. "Do we understand one another?"

"Perfectly."

"Good, then there's nothing more to say."

I take this as my cue to leave and make for the door, slipping the envelope into my jacket pocket. A smile tweaks my lips. All being well there'll be a quarter of a million landing in my bank account on completion of the hit.

"Oh, Anna?"

I pause with my hand on the doorknob. "Yes?"

"Do a professional job, won't you?"

"Of course."

Chapter Two

I DON'T OPEN THE LETTER until I get back home. In my line of work you have to be about a thousand times more careful than in an ordinary job. This isn't a case of trade secrets leaking or deals going public—these are people's lives.

I live in an ex-council house on a modest street in one of the inner suburbs of the city. There's a strong multi-cultural flavour to my area, but I like that. Nevertheless, a single white woman who occasionally goes out dressed in designer trouser suits does stand out somewhat. No one's ever tried anything, and if they did it would be the last thing they'd do. And I'd have no doubts on which side the jury's sympathies would fall.

The most important thing for any hired killer is to remain anonymous, to slip into the background and I play my part of hard up unemployed admirably, if I say so myself. The second half of that is that, for a hired killer, I don't actually make an enormous amount of money. Don't think that I wouldn't prefer to blend in somewhere in Kensington.

My garden gate hangs crooked and I have to almost bend over double to force it open. When I do, I step along the cracked path up to my front door where the racing green paint is peeling away. I scrabble for my key, withdrew it then slip it into the rust-covered lock. And then I've arrived inside, my home. Not much but it's mine. One of these days I should really get round to doing the place up—a splash of paint here, a squirt of lubricant there.

First things first, I squeeze out of my knee-high boots, leaving them in a disorderly pile then jiggling out of my jacket as I step into the kitchen. There's a voicemail message blinking at me from the base of the phone so I press the green button and a male voice—Bob, my live in lover, as I christened him—announces the time and date of the missed call. Then my ex-husband, Arnold, speaks.

"Annie? Annie? Are you there?"

God I hate that name. Hated it when we were together, hate it now. I screw up my eyes and withdraw a packet of cereal and a bowel from the cupboard beneath the sink.

Arnold continues, "Uh, was hoping to catch you before you went out, I was checking through the bank statements today and I've seen that the money hasn't arrived yet. That's fine, but I really would like to get it soon. You see Josie needs a new pair of smart shoes, for school, and Ben needs a whole new kit for football."

My heart bobs a little, hearing the names of my children.

"Anyway, give me a ring back when you've put the money in. Bye."

The voicemail beeps and Bob informs me that I have no more messages.

I've completely forgotten about that money. I'm overdrawn at the moment so a direct debit's out of the question. I go over and check my purse. I've got two hundred pounds inside. That should cover things for the time being—at least the shoes and football kit —I can send the rest over after I've got paid for the hit tonight.

I sigh and check the clock. If I get going now I can make it to Arnold and the kids' house then be back to prepare for tonight. Feet aching and a migraine seeping its way into my skull, I do a quick change, jettisoning my trouser suit—hanging it up carefully in its plastic covering so I won't have to make another trip to the dry cleaner's too soon—then put on a t-shirt and jeans, before jabbing my feet into a pair of battered trainers. Then I'm out the door and on my way.

———

Arnold and the kids live a thirty-minute Tube ride from my house. We separated five years ago, just after I got out of the Army. We tried living together for six months but it just didn't work. It didn't work for me, Arnold or the kids. I guess everyone got used to me being gone. And soon after I started accepting money for hits.

As I stare out the window, at the gloom blurring past, I wonder again whether or not I made the right decision all that time ago, in leaving my family, returning to the Army. I mean, what young mother, in her right mind, leaves a baby daughter in the care of her father, a young boy, to go off and get shot at? But that's just how I am, how I've always been. I'm thirty-five now, so I can't see that changing.

I get off at the stop and trot up the steps, through the Underground station, and emerge on the street, blinking like a mole that's come up for air. I pace my way along the pavement, headed for the estate, preparing myself for the encounter, telling myself over and over again that I won't cry and that I will just get in there, then get out again. Be back home with my mind on my job.

Almost too soon I arrive at the front door. I give it a couple of smart knocks then listen to the bustling activity inside, the footsteps on the stairs. Before I'm fully-prepared, the door swings open and I'm confronted with my son, Ben.

He's wearing a pair of cargo shorts with white socks pulled up over his ankles. He looks me up and down then smiles faintly. "Hi, Mum."

Over the past few months he's been changing, ever since he started secondary school, he's become uncertain how to act round me—knowing that this situation isn't normal, that almost all the other single parents he knows are mothers, not fathers.

"Dad home?" I say.

Ben rocks back on his heels and calls out into the house for Arnold. He turns back to face me, scratches his neck.

"So, I hear you're going to be playing football."

"Yeah," he says, nodding.

"I didn't know you liked football."

He shrugs. "I don't really, but my best mate Kevin's doing it so . . ." His words trail away as if he's already explained it all.

Feeling unsure of myself, I reach forward and touch him on the arm. "It's good to see you, kiddo."

"You too, Mum," he says, flinching a little at my touch then looking over my head, up and down the street.

Arnold bounds downstairs and arrives behind Ben. He rests his hands on his shoulders, then says, "Got some homework to do?"

Ben rolls his eyes. "No."

Arnold grins. "Go on, get it done, if it's all right when I check it I'll let you have half an hour of video games later."

Ben gives me the hint of a smile, says, "Bye, Mum," then shuffles off upstairs.

Arnold leans against the doorframe. "I thought you were going to call."

I stuff my hands in my pockets. "Sounded a little desperate, so thought I'd come down."

"How's the job search going?"

Of course Arnold has no idea that I'm an assassin, no one does, except my employers. "Oh, pretty much the same. Sending CVs here, sending them there, but nothing yet."

Arnold grits his teeth. "Yes, just perseverance, really, isn't it?"

"Is Josie about?"

"No, she's round a friend's house."

"Okay."

"I'd have told her to stay if I'd known you were coming."

"Yes, I really should've called."

Arnold crosses his arms. "So, have you got the money?"

"Can I come in?"

Arnold's eyes darted about their sockets before returning to mine.

He's hiding something. What I'm not sure.

"Bit tied up at the minute," he says, finally.

I dig into my trouser pocket and produce two hundred pounds in cash. I hand it over to him. "There you go, that should keep you ticking over for the time being. Should get the rest to you by the end of this week."

Arnold takes my money. "Look, Annie—"

"Please, don't call me that."

"Anna, I've been thinking about this money. I mean, things

aren't as bad as they were before. I've picked up a few more hours, in fact I got a raise so I'm really on decent money now. If you're finding it difficult to pay, we can cut back on what we agreed. No problem for me. It's just . . ."

But his words saunter off into the background, because I hear another set of steps on the staircase, then a female voice, "Who is it, dear?"

My stomach sinks.

All I can see is a set of legs, clad in blue nylon tights.

A lump appears in Arnold's throat, he looks to me, then replies to her, "I'll be done in a minute."

The legs slink further down the staircase, to reveal a tight midriff, a firm bust and then, last of all, the face. She has cropped black hair and china doll features, sparkling blue eyes.

I should've known. We've been apart for five years. Arnold was sure to move on. It's only logical that he's found someone else. After all *I* was the one who left *him*. But still my tongue sticks to the bottom of my mouth. "I . . . I . . . ."

The woman sidles up to Arnold, rests her head on his shoulder.

Arnold's mouth hangs open.

I pivot and trudge off down the path, back out to the road.

As I go, I hear Arnold's words following on my heels, "I don't suppose you and Kate have ever been introduced. It's . . . ."

I march up the road wiping tears from my eyes, only when I turn the corner do I permit myself a few sniffles. And then, down in the Underground station, the emotion's gone—bottled up. Now my mind's on the hit tonight.

Utterly, completely focussed.

Chapter Three

WHEN I GET BACK HOME night's setting in. Lights are on in most of the houses. Hip Hop music blares from the upper windows of my neighbours' house. They keep the windows wide open so the whole street can hear.

I return to the kitchen, slip open the envelope and dish through the information: Forty-Two Elms Close, New Throms-brook. Then there's the picture of the girl, she looks to be in her early-twenties, blond hair—in fact there's a pang of panic when I think it might be Candy, but after a second glance it's not, Candy has a much better-defined nose, none of that wonky nonsense, if there's one thing that Brian won't put up with its imperfections.

In the photograph she wears a slight smile, she's squinting slightly. I wonder whether this picture has been chopped in half, whether her lover was once featured in some way. There's no way of knowing and, of course, it's not really important—not for me, anyway.

After sorting the photograph and the map apart, laying them

on the table, I head outside into my boxy overgrown garden which is overlooked by just about the whole street, and I retrieve my boots from where they rest, drying out. A week ago, my last hit involved a house out in the countryside and I ended up having to wade through a stream. The recollection of that freezing water sends a shudder up my spine.

As I snatch up the boots I hear a faint meow. I look round to see a tortoiseshell cat down on her haunches, pressing herself up against the wooden fence. One of the neighbours' cats. I've never been a cat person, or an any kind of animal person. Animals depend on you and I can't offer that. All I can promise is to look after myself.

The cat has a streak of mud in her fur and her eyes are wide, gleaming in the fledgling moonlight, glaring right at me. I consider leaving out a saucer of milk but decide against it. No doubt this little lady tries this act on with all the neighbours, probably gets home with four dinners in her tummy from all the doting old ladies.

I step back into the house and slide the French door back into place, taking care to lock both catches, top and bottom. You can't trust anyone round here.

I go up to my bedroom and remove my killing gear, as I call it. It's an all-black outfit, waterproof trousers, a support vest, a fleecy jumper, a jacket, leather gloves and then the balaclava. I change into it then glance at myself in the mirror, feeling like a totally different person. I don't know what it is about clothes but they bring about a change in me—it's as if I've shrugged off my skin and put on a new one.

I take off the balaclava and gloves for now, stuffing both into my jacket pockets. Maybe I do live in a rough area but that doesn't mean that people who walk round in all-black with balaclavas and leather gloves don't attract attention.

As far as making this look like a suicide is concerned, I've got some ideas. I stoop down and drag out a cardboard box marked 'Memories' and unfold the flaps. Inside I have a shoebox which contains a handgun, replete with silencer. I leave that. I always try to avoid carrying a gun unless it's completely necessary, if I believe that I might face some kind of resistance. This girl should be no problem.

In the cardboard box there's a key taped to the side—but the less known about that the better—then I've got some other items: a knife, snuggled into its holder, a long coil of rope, and a lock-picking kit I've had since I was a little girl. I take the knife, rope and lock-picking kit, putting both into my jacket pockets alongside the balaclava, then I nudge the box back inside with my foot.

I wait till just past midnight before descending the stairs, grabbing the envelope of information as I head out of the house.

———

New Thromsbrook is a typical rich neighbourhood. A row of semi-detached houses, all huddled together, for safety's sake rather than economy. The road's lined with parked up estates and hatchbacks, no doubt they have some finer cars but I'm sure they're tucked up in a garage somewhere, watched over twenty-four hours a day. Even rich people aren't stupid enough to leave their pride and joy on the roadside overnight.

Number Forty-Two isn't remarkable in any way. It has the same well-pruned hedges and faint blue light illuminating its front door. I note that upstairs the curtains are drawn, lights all off. I glance up the street, see no one around, pull on my balaclava then sneak round the back, keeping to the grass verges to deaden the sound of my footsteps. I have to vault over the side gate, which only comes up to my waist, and then I'm in.

The back garden is twice as big as the entire plot of my house. There's a trellis with vines climbing up it and a seat swing beyond it. I crouch down and run my palm over the grass. It's thick and plush, like carpet. Someday I might own a house like this. When I'm through with the killing.

I think about how many times my target and her beau have perused this garden, perhaps even making love on that swing seat in the dead of the night. I wonder whether she really felt passion for him, if she really believed that someday she might be more than a mistress. I suppose that, to a certain degree, they must all feel that way. It can't all just be for the money, the sense of protection, can it?

I take deep breaths, bringing my pulse under control, trying to ease myself into the job. I have to forget all sentiment, forget that this person who I'm about to extinguish is another human being. It's just another job. Just another job.

I slip on my gloves as I approach the back door of the house to examine the lock. It's fairly new but easily cracked. It always tickles me when people don't properly research their choice of lock, just going for the most expensive. But, as those of us in the know realise, expensive isn't always best.

I work at it with my lock pick and, within a matter of seconds, I spring the mechanism. Another glance round then I step into the darkened, silent house, pulling the door to as I go in.

I emerge into a kitchen. The dishwasher gargles away. I step forward, keeping my tread quiet, as I've been taught. Somewhere to my right the central heating clicks on. I flinch then scold myself for being so reactive. I have to keep my mind clean, respond stoically and act rationally. Those are my professional secrets.

In my mind I recall the memorised map. The girl's bedroom is up the stairs, first room straight ahead. So simple. I leave the kitchen, stepping into the hall, and grasping hold of the banister with my gloved hands and ease myself up each stair, taking my time, eyes fixed on the door at the top of the staircase.

About halfway up one of the stairs creaks. I stop and listen for any sound of stirring. Hearing nothing, I proceed until I reach the bedroom door. With another deep breath, I touch the doorknob and turn it gently. The base of the door shuffles over the carpet as I push it open. My mind is quiet now, acting on instinct. No one can get in my way.

A sliver of moonlight infiltrates the bedroom, curving its way in round a gap in the blinds. A four-poster bed occupies the majority of the room, with netted curtains obscuring the view of the sleeper. I stalk closer, drawing out the rope from my pocket.

My heart beats against my tonsils as I stand over the bed and look down. It takes my mind several minutes to process the information. The girl's not in bed.

The bed's empty.

Chapter Four

DESPITE MYSELF, I'm cursing under my breath, telling myself off for having been so stupid, having got myself cornered like this, being unprofessional. But I talk myself round, tell myself that it's not so bad, that I need to adapt to the situation, improvise. And then, over my shoulder, I hear the unmistakable sound of a toilet flushing, of footfalls on the landing outside. Now I've got a fix on my target's location.

I swoop through the room and stand to one side of the door, peering at it, anticipating it opening, with the rope coiled round my fists, ready to lash out.

The footsteps get louder.

My breath hitches in my throat.

The doorknob turns slightly then, halfway round, stops turning.

I swallow.

The doorknob retreats. On the other side of the door I hear a panicked intake of breath, then a step backward.

I have to react, need to see the job through, finish what I've started. A quarter of a million pounds. That'll see me through my bills, sort out my obligations. And now my mind's corrupted with images of Kate and Arnold, first at the door then imaginings of them sprawled in bed, in each other's arms.

Blood rushes to my temples and I tear open the door.

The girl's eyes are wide and her lips are parted to scream. She wears a flimsy nightdress, her nipples showing through the thin fabric. No doubt her beau informed her decision on buying that one.

I make a grab for her but, somehow, she evades my grasp, dives to my left, goes right beneath my arm and rushes for the stairs. Feeling the air rattle in my chest, I bound after her, almost slipping and turning an ankle as I go.

When the girl reaches the hallway she busies herself at the door, undoing the various latches keeping it in place. But, before she can get even one of them open, I'm upon her dragging her down onto the tiled floor and shoving her head against the hard ground.

She screams again.

I bring my gloved hand down over her mouth and hold it tight there, feeling her squirm beneath me. And I find myself whispering to her, once more my subconscious, my emotions, showing through. "Easy. Easy. Be quiet for me, eh?"

The girl stills beneath my touch, out of energy, nothing left to fight. Her eyes roll in their sockets, looking for something to fix onto but there's nothing, only me. I fill her whole world now.

Now I'm feeling pity for her, all my speculations about her beau, this politician, enter my thinking. And, all of a sudden, she's human again. I know that I can't simply kill her, not yet, I have to know more about this case—know what's the reason for upping my fee ten times the going rate. But all the while my rational brain is telling me that the girl screamed out, that surely one of the neighbours heard, the police might be on their way. That all seems like it's happening outside of us now, though, outside our intimate gaze.

I slow my breathing and loosen my hand from her mouth a little. "Now, if I let you speak you have to promise me that you're not going to scream out, all right?"

The girl lets out a muted moan.

I take away my hand.

The girl blinks a couple of times. Tears gather in her eyes, turning them watery. Her voice is ragged from her struggle. "You're . . . you're here to kill me, aren't you?"

People say stupid things when they've stared into the abyss. But, having been in that position myself, I can't judge. "Yes."

The girl nods then her eyes slink to the base of their sockets.

"You seem awfully calm about it," I say.

A rogue tear snails its way down her cheek. "Nothing I can do, is there?"

I consider her question honestly. "No."

"I know who sent you."

"Who?"

She smiles faintly then sniffles. "Don't you know who's paying you?"

"Of course I do."

"Then I don't need to tell you."

I rack my brains, thought over the many promises I've made over the years, never to give away who I work for, not even to someone who's about to be dead. Not wanting to give away Brian's name, I say, "Who's your lover boy?"

Her smile widens. "You really don't know, do you?"

"I'm working through an intermediary."

"That figures, last thing he'd want is to get his hands dirty."

"I suppose that's why he wants me to take care of you."

She sniffs. "Don't worry, you don't have to feel guilty. It feels like I've been dead for ages now. If it weren't you it would just be someone else. In a way I'm glad that at least you've got the courage to face me, before you kill me."

A shiver runs down my spine. I think about how I was sleuthing round in her bedroom, with no qualms whatsoever about doing her in while she was sleeping. But, in her final minutes, I have no intention of breaking her illusion of me as a direct person.

"How much are they paying you?" she says.

"Quarter of a million."

She lets out a nervous giggle. "That's all I'm worth? A human being for a few zeroes?"

"That's just how the game works." Then I check my words. "Why, does whoever's paying me have more to invest in killing you?"

"Oh my, yes."

"Who is he?"

From beneath my hold, she shakes her head. "You really don't want to know, it'll only implicate you. Ignorance is bliss." She giggles deliriously. "I know it's just an old cliché but it couldn't be truer in this case."

"Tell me, I'd like to know. He's a politician, isn't he? Someone high up in government?"

"You know, I've had other gentlemen lovers. I bought this house myself, don't think that I took any of the money from him. I'm an economist. Still paying the mortgage here. But I've always felt attracted to older men, men with power. It's just a rush for me."

Unable to understand that point of view, letting anyone else feel like they have control over me, I say, "I can imagine."

"The reason I got involved with him was pure business. Nothing else. Of course, one thing led to another, and I succumbed to his charms. It was strange. He seemed so innocent, he's so sexually basic, and yet he drew me in."

I can believe that. Most of the people who move in Brian's circles are overgrown schoolboys.

Out of nowhere, she sobs. "I fell in love with him. He fed me the usual lines about how he was going to leave his family, but I actually believed him, he wasn't like the others. And then . . . and then . . ."

"Then what?"

"Oh, just kill me already, please! I've had enough, I'm tired of living. Please, put me out of my misery. Just imagine I'm some old lame bitch that needs to be put down." She reaches for me grabs a clump of my shirt in her fist. "Do it!"

I lean back for a moment, unsure whether I can go on. I've just about thrown out every rule I've ever worked to. Now that I've humanised the enemy there's no way back. I fell into the same trap in the Army. And that was the beginning of the end. Are all my old mistakes catching up with me?

She gazes deep into my eyes, yanking me closer to her. "Do it, for God's sake!"

"Did he get you involved in his business dealings?"

She rolls her eyes. "God, I don't want to talk anymore. Is this how you kill your victims, talk them to death?"

"It was wasn't it? He got you involved in something you

weren't supposed to know about. This isn't about his image at all, is it?"

She spluttered laughter. "It has everything to do with his image. Please, was there ever a politician that wasn't interested— first and foremost—with his image? No, everything hangs on it, everything is at stake. He wants to be Prime Minister." She coughs a couple of times, choking on her tears. "And he'll get there, you believe me, he'll get there. When he does he'll have the whole world in his hands. No one will be able to stop him, not even Brian Mathewson."

When she mentions Brian's name that's when I have to draw the line. One rule too many broken. I lurch forward and lasso the rope round her neck. "What's your name?"

Gasping for air, she says, "Liz . . . Elizabeth."

I pull it tight against her throat, watching her eyeballs bulge, her pupils shrink, until they resemble peeled boiled eggs. Moments later her shoulders sag and her final breath sighs out from her.

Chapter Five

AS I LIE IN BED staring at the ceiling I can hear non-stop meows from my back garden. After several minutes tossing and turning, I throw off the duvet and shuffle over to the window to look out.

The tortoiseshell cat is still hunched up against the fence. I'm sure that she's staring right up at me, saying something that I have no means to comprehend.

I tell myself that she'll be gone by morning and click on my TV to watch the early morning news reports. The clock in the corner of the screen informs me that it's just struck half past three. It doesn't matter to me. Tomorrow I can sleep in as long as I want. It's not like have anywhere to go.

I click the volume up a few notches to drown out the sounds of the cat's meows and try to concentrate on the words spilling from the news reader's lips. She's a middle-aged woman with thinning black hair and lashings of blue eye shadow. She looks tired, desperate, as if clinging to her journalistic dreams against all odds—taking whatever timeslots are flung at her. Isn't that just the way of the world?

She informs the viewer of a new school policy being implemented nationwide. The pre-recorded footage reeling through images of schools, classrooms stuffed full with kids attentively observing their teachers. After a while the Secretary of Education, Simon Snarkly, appears on the screen and sums up the proposal, its benefits and, most important of all, its cost. His forehead gleams dully in the studio lights, and the carefully-crafted words fall from his lips effortlessly.

I wonder whether this man is, was, Elizabeth's lover. He has that boyish charm, the public-school look which she pointed to. I think over her words, whether she was speaking frankly, because often those who find themselves caught in dire situation—find themselves fighting for their life, or speaking their last words—have a propensity to exaggerate their own role in matters. I suppose to her, this politician, whoever he might be, was convincing. Probably how he managed to get a Cabinet job. Liars always rise to the top, just as long as they don't get found out.

And then my thoughts turn to Elizabeth herself. Tomorrow they'll find her dead, supposedly hanged. Just another corporate casualty. Like always, doubts seep in, that I've somehow left evidence that will give me away—that everything will lead back to Brian. One thing's for certain, should anything get back to Brian, implicate him in any way, my life is over. He has contacts in prisons—male or female, it really doesn't matter—and it's assured that he'll have his vengeance, at any cost.

Finally, feeling my eyelids droop and my brain losing its sharpness, I click off the TV and roll over, pulling the blanket up over my head to ward off the early-morning sunlight creeping round the edges of my curtains. And I fall asleep with the quiet, almost defeated *meows* in my ears.

———

I sit at the kitchen table at breakfast, munching on my cereal when my mobile buzzes. I check the caller ID and see that it's Brian. He's up early this morning. I put it on speaker phone.

"Anna?"

I swallow my current mouthful. "Present."

"Cracking job last night. Just got off the phone with my contact within the police, says there's no signs of this being treated suspiciously." He chuckles. "Funnily enough they seemed to imply that she wasn't the happiest of souls, had every reason to do herself in—had just lost her job."

My stomach dips and my appetite deserts me. I drop my spoon into my bowl. It clangs against the edge.

"Anyway, just calling to say that the money should be in your account by midday. Give me a bell this evening if it still hasn't arrived."

I think about the girl's dead face last night. Her blank eyes staring up at me. She had told me to do it—Brian's hunch was correct, that the girl hadn't wanted to keep on living. It would take a pretty despicable person to run someone down like that, or call for a contract on their head, for that matter.

"You still there?" he says.

"Yeah."

"You're awfully quiet this morning. Have a few drinks to celebrate? I know that I did."

"No, I just didn't sleep too well."

"All right, well get yourself rested up because it looks like there might be a few more where those came from. Speak soon, bye," he says, hanging up.

The idea of returning to work makes me sick to the stomach. I wonder whether I've lost the resolve for my job—last night I crossed so many lines, almost messed the whole thing up.

When I take in my mobile screen I see that I've got three new texts. I scroll down and scan the senders. All of them are from Arnold. I sigh. No doubt he wants 'to talk' about this situation with Kate. It's so stupid because I'm not angry, not really, it's just that it caught me off guard. I make a mental note that, from now on, I'm going to call ahead.

I dunk my bowl in the sink, which is overflowing with dirtied plates. Maybe once I get the payment through I'll invest in a dishwasher, after I've sent the direct debit to Arnold and the kids, of course.

I look out through the French doors at my sad little garden and think how nice it would be to plant a few flowers out there, to sweep the paving slabs. In fact, I resolve to get down to it today. It's just what I need to take my mind of things, get organising, cleaning.

After I've put on my tracksuit and the battered trainers, I slip outside, relishing the fresh, cool morning air on my cheeks. I step over to the tiny plastic box where I keep the few tools I own and I flip the lid. Inside there's a hand brush, its bristles bent and ruffled, but it'll do the job. I also take out a short shovel.

As I rock down on my haunches and brush up the dirt at the base of the French doors, I hear a familiar *meow*. I look round, unable to make out where it's coming from. The cat's no longer in the place she was the night before. Then my gaze rests on an overgrown bush, up against the fence, and I see her feline eyes glowing within. What's this cat's problem?

I set down the brush and shovel and approach the cat.

She slips back a little into the bush as I get closer.

I look in through the tangled undergrowth. "Hey there, what's the matter?"

The cat remains where she is, just watching me, refusing to leave her place of safety.

"If you're not going to come out then why've you been crying all this time, huh?"

The cat cries out again.

I look round, as if the owner might be nearby, looking over the fence, watching to see if I touch their property. Ascertaining that no one's there, I stick my arm into the bush and my fingers stroke the cat's fur.

She trembles beneath my touch.

"Here, kitty, come on out. We'll find out where you've come from. You're lost, aren't you?"

The cat meows again.

This time I seize hold of her fur, just behind her neck and tug her out of her hiding place.

She digs in her claws but doesn't try to scratch or bite.

Once she's out in the open I look over her, noting the clumps of mud stuck in her fur and the dust covering most of her body. I inspect her neck and find no collar.

She sits back on her paws, watching me.

"What am I going to do with you, eh?"

She just stares at me, like she's just happened to choose me out of seven billion people.

I can't exactly turn her out of the house. She'd probably just come back anyway, sit around mewling in the garden—it would drive me nuts to hear that all night, every night. So, I scoop her up in my arms and carry her inside.

Her bony body juts into my chest and she emits a quiet purr.

After giving her some food and having lunch myself, I check my balance to see that, indeed, I've got quarter of a million pounds in my bank account—it's written out as being from Mathewson Media for 'Services Rendered.' I suppose there's nothing technically incorrect about either of those statements.

I take the cat to a nearby vets where she gets her injections, and the vet looks her over, checking for any signs of illness. Other than being underweight, the vet files a clean bill of health. I return with the cat to my house.

I give her a bath and then we spend the afternoon on the sofa watching films on TV. We watch some film about a girl moving to New York. She finds work as a cleaner before meeting a rich businessman to look after her. It all ends happily in a white wedding and they have triplets. If only films were a little more like real life.

In the evening I decide to give the cat a name. The first name that comes to mind is Lizzie, and before I can think of something more appropriate than my ultimate victim, it's already stuck and I can't imagine calling her anything else. So, Lizzie it is.

We watch the news until my mobile buzzes on the kitchen table. I think about not answering, knowing that I'm not mentally ready for another hit. I need some time off. But I know I have to be professional.

It's not like I'm so rich I can turn down work.

Chapter Six

I PICK UP, expecting to hear Brian's voice on the other end, so I'm surprised when it's Arnold who speaks.

"Annie?"

I think about hanging up, right then and there, but for some reason some stupid sentimental mechanism overrules me—tells me that that would be heartless. "It's 'Anna,'" I say.

"I wanted to talk about what happened yesterday.

I close my eyes, massage my temples. "Really, it doesn't matter. Forget about it. I don't know what I was thinking. I shouldn't have walked away. Sorry."

Arnold breathes into the phone, sending a crackle through the speaker. "No, I should've told you a long time ago about Kate, much before she moved in with us. But I guess I can't change that now."

"It's all right. I understand you've got your own life."

"Only because this is the way you wanted it."

"Was there something else?"

"The money. I was phoning about the money."

I chew on the inside of my cheek. It tastes rubbery and feels smooth. I've been so preoccupied with the damn cat that I completely forgot about the direct debit. "I'll do it right now. I promise. Should be with you first thing tomorrow."

A long pause on Arnold's end. "You know, when I said that I wouldn't mind if you cut back on the payments I wasn't joking. Don't feel like you're obliged or anything. Just pay whatever you can, whatever you think's fair."

I hate it when Arnold's reasonable, it makes him impossible to hate—even though I know that he's with another woman, another woman raising *my* kids. "I'll send the money over," I say, then hang up.

———

Later in the evening, with Lizzie sleeping in my lap, I skim through the internet, checking my emails, responding to a few old ones from Army friends. I've been putting them off for ages, never wanting to reminisce. That part of my life is over with now, and it feels like I've sealed it off in a corner of my mind—no need to revisit.

The car purrs away, sending vibrations through my thighs. I look down and see her head lolling over my leg. I have no idea how she can be comfortable lying like that.

Once I've finished with my emails I decide to pull up an online encyclopaedia entry on the current United Kingdom Cabinet. There's a long list of names, each with their assigned office. I scan down them. There are over twenty of them. Three of them are women. When I cast my eye over the names I concentrate on Simon Snarkly, Education Secretary. No matter how hard I try, I can't get past him, sure that he was Elizabeth's lover.

I bring up his own entry on the encyclopaedia and I skim his biography. Simon Snarkly was born in East Thwapping to Margaret and Roger. His father comes from a poor family and worked his way up to becoming an iron magnate. His mother was from old money, but probably couldn't find any other aristocracy to marry into so settled for Roger Snarkly.

Simon Snarkly went to Fryson's Independent School—the most exclusive in the country—where the article states that he was a competent sportsman, if not captain or anything. However, he was chairman of the debating society. After school he went to Oxford where he studied political sciences—seemingly already looking to carve out a political career—then joined the Conventional Party after graduating. He's been working his way up ever since.

I reach the end of his professional specifications and move onto his personal life. It states that he married ten years ago, to Victoria Roberts. They have three children, all boys, eleven, nine and seven. I wonder whether Snarkly ever actually sees his kids, then realise that's rich coming from me. He probably makes more time for his kids than I do.

There's nothing in his personal life about any affair, or suspected affairs, but I'm sure that since Snarkly has had Brian on the case he's had people watching this site twenty-four seven with their fingers hovering over the Delete button. Brian is expensive but he does a thorough job.

Not having garnered anything from the entry that I wouldn't have been able to fill in for myself, I close down the browser and turn off the computer.

I wake up in the middle of the night following a dream involving Elizabeth. My hands were on her throat, pushing down, and her final breath slipped from her lips as a wispy blue cloud. I watched it float over my head, up to the ceiling and out of sight.

I'm sweating. The sheets are stuck to my skin. I peel them off then sniff the air.

A rancid odour fills my bedroom and, for a horrible moment, I think that I've wet the bed. The dream wasn't that disturbing, nothing out of the ordinary following a hit. I flick on the light then step out of bed, finding the sheets clean, apart from my sweat.

I continue to smell the air, trying to locate the source of the stench. My nose leads me over to the corner of the room where I find a neat little pile of poo, like muddy worms. I look over to my bed where Lizzie sleeps on, her ears twitching as she dreams.

In all the excitement of becoming a cat owner I've forgotten to put out a litter tray. I stoop down low and snatch up an old newspaper from the carpet. I scoop up the poo and fold it inside the newspaper, before dropping it into the bin.

I dig through my wardrobe looking for something to use as a makeshift litter tray. All I have staring back at me is the box with my weapons. I glance over at Lizzie, wondering whether she can hold on till tomorrow. Best to be safe.

I remove my handgun from the shoebox. I put the gun alongside the knife and lock-picking kit in the main box. It's not like it really needs its own compartment anyway. I tear up some newspaper and place it inside the shoebox, hoping that Lizzie will know what to do—take pity on a novice cat owner.

With that done, I get back into bed, feeling Lizzie's warmth pass through the covers and into my toes.

———

In the morning I have an appointment with my therapist, paid for by the Army. I have to admit that the first time I went there I thought it was a colossal waste of time. But, after the first couple of compulsory sessions, it's became something of a crutch. I'm not a social person, I spend most of my spare time alone, so in the sessions I can get out all the thoughts and feelings I've kept bottled up for the past week.

My therapist is called Julie. She wears round glasses and her hair tumbles down to her shoulders in ringlets. She has a delicate face with piercing green eyes. Her office always smells of the fresh flowers, which she keeps by the window. I asked her about them once and she told me that her husband gives them to her every week.

During the sessions I actually lie down on a sofa, head back on a pillow and spill my guts. Although everything is confidential, I'd never consider telling her my darkest secret—getting into what I do to pay my bills.

Today I breeze in and assume the position.

Julie greets me with a smile and crosses her legs.

I get the feeling that Julie might have a hunch that I'm a lesbian, that I might be hitting on her. Maybe I should think about throwing in more about my current life—making up stories about bringing a bunch of men home. But the point of these sessions is to make me feel better, not her.

Julie smoothens a crease from her skirt. "Why don't we take up from where we were last week? The party?"

A smile crosses my lips in recollection. "Okay," I say. "Did I tell you the part about the poker game already?"

"Yes, you'd just reached the part where you and Luke had just kissed."

Trust Julie to remember the romantic bits. "Right, well after that things kind of turned a little more heavy."

"'Heavy?'"

"Yeah, I mean, we were in the locker room one minute, him pushing me up against the metal, shoving his tongue down my throat, and next thing I knew we were in a storage room naked, lying beneath a rough survival blanket."

"And why do you think you agreed to get involved with Luke?"

"I dunno, I was drunk."

Julie gives me one of her trademark glares, kind of the equivalent of a parent tickling a child for information, until they submit and give it up.

I shrug. "Maybe I was lonely." My voice goes quiet. "I don't know."

"Loneliness might have been a viable reason."

A smile curls the corner of my mouth. "But the reason I got into the Army in the first place was to get away from my family, to be alone."

"Sometimes we don't know what we want."

"That's profound."

Julie smiles, glances at her watch. "Have you been in contact with Arnold this week?"

My cheeks flush when I recall that meeting with Kate. I can't believe I acted like a hopped up teenager, hot footed it out of there without even saying goodbye. "Yeah, I took some money round."

"Have you missed him at all?"

"Yes," I say, then think a little more. "No, not really. Actually, I just got a cat. I called her Lizzie. So she's keeping me company."

"Animals can be good to help you see beyond yourself, to care for something else."

"Maybe."

"But there are things that only humans to provide."

I resent that insinuation, because I *know* that I don't need anybody. "I feel all right alone. I'm sure that it's the right way to live."

"There's no right and wrong way to live your life."

"I meant the right way for me."

There's a frosty silence between us, as often happens when our obvious personal differences get flagged up, and I shoot down whatever suggestion Julie's floating at that point.

Julie re-crosses her legs to the other side.

I catch a quick flash of her white underwear and she sees me looking. Great, that's not going to help much in persuading her that I'm not after her.

"I sense there's something on your mind," she says. "In relation to Arnold."

That's not much of an insight. There's almost always 'something on my mind in relation to Arnold.' I may not be vying for Mother of the Year but my kids aren't ever far from my thoughts. I have to be honest with myself, tell Julie the truth. "When . . . when I went round to Arnold's, to take the money, I saw that there's another woman living with him."

"And how did that make you feel?"

Against all odds, the numbness hollows out my chest and tears sting my eyes. I don't bother to wipe them away, knowing that I'm safe here. No one except Julie will see me. "Like I've been replaced," I say.

"But you've always said that it was your decision to leave."

"I know, I know, but some days I feel different."

Julie presses her lips together so they form a single crimson line. She plucks up a box of tissues on the coffee table and hands them over to me.

I thank her and take them. After I blow my nose and dab away the tears I'm ready to confront her again. "I don't mind that he's found someone else . . . it's just that it seems like there's no way back any more. No backup plan."

"Anna, you can't rely on people to always be there, never changing. That's the nature of the world. People get older, form new relationships."

"I suppose you're right."

Julie steers the conversation away from my post-marital problems and back round to the cat, asking me more about her and whether it's filled me with a sense of responsibility—well-being—although I really haven't a clue since I've only just taken her in, I answer all her questions in the affirmative, wanting to end the session on a positive, not just for me but her too. I don't want Julie to feel like she's wasting her time. And, most of all, I don't want to lose her.

As I'm walking to the Underground station following the session my phone buzzes in my handbag. I scrabble for it, see that it's Brian calling and answer.

"Got a job for you," he says.

Chapter Seven

I ARRIVE AT BRIAN'S OFFICE within the hour, after going home to change into my smart clothes. There's one thing that's important in this job, and that's keeping the appearance consistent—unsuspecting. Would someone ask questions of a well-dressed woman strutting into Brian's office? No. Would someone ask questions of a woman wearing a tatty pair of jeans and a t-shirt? Definitely.

Another factor which makes my dress important is the security cameras all round Brian's building—filming every location except for Brian's office itself. If someone were to scan through those, perhaps following a hit gone wrong, they would only have to pick out the badly-dressed woman, slouching her way to a meeting. My clothes offer me invisibility.

Just another city girl.

As I pass Candy's desk she uncreases her frown and smiles vacantly at me. Then she returns to her scowling at her computer screen, her two-fingered typing.

I go right on in without knocking, as usual.

Brian's standing over by the window on a conference call, the face of a Middle Eastern man wearing a keffiyeh. He looks about eighty and has grey stubble sprouting all over his cheeks.

I consider backing out of the office, not wanting to intrude on anything, but, on the contrary, Brian beckons for me to come closer, without turning to look at me. I sidle up alongside him and stand at his shoulder, eyeing the screen, not quite trusting it—apart from a TV, a mobile, and a computer, I try to keep technology as far out of my life as possible.

"Allow me to introduce you to Abdul-Hakam," Brian says.

I do my best approximation of a curtsey, not knowing yet whether this man will be my employer—if I'll have to conform to his expectations of women for the duration of the contract. "Anna Harris," I say. "Pleased to meet you."

Abdul-Hakam screws up his eyes and looks over to Brian. "She's a woman."

Looks like my gut-feeling might just prove correct.

Brian snorts, as if it's the funniest joke he's heard all day—and, with the sheer quantity of phone calls he takes every day, the amount of clients he has to placate with fake laughter, that's quite a statement. "Don't you worry about that, she's perfectly competent."

I give Brian a nudge in the ribs.

Brian continues, "If you're looking for results, she's just the person you're looking for. I've never had any issue whatsoever with her. Satisfying outcomes every time."

Abdul-Hakam cocks his head and looks at me with one eye shut, as if he's eyeing up a wife he's planning to buy. Finally, he slumps back from the screen and sighs. "Well, if you're totally sure about her then I suppose I trust your judgement."

"Absolutely," Brian says.

A slight tremor passes through me, like a teacher's just handed me a glowing comment in front of my parents.

"You'll explain the intricacies?" Abdul-Hakam says.

Brian nods. "Yes, we'll go over all that."

"I cannot have any of this business come back to me, you must understand. I have a good working relationship with the authorities and I do not wish to jeopardise my chances of entry into the country further down the road."

"I fully understand," Brian says.

Abdul-Hakam gives me another cursory glance and then the TV screen flicks to black. Only mine and Brian's reflections stare back at us.

Brian stretches his arms to the ceiling then turns to me. "Jesus, where were you?"

"Had to go home, get changed."

"I've been here for over an hour. You ever tried to entertain someone for that long? I mean there're only so many jokes you can make about the weather."

"I don't suppose it's too difficult. Did you talk about football?"

Brian beams. "We did actually." He forms a double-barrelled pistol from his fingers. "You know men."

"It's more of a disability than a skill, to be honest."

Brian swipes his tablet computer from a side counter and whips through the options, getting to a cache of electronic documents marked with a serial number—nothing more, no names. "Now," he says, "owing to your tremendous performance last time round, I'd like to offer you another job, this time seething with even greater intrigue and danger."

"And will I be party to what 'intrigue and danger' involves this time?"

Brian chuckles. "Oh, no." He flips through a digital document until he reaches a photograph.

It's a businessman, dressed in a grey suit. He looks extremely serious, as if focussed on some vital presentation. Perhaps that's when they took the picture on the sly. I have to hand it to Brian, he can sneak a photographer into just about any co-ordinate on planet Earth.

He hands the tablet over. "This is our target."

I take the tablet clumsily in my fingers, worried that I might drop it or something. Brian could easily afford a new one, but it's damaging the information stored on it that I'm worried about.

Under Brian's guidance, I flip through the pages, taking all the information into account—the maps and intelligence on his situation. The hit's planned for between two and five am tomorrow morning. And there I was, hoping I might get a quiet night in in front of the TV, glass of red wine, cat in lap.

Though minus the red wine, of course.

"Got it?" Brian says, reaching for the tablet.

"Uh, yeah, I think so."

He replaces the tablet on the side—I hope he's got a strong password on it, and I'm sure, knowing it's his neck on the line, that he does.

I stare at the tablet, as if it's some kind of alien technology, freshly-arrived in the middle of an asteroid. "Are you going to give me a copy of the info?"

"Not this time," Brian says, all trace of a smile gone. "It's too sensitive to let it out of the office. This isn't just some dizzy whore. It's much deeper than that."

"Then what?"

Brian taps his nose, flashes me a smile.

Good thing I've got a good memory for details and faces. I've mentally jotted the address and likeness of the guy. "So can you tell me why this is going to be trickier?"

Brian clasps his fingers over the back of one of his high-backed chairs. "Wife and kids are going to be home."

My heart skips a beat. "What?"

"Thought you'd like that."

I stop and consider for a moment, try to put my personal judgement to one side, to stay professional. "It makes things a little more complicated."

"That's why I'm paying you the same as last time."

I had the feeling something like this might happen. That Brian would feed me an easy job with a higher fee and then sucker me into more and more complicated, more sensitive, contracts. "What if I say no?"

Brian's mouth straightened out. "I wouldn't advise it. I've got some friends in the police who might be interested in your nocturnal activities."

"What nocturnal activities?"

"Your drug-dealing."

If I wanted I could respond with a similar threat, tell him that anytime I want I can go to the police and give them what I know about the shadier side of Brian's operations. But that would be a dire mistake because I know that when Brian says he's got friends he's not lying. Very few people are above the law in this country, and Brian might just be one of them.

He brightens, reaches across and pats me on the knee. "So, what do you say?"

I peel off his fingers one-by-one then head for the door. "I'll do my best not to disappoint."

———

Back home, I rummage through my clothes, throwing them onto the bed, going through the motions. I eye the gun and decide that I'm taking it tonight. This is one of those occasions that could go badly wrong—so badly wrong I don't even want to think about it. Whenever there are other people involved it turns everything on its head. If there are children it changes everything. The terms of the assassin are to take out whatever gets in the way, without discretion. I abide by no laws except my own for those moments in time. Anything less could get me caught, or worse.

Lizzie paws through my jumper and then curls up on it, resting her head on her flank and closing her eyes. I have to disturb her a few seconds later, to pull it from beneath her and yank it down over my head. It still smells of the sweat I expended during the last hit. I'm sure I can smell a trace of Elizabeth's perfume there too, but I try not to think about it. I would've washed my clothes if I'd guessed another hit was coming my way. Usually there are weeks between contracts, sometimes months. But, on the bright side, I'll be halfway to being a millionairess after tonight.

I fit the silencer to my handgun and strap it to my thigh so it's invisible to the average passer-by. It'll be no good taking it out in a rush but I don't plan on doing that till I get to the target's house.

Lizzie cranes her neck up to me, expectantly.

I reach down and stroke her head, give her a scratch behind the ears, then head out into the night to kill again.

Chapter Eight

FREEZING COLD DRIZZLE STREAMS DOWN. My nose starts running when I get about a hundred yards from the house. I sniffle away, knowing that I've caught a cold somewhere. In this business, where the slightest sound can give you away, it can be a killer. I wipe the snot with the sleeve of my jumper then venture onward, keeping sight on my peripheral area—checking no one's following—and trying to act as casual as possible. Just a woman walking alone at night, all dressed in black.

When I get to the target's back garden, I take another quick look round then vault over the short wall and into the bushes, taking care not to rustle them—not wanting to warn anyone who might be watching from the house.

I lie down on my stomach, caking myself in the newly-formed mud, and survey the house. Its outline is dark against the moonlight. I look over the windows. No lights. That would suggest that everyone's sleeping, but I know better. I've got on in this game long enough never to assume anything. When I started all this I never imagined I would be asking a target's name, just before I killed them, or got myself interested in the finer details of my employer's wishes.

Keeping to the edge of the garden, I inch my way forward on my stomach, telling myself to take my time, not to make any sudden movements. I'm convinced there are motion sensitive lights in the garden, but I'll be just fine if I go slow.

About twenty minutes later I'm drenched, but standing at the porch of the house, a matter of inches from the back door. I suppress the urge to sneeze and wonder about my point of entry. Before I was one hundred per cent certain of the locations of the bedrooms but now doubts have crept into my mind. I can't remember whether the master bedroom was directly above the utility or if it was the children's. I silently curse Brian for not having given me a hard copy of the information. But I know that it was my pride that stopped me taking a second look. There's nothing for it now, though, I have to push forward.

Getting in takes me longer than it did with Elizabeth. There are three locks on the door. That tells me a lot about the person. They aren't just being sensible, they're being overly-cautious. They have expectations that someone would want to get inside their home. That means they'll be on guard, sleeping light, stirring at any sound.

The first two locks are really no problem, but I really have to jimmy the last one hard to get a grip on the springs then, all at once, it gives, opening with a light *click*.

I decide to leave the door open, not wanting the locks to snap back into place. I may have to leave the property in a hurry, you never can tell. I just hope no insomniac neighbours overlook their garden, eager to phone at a mysteriously open back door in the middle of the night.

I step forward.

A panel beside the door flashes its green display and croaks. It's counting down seconds, starting from thirty. A burglar alarm.

I reprimand myself again for being such an amateur, then clear my thoughts, try to get my mind back on the job. I confront the panel, flip open its front to expose its rubber buttons.

The count reaches twenty.

My fingers shake as I consider my options. I could back out, go back into the garden, let the alarm go off, then wait for someone to come down and reset it. They'd probably think it was a cat. Or they might call the police.

This hit needs to be done tonight, or I'm sure Brian will make plans for another assassin. And he won't just let me forget what happened, allow me to slip away into the twilight of retirement. I'm sure he has a full alphabet of plans for me—punishments if I fail at my task.

The count reaches ten.

My brain moves fast and, before I've even informed my fingers, they're stabbing in the digits: one, one, one, one.

The electronic croak ceases and the green display stops flashing. Its message reads 'Alarm Deactivated.'

I exhale and allow myself a few moments to regain my composure. I listen for any sound in the house, knowing that the croak wasn't silent. With four people in the house the chances are up that someone might have overheard, might be lying awake, staring at the ceiling wondering what that sound might've been.

With my pulse returning to normal—cold-blooded killer mode—I stalk through the shadows and into a corridor.

I emerge in an enormous hall. I got no sense of the size of

the house, coming in through the back garden, but the hall has twin staircases, one snaking off to the right, the other to the left, like in a film. I never really believed houses like this existed.

From what I can tell staring through the gloom, paintings adorn all the walls. Portraits, shadowy figures glaring down at me, challenging my presence there. The whole place stinks of polish and has more of an essence of museum about it than home. Each to their own, I guess.

Rain pitter-patters down on the roof tiles, turning the hall into an echo chamber. That sound reminds of being back in the Army, staying out in a tent, at the beginnings of a typhoon. The rain would always start lightly before pouring down.

I take care to step on the central carpet which occupies the staircase, keeping my footsteps silent. If the target had really thought carefully about security he would've taken away the carpets—a gift to anyone who wants to get around a darkened house unheard.

At the top of the stairs I pause and listen again for any stirrings. With nothing registering, I proceed along the landing, to what I've earmarked as the target's bedroom.

Dank moonlight beams in through the rain-splattered corridor windows. I keep my movements fluid, so that any passing observer might think that it's simply someone getting up in the middle of the night to get a glass of water. Nothing says suspicious more readily than someone lurking by a window.

When I get outside the door, I crouch down and pat my thigh for the handgun. I release it from its binding, twitch off the safety then hold it down by my side.

I reach for the doorknob and turn it in a single motion, feeling the mechanism tick beneath my grasp. Gently, I shoulder barge the door open and then slip inside, bringing the door shut again as quickly as I opened it.

The room is dark. Unlike the corridors, no moonlight enters. There must be a blind covering one of the windows. I stand at the door, waiting for my eyes to adjust to the gloom, but no matter how long I hesitate no focus arrives. Whatever's covering the window is a serious piece of kit. Blackout blinds. It figures that the target's just as serious about having no one see into his bedroom after lights out.

As time passes I know I'm going to have to take some chances. Keeping my hand against the wallpaper—it's the expensive kind that feels weighty beneath the fingertips—I guide my way round the room, taking care with my feet, not wanting to come across a loose shoe or some solid object that might catch my toe, cause me to cry out. If my target wakes this could get messy.

I stop and listen. I can hear breathing—a steady push and pull of lungs, a pair of lungs actually. The target and his wife sleeping. A fleeting thought crosses my mind, that if the wife wakes, as she surely will—even with the silenced shot—will I have the nerve to do her in too? I would be orphaning the children.

Now I'm so close to the sleeping bodies that I have only to reach out to touch them. I shuffle my way toward them so that I'm right overhead the first sleeper. Without light, not being able to distinguish between them, I might have no choice but to do them both.

From outside the rain drums harder and then, from nowhere at all, there's a flash of lightning. It illuminates the room, penetrating the blackout blinds. Below me I see the face of a sleeping boy. This is the children's room.

I retreat to the corner of the room, anticipating the inevitable.

The clap of thunder reverberates the foundations of the house, sending tremors up through my body. It hangs in the air for a second or more before fading.

The boy's breathing quickens and then he coughs himself awake.

Outside there's another flash of lightning. It shines through the room, revealing the twin beds. The boy sitting up, against his headboard, leaning over to the still-sleeping girl.

Mercifully, the light fades and the thunder claps again.

My palms sweat on the grip of my handgun. I know I have to do it if there's no choice, if I can find no other way out of the room. But my muscles lock tight, telling a different story altogether.

Amid another flash of lightning, the boy nudges the girl and speaks to her softly. "You hear that? There's a storm."

"Go back to sleep," she says.

From the tone of her voice I assume that she's older, more wizened, less affected by childish fear. In my head, I repeat her command, hoping that the boy does it. For all of our sakes.

The thunder rolls this time. There's a shuffle as I imagine the boy sitting back in his bed, eyes wandering through the gloom. I pray that the storm blows over, that I can steal out of the room—like I never even came in here in the first place. But, when the lightning inevitably returns, the boy's staring right at me, eyes ablaze and mouth torn open in terror.

Chapter Nine

AS THE BOY'S SCREAM SHRILLS through the air I forget myself completely, feel like I've left my body behind and see myself from above, witnessing the scene in third-person. No way can this be happening to me. I can't have made such an elementary error. Why couldn't I have just remembered the right room?

One of them flips on the bedside light and both of the children stare at me, both shouting and pointing. They shout out for their parents to come.

As a reflex, I bring the handgun up, stare along the sight, aim at the boy's forehead. My finger relaxes on the trigger, I know what I must do, but I simply can't.

A sob escapes my lips and my hand shakes.

There's another thunderclap and the door to the children's bedroom swings open. The man, my target , stands there, his eyes wide with fright, hand still resting on the doorknob, unable to process the scene against the still-present blur of sleepiness—unable to sort the reality from the fantasy.

I swing my arm round and squeeze the trigger. My bullet catches him in the chest. He staggers backward, falling back into the corridor. I tread toward him, looming over his fallen frame. As I line up the headshot, a door squeaks open at the end of the corridor. It distracts me only for a moment, but that's all the target needs. He swipes his leg out, catching me round the back of the knees.

I tumble on top of him. My gun clatters away into the darkness.

There's another scream, this time a woman, the target's wife.

I wrestle with the target. He's clearly hurt, fighting for his life, but he manages to snatch hold of my wrist, to just keep me from reaching the gun. It's only inches from my fingertips, but still too far.

Through throaty gasps, the target says to his wife, "Call . . . call the . . . police!"

I manage to shuck off his hold for good. I stumble forward and snatch up the gun. With it back in my grip, I take aim at the target's head and shoot.

A light *zip* flies through the air and the bullet catches the target. At first I think something's gone wrong, as if the bullet's just passed right through him and gone into the floorboards, but then he shudders and drops back. A pool of blood forms around the back of his skull.

The little girl shouts out and rushes for me, arms flailing.

I sidestep her, but she somehow catches the gun in her rage, sending it flying from my hand. I consider searching for it, but there's no time. I make off down the landing, spinning round the corner when I reach the stairwell. I can hear the hysterical sobs of the target's wife as she loudly explains the situation to the police over their bedroom phone. I know that I must take everyone else out. They've all seen me here. Not my face, because of the balaclava, but they've got the gun—and they know it murdered their father.

Panic's got a hold on me now and all I can see to do is get the hell out of the house, run as fast as I can, get back home and slip under the covers, as if nothing at all has happened. I'll write off tonight as an unmitigated disaster. Nothing else to be done.

I'm back in the kitchen before I've even got my thoughts straight on where I'm going—survival has kicked in, it's leading me by the hand. I just have to trust my gut, that's all that can save me now.

The grass is damp as I sprint for the end of the garden. The fence fills my vision. Just a hop over there and I've almost escaped. When I reach it my hands are shaking so much that I can hardly get a grip on the wood. I slip several times on the damp surface, but I manage to vault myself over.

I land badly on the other side, failing to bend my knees. A jolt passes up my spine, tweaking a muscle at the base of my back. I think nothing of it till I try to break into a run again. Then the pain is unbearable. It makes my teeth chatted. But I have to keep going. Just a little further. I can think about the pain later.

In the distance I hear the sirens, ripping through the night sky. Several cars, not just one. The key to getting half the force out is to mention a gun—a handgun probably gets them out in double time.

Before everything had burst apart, I'd planned to walk back home, like always following a hit, give myself some space to think in the cool morning air. Now, though, I needed a fast escape, a way to get out of the area quickly.

Another sound joins the sirens.

The pain seizes hold of my body and I have to stop dead, lean up against a nearby tree. My heart is almost popping out of my throat. I concentrate on the new sound. It's a consistent slicing and pound of air. I rack my brains trying to place it.

And then it gets so loud it's unmistakable.

A helicopter.

Paying no attention to the mind-numbing pain, I break into a sprint, not caring who sees me now. If that helicopter gets me in the sights of its thermal camera that's the end. I'll never shake it —not on foot. I have to find some cover, that's all that can save me now.

I try to resist the temptation to glance over my shoulder—an old Army trainer's voice shakes through my skull, shouting at me for doing it, telling me it'll just slowing me down, the first admission of defeat, weakness.

I pick out a cul-de-sac and rush down it, hoping some opportunity will present itself. That's all I have now, hope. All my professional skills will count for nothing if I can't find a hiding place.

The helicopter blades beat louder.

I wonder whether they already have me on their screens, if they're simply holding back, feeding my location to the police, biding their time and considering how they're going to play this dangerous and armed individual. Well, they can scratched the armed part for a start because I'm not—except for my trusty knife.

Trying to stay positive through the pain and resilience of the chase, I dash down an open side gate and into someone's back garden. I notice a dog kennel nestled in the corner of the garden and make for it, hoping that its occupant isn't home.

With no time to think before acting, I dive down and fling myself into the shelter.

The helicopter blades are louder. Overhead almost, I'm sure.

Inside the kennel it's fairly roomy—roomy enough for me to bring my knees up to chest. I notice the door and I bring it shut.

Despite what you might've seen in films, thermal cameras cannot see through glass, foliage, water or, thankfully, in my case, wood. But that didn't rule out that they had already caught sight of me, watched me sleuth into the kennel. All I can do now is sit tight and wait. I've done my part now it's fate's turn.

My mind flickers back to happier times, and I realise they're all with my family, back at home. Images of us gathered around a birthday cake for Josie's third birthday. Kids threading themselves beneath the table, popping up everywhere. For all the happiness, all I remember of that day is shouting myself hoarse, constantly telling children off. That night I'd needed to drink a bottle of wine just to calm down. That was when I was still drinking.

The helicopter is hovering overhead.

I get the horrid sensation that I can feel its air pushing in through the kennel, chilling my skin. I have the urge to just run out, to give myself up, for this all to be over with. But I can't just give up. If for no one else, and I know this sounds sadder than anything, I want to get out of this for Lizzie the cat. There'd be no one to let her out of the house. She'd starve to death.

At first I'm convinced my mind's playing tricks on me, that my imagination is dangling hope in front of me when there clearly is none. But, no, when I concentrate, listen closely, I hear the helicopter leaving me, going off somewhere else to look.

I suppress a cheer, knowing that this might still be part of their tactics. As far as they're concerned I might be armed. Maybe I'll come out firing, trying to take the helicopter down with me. I don't have any experience with police tactics but they can't be a million miles away from Army ones.

So, I just sit there in the kennel, the stench of wet dog filling my nostrils, making me gag, as I keep my ears alert for any sound outside. All I can hear now is the wind and rain, the light wail of sirens fading into the distance. For the first time since my escape from the house, I dare to hope.

I have to remind myself to breathe, although when I do I try to get it over with as quickly as possible, not wanting to miss one aural detail. After what I presume to be an hour or so later, I hear nothing. Not even the sound of the helicopter. The search has moved on. I'm home and dry. For now at least.

I consider my options. I could make a break for it, rush from the kennel, head back home. But I can't chance running across a police car. I'm sure every officer on duty is on the lookout for a woman dressed in black. No, I need to lie low just a little longer, until this all dies down. My only constraint is to get out of the kennel before the people who live in the house wake up.

My back is killing me, sending wave upon wave of pain through my spine, and up to my brain where it becomes a searing burn. Maybe, if I get through all this, I'll need to add a chiropractor to my monthly expenses.

Fending off the pain, or at least keeping it to the edge of my mind, I bed myself down and close my eyes, keeping my ears alert for any extraneous sound.

———

I can see the early-morning light curl through the cracks in the kennel. I only dare open the door when I'm absolutely certain that no sound lingers in the air. I poke my head out. Total silence. No trace of the frantic manhunt which took place the night before—which is probably still taking place, away from here.

As I leave the kennel behind, rise slowly to my feet, feeling pain rush through my nerves, dulling my senses, I see that utter stillness grips the houses round me. It's like I've stepped onto some other plane of reality, or like I'm dreaming. I recall my Army training—what Julie's told me over and over during our sessions—about the effects of trauma. How it plays tricks with the mind. I tell myself to be wary, to take extra care.

I walk along the empty street, arriving back at the main road. I look back along it, toward the target's house. Although I can't see it from where I stand, a shudder passes through me, knowing that right now, as I stand here, forensics are bustling through the house, studying the tread of my boots, swiping up my DNA off the handle of my gun—I never took enough care with it back home, handled it too much without wearing gloves, never entertained the thought it might escape my possession. I wouldn't be surprised if the forensics were taking samples of the air I breathed.

Any moment I'm expecting a group of officers to burst from a nearby hedge, guns all trained on me, to shout for me to get down on my front. But I know that's just the trauma too, still snaking its way through my veins, trying to turn me into my own worst enemy.

When I get back to my street, there're some of my neighbours bobbing round in their drives, starting cars, kissing their wives, husbands or children goodbye, before heading off to their private worlds of work—just as I am returning from mine.

I keep my head bowed, like a penitent nun, and arrive outside my door, savouring the sweet *snick* of my key entering the lock.

It's a sound of imminent safety that I'd convinced myself I'd never hear again.

I close the door behind me and press my shoulders up against it, closing my eyes, trying to get my warped mind into some kind of shape.

What a night.

In the kitchen, I flip the switch on the kettle, drape a teabag into a mug then sit at the table, head in my hands, thinking of those kids' expressions, the panic as that girl attacked me. And, despite myself, I wonder about the target, whether or not he was a good man, a good father. Was he like all those other overgrown school boys, sneaking round with several mistresses, or was he different? I will never know.

The kettle boils and I pour the hot water into the mug, watching the tea mingle with the water in brown clouds. As I slip the teabag out, plop it into the sink, I hear a sound off in the house. A light *shuffle*. I stop dead to listen closely.

Lizzie rubs her bony body along the doorframe as enters the kitchen.

I allow myself a brief snort of laughter—it feels alien, weird, after all the seriousness of the past hours. I scoop her up in my arms and she purrs against my chest. "Did you miss me?"

She purrs harder, rubbing her delicate head against my leathery skin.

And then, without warning, a tear seeps from the corner of my eye, lands in her tangled fur. I grip her tighter to me, knowing that she's all that I have in the world.

Upstairs, I hear the *creak* of bedsprings.

My heart sticks in my throat. I let Lizzie down and feel for the knife at my belt. I withdraw it from its sleeve and slip into the hallway to investigate.

Chapter Ten

I CLIMB THE STAIRS keeping my neck craned upwards, watching for any motion, ready to strike. I should have the upper hand, the element of surprise, since whoever's in my house clearly hasn't realised I've come home.

There's a loud yawn from my bedroom.

A brief moment of fear grasps me. I know it's just a combination of a sleepless night and the recent events I've witnessed, but it takes me all the same. And I hesitate, have to push myself forward.

Lizzie weaves in and out between my legs, still purring her head off. Some guard cat she is.

I get myself up onto the landing, taking care to stay out of view of the doorway to my bedroom. If the intruder gets just one glimpse of me then it's all over, I will have lost my advantage. I pass the danger point, slide along the wall and then burst into my bedroom, knife bared, ready to fight off whoever's there.

It's a man dressed in a crumpled blue suit. He's sitting on the edge of my bed, putting on a pair of brown shoes, doing up the laces. He shoots me a glance then continues dressing himself. "You didn't answer when I rang, so I let myself in." This time he straightens up, gives me a wink and a smile. "Hope you don't mind."

It's Adam Alderknot—or AA as he likes to be known. A fellow assassin, also ex-Army. He got me into this whole killing business, got me in touch with Brian. In fact I took his job, and he got a promotion, pushed out into international jobs—higher stakes.

"What're you doing here?" I say.

AA rolls his shoulders, getting the stiffness out. "I would've thought you'd invest in a fancier mattress considering your pay rise." He looks to the knife. "Do you mind?"

I linger a moment then return the knife to its sheath, but I stop short of buttoning it closed.

AA says, "I know you're under strict orders not to give away any details of the job but it's fine, you can trust me. Brian sent me."

"He did?" I say, not trusting him.

"You left an awful mess back there."

Still unsure about how much he knows, and not wanting to give anything away, I stay silent, waiting for him to prove himself.

AA has slick black hair—I think about the grease he must've left on my pillow—and firm, high cheekbones, almost feminine. I'm sure that he's got some Eastern European blood in him, but I've never got any personal history out of him—as he hasn't got any out of me.

He gets up, fastens the middle button on his jacket. "All I came to tell you was that it's all taken care of. Nothing to worry about."

"'Nothing to worry about,'" I say, feeling ditsy echoing his words.

"Brian's shut them all down, had them all report that it was a gas explosion, evacuated the whole area."

"You mean the police were in on it?"

"They were looking for you, Anna, sent a bloody chopper to bring you in. You certainly took your time, had us all worried, thought you'd fallen in a ditch or something." He looks me over. "By the looks of things you did."

This is too much to absorb right now. I need a shower, to get some sleep. I can't comprehend that those same people I was running from throughout the whole night were really trying to save me.

AA buttons the cuffs of his jacket. He brushes some lint from his lapel then says, "Well don't just stand there, I'm bleeding starving. Get us some breakfast, will you?"

———

Over coffee, cereal, some eggs, bacon and toast, AA fills me in on the intricacies of the media blackout. It seems that Brian's pulled just about every string he can get his manicured hands on to keep this quiet—not content to get the TV channels onside, he's called up every editor in charge of every major publication in the United Kingdom. I knew that Brian was powerful but I really had no idea.

AA blows on his coffee, sending steam coiling out over the lip of the mug. He takes a sip then sets it down. He meets my eye. "So what do you think about old Brian Mathewson now?"

"He's my boss. An employer."

"You don't think this is all a bit much, that he's taking just a few too many liberties?"

"What do you mean?"

AA rocks forward on his chair, leans over the table so his tie dangles down, and he mock knocks on my forehead. "Hello? Anyone home? Were you listening to anything I just said?" He sticks his tongue out the corner of his mouth, like he does whenever he's giving something serious thought. "You don't think there's anything morally wrong in what he's doing to this country?"

"I'm not really in any position to pass judgement."

AA chuckles. "Me neither, but I can't help gossiping. Nature of the business. Problem with people like us is there's no water cooler for us to have a good chinwag around. So we have to make do with what we can get."

Feeling uncomfortable with this conversation, with the direction it's headed, I collect up the empty plates and dump them in the sink. Perhaps I can get a dishwasher delivered today, save me having to scrub for an hour. God knows I've got the money now.

"So? What's your opinion?" AA says.

"Like I said, I don't have one. Brian pays me well for what I do, pays me not to think."

"But you do, don't you? I know you do. Don't tell me that you've never cornered a target, got talking to them, asked for details on what's really going on."

My mind's eye summons up Elizabeth, writhing below me. I turn on the hot water tap, filling the sink with steaming water. "Never."

AA whistles. "Well, check out Little Miss Professionalism. Lips sealed. No questions asked, no answers wanted." He drums his fingers on the table. "So last night was just a fluke, was it? First mistake you've made on the job?"

I squeeze my eyes shut, scrub at some egg stuck to a pan. At this point I just want AA out of the house, to give me some time alone so I can bring myself round. "Yes."

"I don't believe you."

I glance back over my shoulder. "That's a pity."

"The name Simon Snarkly mean anything to you?"

A chill passes up my spine. I drop the pan and it clangs against some cutlery.

AA laughs. "You'd be a terrible poker player, you know that?"

I fill the pan with hot, soapy water and set it to one side, take a look at the rest of the plates and realise I can't bring myself to do any more, not right now. I return to the table, taking my seat opposite AA again.

Lizzie enters the room and leaps up onto my lap where she turns several circles before curling up and going to sleep.

"Nice cat," AA says. "Kept me warm all night."

I scowl at him as I comb my fingers through Lizzie's fur.

"So you're telling me that Elizabeth Newman didn't tell you anything about Snarkly, not even hint at what's going on?"

"No."

"Then she didn't tell you that she wasn't just his lover, that there was more to Brian's briefing that first appears? That, in fact, she was complicit in Snarkly's plan for global domination."

I sniff a laugh at AA's 'global domination' remark. All this politics just reminds me of a spoof superhero film. Sometimes it's scary how closely fiction and fact relate.

AA continues, "And you've got no questions about your employer for the latest hit? Abdul-Hakam?"

Another chill up the spine. I twitch.

Lizzie stirs in my lap, looks up at me, then resettles and resumes her slumber.

"None," I say.

"My goodness, you are a well-behaved girl."

Despite my front, I'm almost trembling for more information, but I know that I can't know more—that it's beyond my job description to know any more. The worst of all is it could affect my professional performance, if I get to thinking of the consequences of my role in all this.

AA cracks his knuckles. "Brian wouldn't have pulled all those strings last night for you, just to save you from going to prison. He wanted to make the whole situation look like a cover up."

"What?"

"Oh come on Anna, dig your head out of the sand, just a little bit, just for once, 'gas explosion?' Who in their right mind will really believe that when the evidence gets out."

"What evidence?"

"There's always evidence, CCTV, officer statements, I'm sure that a neighbour or two saw or heard something that disproves it."

"But why? Why would Brian want it to look like a cover up?"

He grins. "See, I knew I'd bring you down to my level eventually. Now we're speaking frankly." He props his elbows on the table. "I've been wondering that myself."

My mobile buzzes across the table.

I startle at the sudden movement.

"I'd best be off," AA says, glancing at the screen of my mobile then making for the door. "Thanks for breakfast." He nods at the mobile. "I'd answer that if I were you."

When I examine the caller ID I see that it's Brian.

Chapter Eleven

MY HANDS SHAKE as I bring the phone to my ear and answer. "Hello?"

"Anna?"

"Yes."

Brian sighs. "Jesus, girl, I've been calling you all morning, trying to get through."

"I just got in, an hour or so ago."

"Do you mind telling me what on Earth happened?"

I reel through the story from my perspective, stopping short of telling him about AA's visit—I'm sure he's not all that interested in that part, considering he's managing a media blackout of the target's house.

After I finish up my explanation I'm sure that's he's going to give me a dressing down, instead, though, he says, "Good job, well done."

"You're . . . you're not angry about how it went down?"

"A few rough edges, here and there, granted, but it's all taken care of now."

I have a horrible sinking feeling in my stomach. I know that I have to hang back, stay detached, but I can't help myself asking. "And the children, the wife?"

Brian's voice firms up. "Like I said, it's all taken care of."

Blood rushes to my cheeks and I get caught in a dizzy spell. My fault. It was all my fault.

"Now, listen," Brian says. "I've set up an appointment for you, on the company account, at Yawley's. They're going to give you the best massage this side of China and sort you out with a swim and sauna. Then we'll talk, okay?"

I feel nauseous. I have to get off the phone right now, get to a toilet bowl. "Okay, thanks."

Brian clears his throat. "Anna?"

"Yeah?"

"You did a perfect job, don't worry about the details," he says, then hangs up.

I drop my mobile on the table and rush to the toilet.

————

Yawley's is just about all it's ever promised to be. I remember a while back, waiting to go into Brian's office, overhearing a pair of silver-haired media executives strutting past me talking about the place like it was some kind of heaven. Then I thought they were exaggerating, the executives often do, but actually being here, feeling the steam wash round me, the masseuse's nimble fingers finding all the tense spots in my back and tweaking them away, I realise that I've never really understood the definition of the word relaxation.

I lie with my face down, poking through the hole in the massage bed. My whole body is relaxed and my mind, for the first time in days, is totally blank. Before coming here I had to call and cancel my appointment with Julie. She sounded concerned until I told her where I was going, then she wanted to know who had got me in.

Somewhere out of sight a cinnamon-scented joss stick smoulders away, destroying all concept of the smell of sweat or body odour. Everything here feels so naturally clean, as if the place is cleaned with citric fruits.

My masseuse, called Michael, finishes up the massage. As he walks away from me I can see his well-defined flanks where his damp t-shirt sticks. I bite on my lower lip to prevent myself declaring my undying love for him.

I have a shower then put on a swimming costume, as provided by Yawley's. When I got the option of bikini or 'something weightier,' I went for the latter option. It's not that I'm self-conscious of my body—that I've had two kids—but more to do with not attracting unwanted male attention. I'm certain this is a major place for women of a certain ilk to get picked up by millionaire playboys. And I just don't roll that way. I'm an independent woman, thank you very much—having half a million in my bank account at the present time builds my confidence sufficiently to declare it out loud.

Once I've put on my swimming costume, a curve-fitting black design, I grab a towel and make for the pool. It's pretty empty at this time, it being the middle of the working day. There're only a pair of men at the other end, resting with their elbows propped on the side of the pool, chatting—no doubt completing some multi-million-pound deal.

I squeeze my hair beneath a rubber cap then slip into the

water. Just like everything else at Yawley's it's perfect. The temperature is somewhere in the sweet spot: between the late-twenties and early thirties. And, I kid you not, the water smells of rose petals.

I swim a length of breaststroke before speeding up, going with a front crawl. As I come to the end of a length I notice the men staring at me, gawking. I try to put it out of my mind, but every time I return to their end of the pool I feel their eyes on me, perving on my body. It poisons my good spirits and bothers me no end until I decide I've had enough. On my next length when I look up, sure enough, both of them are gaping at me. I draw to a stop, rest my hand on the side of the pool and look them both in the eye. But, before I speak, the words are stripped from me. I realise that one of the men is Simon Snarkly: Education Secretary.

————

I try to pass it off as nothing at all, I turn in the pool and face the other way, as if prepared to swim another length, but Snarkly calls out to me. "Hey? Everything all right?"

What a smooth customer. I tilt my head back, give him a weak smile then say, "Fine, thanks."

"You're fast."

"What?"

"You swim quickly, got a good, solid front crawl on you."

I really have no idea how I'm meant to take that comment. It feels like I'm having an awkward conversation with a PE teacher out of school—I wonder whether, being Education Secretary, Snarkly actually has any education credentials, if he's ever actually taught anyone in his life.

I settle on a simple, "Thanks."

Snarkly says something to his bald companion, who nods to him then gets out of the pool, heads toward the changing rooms. After watching his companion disappear, Snarly hauls himself toward me.

He has a well-defined body—not as nice as Michael the Masseuse's, of course, but fine, all the same. He must be in his forties and he still has a thick head of curly hair. The only aspect which gives his age away are the wrinkles round his eyes, that testify to more than a few late nights, work stress.

"What's your name?" he says.

Wow, he really does have all the lines. His wife must feel so lucky. "Hannah," I say, without thinking.

That's my reflex name. Whenever anyone asks my name, and I don't want to give it, something subconscious gets triggered and I give them Hannah.

"Hannah?" he says, batting his eyes. "That's lovely. I used to have a grandmother called Hannah."

I bet he didn't. I decide to change the subject, get round to making an excuse to leave. I don't want to accidently hint at the fact that I was the one who he paid to take care of his late mistress. "Who was that?"

"Who?"

"The person you were talking to, the bald guy who got out of the pool."

"Oh, that was my bodyguard."

Now he's got my attention. "Bodyguard?"

He gives me a sly smile, then examines his knuckles. "Don't you recognise me?"

I wait a beat, so that he might actually buy the fact that I'm giving the matter pause for thought, that I haven't known exactly who he is all along. "Uh, are you a politician?"

His grin widens, revealing perfectly-set teeth—a computer-designed smile. "That's right," he says.

"I . . . I'm sorry, I don't remember your name. I'm not really that interested in politics."

He rolls his eyes. I notice a birthmark on his neck, I suppose surgery couldn't take care of that imperfection. "Perfectly under-standable," he says. "It's not like we run the country, or anything."

A sliver of a second too late I realise I'm supposed to laugh at that comment and, when I do, it comes out forced. However it doesn't seem to much bother Snarkly. Surely he's used to faked laughs, perhaps he's so accustomed to them that he can no longer tell the difference between the fakery and the real thing.

"The name's Simon. Simon Snarkly. Education Secretary."

I do my best wide-eyed impressed look, but really I'm trying to pick my moment, wanting to get away.

"I'm taking some time off this afternoon, well deserved rest and all that. Had a hectic morning in the Commons this morning."

He then goes on to talk for about twenty minutes, without stopping, about his morning, and all the drudgeries associated with it. He really has no idea how boring he is. How self-absorbed and how much of a pompous fool he comes across as. But then, I realise, that he's pinned me as some rich bimbo. That he believes he can use a bunch of long words to bowl me over.

Finally, I manage to pick a moment in the conversation to make my excuses. Aware of his wolfish gaze, I lug myself up the ladder and get out of the pool. As I walk back toward the changing room, he calls after me.

"Say, Hannah?" he says.

My sense of politeness gets the better of me and I stop, turn round.

He continues, "Would you be interested in going for a drink with me, this evening?"

I turn the idea over in my head. Of course it's a terrible idea, not most because this man's married, that I have absolutely zero attraction to him, not after his little diatribe about his 'chums' in the Commons, or that I've recently taken care of his ex-mistress. And yet, my lips do exactly the opposite. "Okay," I say.

"Excellent, what's your number?"

I consider giving him a false one, then reach for an easier option. "You don't have anything to write it down with."

"I have a terrific memory."

I'm sure he does. I give him my number, my real number.

As I get changed I tell myself off for having done it, I analyse my thinking in doing so and realise that it's just as AA said, I'm truly interested in what's going on, what Simon Snarkly has planned—his 'world domination.' And, anyway, I'm sure he approaches a dozen bimbos every day, gets their numbers.

Even if he does call I can always hang up on him.

Chapter Twelve

CANDY'S DOING HER NAILS when I get to Brian's office. She looks up at me and smiles inanely. "You look very pretty today," she says.

Always partial to a compliment, I say, "Thanks."

She almost closes her eyes as she examines me, as if she's using an enormous quantity of brainpower. "Very naturalistic."

I don't think that's exactly the word she's looking for, but I thank her again, then take a seat to wait for Brian. Today he's got some magazines spread out on the table. I snatch up the first, mostly to avoid losing my mind via conversation with Candy, and who should be the feature article but Simon Snarkly?

It's a light-hearted interview, with several shots of Snarkly standing in his home—or one of his homes—his wife and children appearing in a few. Each photograph is carefully orchestrated, Snarkly always standing at a window, with rolling hills behind him or emerging from French doors, glittering in the noon sun. There's no sign of his birthmark, I'm sure that Brian has people making sure those kinds of 'defects' are digitally-removed.

Image, as Brian says, is everything.

The interview reveals nothing I couldn't have researched in five minutes on the internet. Sometimes I wonder whether these things ever actually happen—whether the journalist ever really visited Snarkly or if they simply sent the photographer round and then cobbled together the text using a stray copy of *Who's Who*.

For some reason there's a strange throbbing in my chest when I look over his photograph. I guess I'm not totally immune to the influence of fame and fortune, the idea that some of us are greater than others. I have a funny flush of pride considering that he asked for my number. He chose me out of so many other women. Giving him my number becomes a worse idea by the second.

A few minutes later, Brian arrives and calls me into his office. I smile politely at Candy then go in after him.

———

Brian's back on the whisky today, just a small one, though, no more than a trickle in the bottom of the glass—a little something to get him through to teatime. He swirls the whisky in the base of the glass as he peers at me over the rim. "How was Yawley's?" he says.

My thoughts fill with Snarkly's face. "Fine."

"Fine?" he says, raising his eyebrows. "Is that it?"

"Okay," I say, lightening my tone. "It was pretty spectacular."

He eyes me suspiciously as he drains the whisky. "That's more like it." He looks out the window, over the skyline, probably planning his next strike. "I'd like to get down there more often, but work doesn't allow it."

"No, I suppose it doesn't."

"Recovered from last night?"

A knot sticks in my throat. Those children's faces pop back into my mind. I think that they're all dead now, and that I caused it. If only I had taken care of the target when he'd been alone, no witnesses, Brian might've spared the rest of the family—or would he?

"Yes, I feel much better," I say.

"Good," he says. "Don't want you having a breakdown on me, nothing like that. Sorry to hear that you spent the night outdoors, couldn't really be helped. No way of getting in contact with you, you see. You really had me thinking on my feet, I can tell you."

I cast my mind back to AA in my house, telling me that Brian planned it all along, that he had specifically sent me in there to get things messy. Had the information even been correct in the first place? Had he switched the children's bedroom on the map I saw or had I simply not remembered correctly? I really don't know who to believe.

"You all right, Anna?"

"Hmm, yes, I'm fine."

"Thought I'd lost you there."

"Just a bit tired, that's all."

He nods. "Yes, that's to be expected. I imagine killing is tough work."

He really has no idea. It's easy for him to dish out cash and tell me to kill someone. What he doesn't realise is that it gets easier with every hit. The nightmares remain but the actual act becomes mechanical, automatic. I can hardly remember the moment I delivered the deadly shot to the target last night. What kind of person have I become?

Brian sets his whisky down on the drinks cabinet, then looks over to me, without the trace of a smile. "I'd like you to answer me a question honestly, Anna."

"Okay."

"Have you got any idea at all about the last two jobs you've done for me? Have you garnished any information that might impair your performance on future contracts?"

My pulse quickens. There's only one answer I can give here. "No."

"You're quite sure? I know how it can go. Something incriminating lying round the house that you happen upon: a photograph, documents, an identification badge, nothing like that?"

"No, sir."

"Good, because you know that at Mathewson Media we can tolerate no leaks when a client's confidentiality is on the line. That's the service we provide and if it's broken it must be fixed. Otherwise we'd be peddling in lies, isn't that right?"

"Yes, I suppose so."

He snorts. "I even remember I had someone work contracts for me a while back. He used to speak to the targets, before he killed them. That went on for months before I stopped it."

My throat dries but I have to ask the question. "What happened to him?"

"Hmm, the assassin? It's just like dealing with any employee leaking trade secrets, really, they have to be dealt with."

I've come this far, I might as well keep going. "But . . . but how did you deal with him?"

He snickers to himself then, all of a sudden, becomes deadly serious. "Why, I put another assassin on him. Par for the course."

I turn my gaze to look out the window, hoping that Brian doesn't notice my hands shaking or my eyes darting about their sockets as I wonder what to do.

Chapter Thirteen

A S I TAKE THE TUBE back home I think about AA's visit. Was he trying to sound me out? Was he really there because of Brian, as he said, to try and establish what it was that I knew about the targets? Now I'm panicking because if that is the case then how long is it before Brian decides that it's not worth the risk leaving me alive and sends someone after me?

When I get up to surrender my seat to an elderly lady, my phone vibrates. I reach for it and read the message. It's from Simon Snarkly: Dinner at eight? Tulips?

I stare at the words, turn them over in my mind, wondering whether what took place this afternoon really did happen. This is the evidence. Whether or not AA's curiosity was feigned as means for me to give up what I knew about the targets, it's certainly drawing me to Snarkly—makes me want to know more about this. And, with everyone warning me away: Elizabeth's dying breath and Brian threatening to have a hit put on me, I'm more intrigued than ever. If Brian finds out that I have an idea of what's going on he's going to kill me anyway, so I might as well find out all there is to know—what I'm dying for.

———

It's still late-afternoon when I arrive home. Lizzie greets me at the door, rubbing up against me legs. I feed her then head into the kitchen. If I'm having dinner with Snarkly at eight that leaves me a few hours to go and visit my kids. After last night I just want to hug each of them, check that they're still there—that they're real.

I phone up Arnold, subtly ascertain that Kate's not round, then I pick up my handbag and hustle back out of the house, back down into the Underground.

When I ring the bell, I hear the usual rustling inside, the panicked fumbling of someone to answering the door. I miss that sensation. It's gone forever now. I'm too old to have a new family, and I can no longer return to this one.

Arnold answers. He sweeps his hand through his fringe, like he always does when he's nervous, then asks me in.

Photos of Josie and Ben hang from the walls. There are loads from when they were much younger, just toddlers, one in which Ben's carting Josie around in a wheelbarrow, another where Ben's sitting on the toilet and Josie's walked in on him. Then there are more recent photographs. Among them I'm taken aback to notice one featuring Kate.

Arnold sees me looking. "Again, sorry. I messed up. I should've told you much sooner. The thing is that Kate's been a part of our lives for—"

"I don't want to know about it." I peer up the staircase. "Where're the kids?"

"In their rooms."

"Is it all right if I go up?"

"Make yourself at home."

I shuffle up the stairs, aware that Arnold's gaze is fixed on me. I know that he's still in love with me, pines after me, and that if right now I told him that I'd come back to them I'm sure he'd be the first to welcome me. Kate would disappear, I could take care of that.

When I get to the top of the staircase I hear the noise of a videogame, virtual-reality guns firing and virtual-reality men screaming. I slip into Ben's room and rap on the door.

He's perched on the edge of his bed with a controller in his hand, his back to me. He has a friend alongside him—a redhead kid I've never seen before, but then, why would I have seen him?

Someone dies on screen and Ben clicks the pause button. He glances over his shoulder. When he sees me there I'm certain I see him roll his eyes.

"Who are you?" Ben's friend says to me.

"That's not very polite," I say.

"That's my mum, Kev," Ben says.

Kevin's mouth forms an 'oh' then he looks back at the screen. "Come on then, I'm about to win."

Ben's eyelids droop as he speaks to me. "Is it all right if we just finish this game, then we talk?"

"Fine," I say, feeling a little hurt at him choosing his virtual-reality violence over real-world interaction with his mother, but not all that surprised. "I'll go see what Josie's up to, shall I?"

Ben gives me a non-distinct grunt.

I know where I'm not wanted. Sometimes I wonder whether Arnold poisons the kids against me, paints me as the mother from hell. Then I reach the conclusion that, really, that's not necessary.

I do a pretty good job of it myself. How many other mothers in the country killed a man last night?

I step along the landing, overhearing Josie's voice. If she's got a friend round too then I might as well just head back home. I'll only get in the way.

However, when I reach Josie's door, and look inside, I see her sitting in the middle of her bedroom floor with a doll in her hand. She's brushing its hair and muttering to it, something about being pretty for a ball. I hang back another moment, not wanting to encroach on her, smash her illusion, and then step forward. "Hi there, Jo, how're you?"

Josie turns her attention away from the doll. Her eyes first scan my battered trainers, before rising up to my shins, stomach, then to my face. Slowly, her mouth curls at the edges, trans-forming into a smile. She rushes for me, clings to my legs. "Mumma!"

I prise away her fingers and lift her. She's much heavier than I remember. "Did you have a nice day at school?"

Her eyes wander as she considers the question, before her mouth swings round to a frown. "No."

"No? Why not?"

"Francesca called me a smelly-welly."

"Who's Francesca?"

She scans me as if trying to tell whether or not I'm joking. "She's my best friend."

"Of course she is. That's where you were last time I came to visit, I reckon."

"Dunno, don't remember."

I set her back down on the ground. "What's a smelly-welly, anyway?"

She pouts then shrugs.

"Then what're you getting all wound up about?"

"I don't like it, that's all."

"Why don't you tell her not to say it anymore?"

"She won't listen."

I think about dishing out useful advice, telling her to give Francesca a good slap, but I refrain, knowing that's bad parenting. "Well," I say, "sometimes girls just fight. And there's nothing you can do about it. Why don't you come up with a name for her?"

"Like what?"

"I don't know, something like: hairy-beary."

Josie sniggers.

"Is that funny?" I say.

She nods.

"Use it on Francesca, then, maybe she'll feel different knowing that she has to take it if she's going to dish it out." I scan her room. "Why don't you introduce me to some of your dolls?"

For the next hour or so, I sit on the thick carpet in Josie's room as she presents me to each of the dolls. Each one has not only a name but a favourite colour, favourite food and a basic personality. She informs me that some of the dolls are angry, while others are happy, there's even one which is jealous.

There are heavy footsteps in the landing and I look round to see Arnold peering over us. "Wondered if you'd like to stay for dinner."

I slip my phone out of my pocket, check the time. "It's okay, I've got plans. In fact, I'd better get going."

Arnold looks like he wants to ask the follow up question: 'who with?' but he remains silent, like the pushover he is. He gives me a parting smile then disappears from the doorway.

I kiss and hug Josie goodbye then move off along the landing to look in on Ben.

He's still immersed in his videogame, him and Kevin chirping back and forth every so often. I consider stepping inside, breaking up their game to say goodbye, then I just duck out, and head down the stairs, not wanting to inconvenience him. If he really wants to speak to me he knows where the phone is.

I dodge round Arnold on my way to the front door, managing to get out without getting into a heart-to-heart, then I'm pounding the paving slabs outside and heading back to the Tube station, to get ready for my hot date with a married man who could get me killed.

Chapter Fourteen

BACK HOME I pick through my wardrobe, selecting and then discarding various dresses. I haven't got that many and most of the ones I do have are several sizes too small. It's weird because it doesn't feel like I've gained much weight, but I suppose that's just aging. It sneaks up on you silently, like carbon monoxide.

Once I've got my outfits down to the ones that fit there's really not much choice: a blue dress or a green one. I go with the blue since I don't have any shoes that'll go with the green. I plaster on makeup and have to admit, looking in my fully-body mirror, that I turn out fairly presentable. Enough for a politician anyway.

I empty the contents of a can of tuna into Lizzie's bowl, give my hands a thorough wash then call a taxi. I don't think Snarkly expects his dates to arrive by Tube. I know I can afford to be a little less thrifty with half a million in the bank, but it does hurt to think about how many Tube journeys I could have got out of my taxi fare. Old habits die hard, I suppose.

Ivy sprawls up the exterior of the restaurant: Tulips. I bet it's designer ivy, that they got it from some exclusive garden shop, the kind that grows exactly how you want it. There are no yellow or brown leaves and I think of the poor sod who has to prune the defective leaves every day.

Inside the restaurant there's the bustle of conversation, the clatter of cutlery on plates and a cacophony of sweet smells—fish, chicken, beef, herbs all mixing together into a single entity. I trot along on my heels, into the entrance hall where a maître d' stands straight-backed over a lectern, a reservations book flattened before him. Not really knowing what to do, never having come to a fancy restaurant like this in my life before, I stand and wait.

The maître d's gaze crosses mine. He smiles politely. "May I help you, madam?"

"I'm waiting for someone."

He gestures with his hand. "Perhaps you would like to take a seat at the bar while you wait."

I look to where he points. A bartender wearing a black shirt and a white apron cleans a glass with a cloth. Between loitering in the entrance hall and propping myself up against the bar, I choose to prop myself up at the bar.

The bartender asks me what I want and I order a tonic water with lemon and ice.

Gourmet water.

About half an hour passes before Snarkly's arrival. A black car with tinted windows rolls up outside the restaurant and a previously-unseen attendant rushes to open the door and stands by Snarkly as he emerges.

I watch as the maître d' rounds his podium with the reservation book and pads up to Snarkly, like an overeager terrier. He gives him a two-handed handshake. When Snarkly asks after me, a look of confusion briefly crosses the maître d's face, then he looks over to me. With the same smile pinned across his cheeks, he marches over and offers his hand, to help me off the stool. "Really, madam, you should've said you were waiting for Mr Snarkly."

"It slipped my mind," I say, sounding giddy and half-believing myself.

Snarkly puckers his lips and swoops to give me a kiss on either cheek, before taking my hand in his and kissing the back of it. "You look lovely this evening."

I'm embarrassed to admit that I blush. Just a little.

The maître d' personally escorts us to a table on the other side of the room. It looks directly out onto the street. As the maître d' pulls back my chair for me to sit, I watch Snarkly's well-polished car slip past the window and out of sight. I wonder whether the chauffeur just drives round, waiting for a call, or if there's some exclusive parking space for the rich, famous and political.

I allow Snarkly to order wine—not bothering to tell him that I don't drink—and I accept all his recommendations for ordering the starter and main course. As the waiter takes note of our orders and leaves us, it sinks in that the person sitting opposite me paid to have another human being killed. And that thought never leaves me as Snarkly begins to hold forth.

"Beautiful day, wasn't it?" he says.

Not really having noticed, I say, "Yes."

"I say, just as I was leaving Parliament on my bicycle—"

"You cycle there?"

"Oh yes, it's all part of this publicity thing, we need to be seen leading the charge for the green revolution. Being a politician is a little like being Head Boy at school. You must set a positive example."

"And does your bodyguard follow you round in the car?"

A frown crosses his lips, as if I've trod over some kind of line, then he brightens. "No, he cycles too. A little way behind, of course."

"What's it like to have a bodyguard?" I say, genuinely interested.

He pouts. "Couldn't say, really. Ever since I was a child I've had someone looking over my shoulder, checking to see that I'm safe."

I recall the write up in the encyclopaedia online. That his father's an iron magnate. "Wasn't it weird not to have any privacy?"

"No, you become accustomed to it."

"Are you really afraid that someone might try to kill you?"

Again, Snarkly pauses before answering the question. "One can never be too careful these days. All sorts of things have been known to happen in the political sphere."

Deciding to push my luck, I say, "You mean assassins?"

The waiter arrives with a freshly-corked bottle of wine. He flashes the label at me before turning it to Snarkly so that he gets a proper look. Snarkly tastes then merely nods. As the waiter pours wine into my glass, Snarkly continues, "It's been known to happen, yes."

"But why?"

The waiter fills Snarkly's glass then leaves us.

Snarkly raises his glass.

Instinctively, I meet it with mine.

Our glasses tinkle together.

He gives me one of his sly smiles. "Let's change the subject, shall we? All this talk of murder isn't good for the digestion."

And, like a good little bimbo, I indulge him.

———

At the end of the meal Snarkly pays, of course. And just like the perfect gentleman, he doesn't even let me get a glance at the bill. I remember going out to a slightly posh restaurant with Arnold for our first wedding anniversary. When he read the bill I thought he was going to have a heart attack. But I suppose for someone like Snarkly who's always had a certain amount of money, and who's never had to scrounge in his whole life, then money has no fixed meaning.

He helps me on with my jacket and then we make our way across the restaurant. I notice a few famous faces who have their heads down in conversation, as if they didn't want to be recognised. Surely the main reason they come here is to be seen.

I have no idea what's going to happen next, although I can already see Snarkly's car sitting on the curb, just outside the door to the restaurant, the footman already opening the back door for us.

As I step onto the street I feel the chilly night breeze and tremble slightly. I feel Snarkly's sure hand in the middle of my lower back. His touch is warm and sure. If in everything else he exudes overgrown schoolboy, his physicality doesn't. My mind snaps back to Elizabeth's words about Snarkly being 'sexually basic' and I wonder what she meant precisely. I realise, with a little fear, that I'm about to find out.

No words pass between us as we ride through the city, the

streetlights competing with the brutishly-white car headlights. We roll beneath bridges, past parks and along populated streets, with patrons falling out into the road, sodden with drink.

I don't know whether it's the wine that's gone to my head—my first drink in several years—or Snarkly's aroma, but I don't think I can back out of whatever he's going to ask of me. I feel like a fly caught in a spider's web, turning over and over, ensnaring herself more and more.

We finally arrive at a large building. I read the placard which stands out in a garden decorating its entrance: Peterton Gardens.

"This is my flat," Snarkly says.

I look out the window, having to crane my neck to see the very top of the building. "Which is yours?"

Snarkly snorts. "I own the whole building—a small investment—but I keep up a residence in the penthouse."

I think back over Elizabeth's words, that I should get away, not pay any attention, not get myself caught up in what's going on. Now it's too late. I've committed myself to Snarkly, at least for one night.

The bodyguard's smooth bald head gleams in the streetlight. He's dressed in a suit and wears a simple black tie. He walks round the car and lets us out. He nods to me, not a trace of a smile, then turns to Snarkly and says, "Goodnight, sir."

Snarkly half-nods in acknowledgement then his hand finds that pit in my lower back, once again, and guides me toward the building entrance.

I try to suppress my show of excitement as we take a ride in a transparent lift. As we rise over the city I can see everything. The whole skyline: St Paul's Cathedral, the London Eye, the Shard and then, a little further away, the Houses of Parliament.

"Nice view, isn't it?" Snarkly says, as if it were the most normal thing in the world.

When we reach the top, his hand returns to its favourite spot and he guides me to the front door of the penthouse. It opens with a card Snarkly holds up to it.

The penthouse occupies the entire top floor of the building and has panoramic views, much superior to the lift. I guess that all the bimbos he brings up here are impressed with it and, just for a moment, I'm taken in by its magic too. And then I realise what I'm getting myself in for, what I've promised Snarkly by joining him up here.

"Drink?" Snarkly says, drifting over to a drinks cabinet—which reminds me of Brian's—where he removes a crystal decanter filled to the top with a colourless liquid: vodka or gin.

Since I've already broken my teetotalitarian streak, I might as well. "All right. Just a small one."

He pours the drinks and then brings mine over. He stands only a few inches from me as he sips on his, looking over me hungrily. "You don't drink much, do you?"

"Huh?"

He smiles. "Your cheeks, they're all blemished, not used to it."

I reach to touch my cheek and, as I do so, he takes hold of my hand, brushes the back of it with his thumb.

"Let me show you the bedroom," he says, then leads me by the hand through a pair of heavy wooden doors.

A king-sized bed stands in front of us. There's an enjoining ensuite which Snarkly waves his hand at. "Take a moment, if you like."

'Take a moment?' I wonder what that euphemism is driving at, whether he thinks I'm going stick in some sort diaphragm from the seventies. Everything about Snarkly speaks of a different decade, maybe a different century.

I close the door to the ensuite and peruse the options. There are female perfumes, creams and deodorants. When I inspect the shower I see that there's even a pink bottle of body gel, surely meant for a woman too. Now I understand that Snarkly has this whole act down to an art.

I stare at myself in the mirror, wondering what I'm doing here. If I wanted, if I really wanted, I could make an excuse and leave. It would be as simple as telling him I was on my period. He would understand, I'm certain. But I've come this far, and if I really want to get some more answers on what's going on then this is the perfect opportunity.

I squirt myself with some perfume and apply a touch of concealer. Then I take a deep breath, pull back the door and head out.

———

Snarkly's lying on top of me, breathing heavily. His breath smells fine, although I imagine that if I hadn't eaten the same, drunk the same as him, it would've been impossible to stand. I get no pleasure as he slides in and out of me, emitting little moans of pleasure, one of his hands clutching my breast, giving it a squeeze now and again. It's all over after about five minutes. Now I know what Elizabeth meant by 'sexually basic.'

He rolls off me and lights a cigarette. He puffs smoke into the air.

I watch it cloud up on the ceiling before disintegrating. "Can I have one?"

"Of course, my dear," he says, leaning over, exposing his firm buttocks, before lighting a fresh cigarette with his own and passing it to me. "Can't say it's fashionable to smoke nowadays."

"No," I say.

We lie there in silence, me trying to think of some way to broach the subject of Snarkly's private affairs, to get a grip on what it is that he's planning, what AA's so hopped up about. I tap ash into the tray located on my bedside table. "So did you pay for all this out of your politician's wages?"

He guffaws. "God no! Really doesn't pay as well as you'd think. No, no, this is all from old money. Father's estate he left me. Not exactly admirable, but it's the truth."

"You can't do anything about the situation you're born into."

"Quite right, I suppose."

It's funny, during the entire evening I've been preparing lies to feed him for when he asks the inevitable questions, what I do or where I live, but he's never asked me anything—only sticking to himself. Perhaps he just doesn't care about maintaining a pretence. I'm little more than a whore to him.

I suck up my pride and tell myself to play the role if I want the information. I draw my hand out from beneath the covers and run my fingernails through his wiry chest hair. "You don't have your own businesses?"

"Oh, odd pieces, here and there." He pauses, thinking, considering, then says, "There is one . . ." His words trail off and he makes no indication to continue.

I can hardly push this without blowing my cover. I have to keep playing this part.

A few minutes later he's snoring, his still-burning cigarette dangling from his fingers, twirling smoke up into the air.

I reach over him, remove his cigarette from his fingers and extinguish it in the ashtray before turning on my side to face the wall. The bed's comfortable and before long I find myself drifting away, making up for the previous sleepless night.

———

I wake to the sound of Snarkly speaking on his mobile. I crook open an eyelid to see that it's morning. Sunlight streams into the bedroom. Snarkly's showered and wearing a fresh suit. I close my eyes, hoping that he will just leave for his day's work, leave me to get changed in privacy. Hopefully I've done enough to convince him that I'm not a common thief—I'm fairly sure he's unaware that I'm a hired killer.

Snarkly gets off the phone, then places it down on his bedside table. He reaches to do up his tie. "That was my publicist. He's coming over for a morning meeting. You don't mind, do you?"

Chapter Fifteen

I YANK the sheet up off the bed, holding it up over my body to keep myself hidden from Snarkly.

"What is it? What's the matter?" he says.

I was acting on instinct and now I've made him suspicious. "I've just remember I've got to be somewhere."

"I can see that much. But, please, don't feel you have to rush out of here, take your time."

"Thanks," I say, fetching my bra and knickers from the floor, still wrapped in the sheet, "but I've really got to get going."

Snarkly shrugs then says, "I'll see you again, shall I?"

I break from my frenzy and study him, almost unable to believe the tone of voice he used to asked that question. He really does think I'm nothing more than just a dizzy whore. "Whatever suits you," I say, stumbling into the bathroom and clicking the door shut.

I'm dressed in my clothes from last night in less than five minutes —it must be a personal record. I slip out through the door of the ensuite, back into the bedroom. Snarkly has gone. I can hear him making another phone call in the sitting room. Maybe speaking to his wife.

I inch my way out of the bedroom, hoping not to make a sound but, before I manage to reach the front door, the latch within reach, Snarkly pivots and holds up a hand, telling me to wait. I count the seconds in my head as he finishes the call.

He covers the phone with his hand, crosses the room and speaks in a hushed tone. "If you wait I'll have the car brought round. It'll take you back home."

That would be an extremely bad idea. I know that the driver will take stock of my address and feed the information back to Snarkly. I wonder how close the relationship between Snarkly and Brian really is. It might well be that, as a matter of course, he gets all his lovers checked out. He already has my mobile number, maybe he's already run that. I can only hope that this aspect of the operation happens somewhere below Brian, that he doesn't do anything as low as running mobile phone numbers himself.

"No, really," I say, answering Snarkly's question. "I'll get a taxi. Hail one off the street."

"It's no trouble. It'll only be a minute or so."

"I have to go right now, I'm late as it is."

Snarkly shrugs. "I'm sure it'll take just as long to stop a taxi as to call up my car."

I move toward the door. "It's okay, I'll take the risk." I pause with my hand on the latch. "Thanks for dinner last night."

Snarkly grins. "Thank you for showing me the wonders of your body."

The combination of the wine, the situation and, most of all, Snarkly's revolting words almost cause me to vomit on his pinewood flooring. But, somehow, I hold it in and slink out the door before he tries to kiss me again.

I descend in the lift, hardly noticing the incredible view, urging it to hurry up, hoping that Brian is stuck in traffic or something. When I reach the reception, I dash through, giving the porter a quick word of greeting. He touches his cap and shoots me a knowing smile. I imagine that Brian has him all bought up too. No leaks get out of this building or I would've read about them online.

As I go out through the doors a car draws up. I notice Brian's profile in the backseat. I turn side on and walk in the opposite direction, along the pavement, heading away from the building. Someone calls out to me. I keep my head bowed. Turning round would mean more than professional suicide, it would mean actual death.

When I reach the corner of the street and prepare to cross, I do dare a look back over my shoulder. Brian's no longer in view, his car's gone too. I look upward to see Snarkly on his balcony, leaning over it, blowing a kiss to me. I blow one back, turn the corner then jump into the back of a cab sympathetically waiting on the curb.

———

I get a hot shower, change into my tracksuit and take up my standard position on the sofa, to watch the afternoon TV films. Lizzie curls up in my lap. As I lie there, my eyes blurring in and out of focus as the actors move about the screen, I think about my riches. I have money in the bank. Enough to keep me going, to do up my house, to help out with my children. And yet I know that I've damaged a part of myself.

Those faces, Elizabeth's, the target's, they come back to me, as if etched on the back of my eyelids. The target's daughter fighting with me wildly, like an animal. Is it worth going on when all I do is cause pain?

Julie tells me that whenever I have thoughts such as these that I'm to call her immediately, to schedule an emergency appointment. This feels like just one of those moments.

I dump Lizzie off my lap and she gives a small *meow* of protest.

I get into the kitchen, pick up the phone and make an appointment for a few hours' time. The secretary asks me all sorts of frantic questions, like if I've had any thoughts of suicide or harming myself in some way—of harming someone else. I tell her that I haven't, then go upstairs to dress.

———

Julie welcomes me at the door just like it's a normal day. But her smile betrays her. It seems painted on, as if she's trying to look through me, into my mind, to second guess what I'm thinking, to try and get a handle on my mental state.

I do my best to act normal, keep my hand steady as I shake hers. Then I take up my position on the sofa, opting not to lie down—I'm still feeling a little strange following the fish from last night.

"So, tell me," Julie says. "What's the problem?"

I tell her about last night, sleeping with Snarkly—leaving out the details, of course.

Most of all I want to tell her about the children's faces, from the night before last, having killed their father before their eyes. That soon after they were killed themselves. But I can't.

When I reach the end, Julie rocks back in her chair and considers me. She drums her fingers against her thigh. "So that's why you cancelled our appointment yesterday. You had a hot date."

"Yeah," I say. "Sorry about that."

Julie doesn't bat an eyelash—the flawless professional, I'm in envy. "And do you think this was self-destructive behaviour? Did you think you were doing yourself harm by sleeping with this man?"

"Like I said, he's rich and powerful. I don't know why I did it, why I went with him."

"It might be that it was just normal attraction. You shouldn't beat yourself up about following your urges."

I really wish I could fill in the rest. Not being able to tell her that I went with him because I want to get my hands dirty with what's going on in the background, work out the intricacies of my job, calculate the dangers I'm putting myself up against. I decide the only way to get close to allowing Julie to help is to feed her a few lies.

I curl my toes up in my shoes in anticipation, because if there's one thing I hate more than anything else in the world it's lying to Julie. "I got a new job."

"Oh?" she says, arching an eyebrow.

"The man, he's my boss."

"I see."

"And, I don't know, I got the impression that there was something going at work, people talking behind my back, not letting me in on the full picture. So I decided that the way to get to the bottom of it—to find out what was really going on—was to accept the advances my boss was making toward me."

Julie smiles faintly. She picks at a hangnail.

"Yeah, I know what you're thinking and, believe me, I'm right there with you. It was a stupid plan. But I've got myself neck-deep in it now. He wants to see me again. And the worst part is I hardly established anything from our . . . our meeting."

"You didn't manage to garner anything?"

"Well, he did start to speak about one matter in particular, but he stopped himself before saying anything."

Julie cocks her head to one side, thins her lips. "Don't you think there might be another way to get hold of the information? Couldn't you ask one of your fellow employees what's really going on?"

Now the lie's starting to break down, I need to get out of this sooner rather than later, before I tie myself up in knots. "No, I don't think they'll talk to me about it."

"You can always try."

I let the matter fall there and turn the subject of the conversation to the old reliable: my kids and estranged husband. Once we're through with the weekly developments, the session's at an end.

Julie wishes me well at the door, her eyes lingering on me longer than normal. I get the impression she's about the impart some kind of wisdom, but she backs off, returns to her steady smile. "See you next week," she says.

I walk through a series of market stalls, taking in the various fruits and vegetables. On instinct I stop and buy a couple of aubergines and some carrots. I don't really know what I've got in mind for them yet, but they just drew my eye.

As the seller bags up my purchases, my mobile rings in my handbag. I reach inside, draw it out and answer.

"Hello, Anna?"

It's AA. I reprimand myself for not having checked the caller ID. I need to get into the habit of doing it more often. "What is it?"

There's a pause, then, "Saw you at Tulips last night."

Chapter Sixteen

M Y BLOOD CHILLS AT AA'S WORDS.
The seller holds out a brown paper bag to me, prompting me for the cash. I hand it over and take the bag, stuffing it down into my handbag. I turn my attention back to the phone call.

AA scoffs. "Knew you were interested after all."

"I've got no idea what you're talking about."

"Come on, don't lie to me, Anna. I was there. I saw you leaving with Snarkly."

My nerves jangle at his name.

AA's voice drops a tone, in conspiracy. "So, find out anything interesting?"

I still have no idea to what extent I can trust AA. A little voice at the back of my mind keeps nagging away, warning me not to tell him anything—that he'll relay the information straight to Brian. But, if that were the case, then why would he even bother to call? Surely he would just tell Brian that I was too close to

Snarkly, and he would have me taken care of. Maybe AA has already told Brian what he's seen, in which case I might as well open up seeing as my goose is cooked in any case.

"Anna?"

"Yeah."

"Thought you'd hung up on me. What then? Tell me, the suspense is unbearable."

As I march along the street, making for the Underground station, I reel through the whole story, not leaving any detail unturned. I figure that the amount I know doesn't really matter. By being seen out and about with Snarkly I've crossed a line, made a mistake that can never be erased.

AA sucks in air after I've finished telling the story. "I had no idea."

"No idea about what?"

"That you were that sort of girl."

I approach the Underground station and I'm of a good mind to hang up on him but, instead, I stand to the side of an advertisement board selling deodorant and wait patiently. If I stay on the line long enough, I might be able to garner a clue as to when Brian's sending the assassin round to kill me.

"I mean," AA continues, "the sort of girl that jumps into bed on the first date."

I smirk. "I'm not usually, but it just seemed the way things were going." I look off over the crowd, looking to see if anyone's following me. I've got that horrible tingling feeling that someone is. "I watched the situation play out and acted accordingly."

"You must've got something thick and juicy, then?"

"No, not really."

"Anna, come on! Open up to me, I'm your friend."

"I've got to go. I'm about to get on the Tube."

"Anna, please—"

I cut the call and trot down the steps. When I glance back over my shoulder I see a man coming after me. I recognise him as the bodyguard, Snarkly's bodyguard. I quicken my pace, trying to lose myself in the crowd thronging through the turnstile and moving down toward the platforms.

I rush down the empty left-hand side of the escalator, snagging myself on tourists' backpacks and bum bags. I reach the bottom and resist the urge to look back, not wanting to give the bodyguard too much of a hint that I know he's there.

As I snake through the corridor, toward the platform, I catch sight of the carriage, the orange lights above the doors blinking and the synthesised voice warning. I break into a flat-out sprint and leap in through the closing doors, stumbling as I land.

An old woman shrieks and passengers leap back, as if I might be a terrorist or something.

The doors clatter shut and I peer out through the glass at the bodyguard, standing on the platform, eyes fixed on mine. I give him a vague smile, pick up an old newspaper stuck between a pair of seats and lean up against the handrail to read.

———

Lizzie's pawing at the door when I unlock it. She sticks her head out through the crack and sniffs at the air. I wonder whether she wants to go outside. I can't remember her going out once since she's been living with me. Something outside must've frightened her, caused her to take shelter in my back garden. I bring the door shut and she retrieves her nose from the space just in time.

Voicemail Bob informs me I've got a message: Arnold

thanking me for the money I've deposited, with an aside about it being much more than he expected.

I allow myself a cheeky grin, thinking that he'd better expect greater and greater payments from now on.

With nothing else to do, I return to my computer and attempt to find more information on Snarkly. As before, there's really nothing at all to find—nothing interesting in any case. Just as I've pulled up a page on his potted school history, I hear the doorbell go. I click through various windows, hoping that whoever it is they'll just go away on their own. But the ringing persists and I have to go and answer, to save my sanity. I leave my seat and pad over to the door.

When I open up there's a black kid standing there. He's about nine or ten years old, at least a year younger than Ben. He thrusts a poster at me.

I accept it and look it over.

"I lost my cat," he says.

I absorb the picture. The first time I cast my eyes over it I'm convinced that I've never seen the cat before. But, when I look again, I'm almost certain that it's Lizzie. I look at the kid.

He stares up at me, waiting for my answer.

I think this over. If the cat does belong to this boy then it asks the question what she was doing my back garden, clearly afraid. She must've been running away from somewhere. And, anyway, I'm not totally sure that Lizzie's the same cat as the one on the poster. It wouldn't be good to get the kid's hopes up.

I smile a touch, then make to close the door. "I'm sorry. I haven't seen it."

The kid bows his head.

I wonder how many houses he's visited today, searching.

"Thanks," he says, as he turns and heads out through my garden gate.

I'm still holding the poster when I return inside, gripping it in my hand, dampening it with sweat. I lay it down on the kitchen table and return to the sofa.

Now I've got that kid on my mind, his round pleading eyes. Maybe I should've at least offered to show him Lizzie, just to check whether or not it was his cat. There's a number on the poster if I change my mind.

I can't get comfortable on the sofa so I venture into the kitchen where I pick up my mobile and find myself selecting AA's number. Snarkly's bodyguard tried to follow me home, I have to speak to someone, know more about what I've got myself caught up in.

Chapter Seventeen

AA GETS ROUND in about half an hour flat. I don't know if he has a helicopter or what, but he always seem to arrive ridiculously quickly. Then I wonder how far away he was from my house, and the old worries kick in, that really he's working as a double agent, reporting to Brian exactly where I am, whether or not I'm to be trusted.

He enters wearing a white polo shirt and shorts, and carrying a tennis racket.

I don't ask where he's just come from mostly because I'm really not interested in whatever high-society sports club he's just left. I've had my taste of fancy with Snarkly and it wasn't all that entertaining.

We go to the sitting room, with a teapot between us.

AA eyes his mug. "Got anything stronger?"

"Not a drop of alcohol in the house, I'm afraid."

He look genuinely shocked. "How do you live?"

"A glass of water at a time."

He swills his tea round the mug, sniffs at it then takes a sip with his eyes screwed up, as if I might've slipped poison in there. He winces a little as he swallows then replaces the mug on the table. "So, what've you curtailed my tennis match for?"

"Snarkly's bodyguard was following me."

He raises an eyebrow. "Really?"

"Yes, he wanted to follow me home, but I saw him. What do I do to make it stop?"

"You caught him?" AA says. "What an amateur!"

"I suppose he's more used to being out in the open, making himself seen so that no one tries anything with Simon Snarkly."

AA interlocks his fingers and says, "Hmm."

"This is a problem," I say. "If he gets back here, has Mathewson Media run the address, I'm sure it'll be flagged up on the system—it'll get back to Brian, anyhow. And he won't blink before setting someone on my case."

"Don't you think I've got a vested interest?"

I consider his remark, and then notice AA's wry smile. "You'd seriously accept an offer from Brian to kill me?"

"Depends how much he's offering," AA says.

I throw a pillow at him.

He ducks and then, coolly, knocks back the rest of his tea. "Do you want my advice?"

"Go on."

"Take extra care from now on."

I roll my eyes. "Thanks, but—"

"Wait, there's more. You should continue to see Snarkly."

I open my mouth to speak again.

AA holds up his finger. "Uh-uh-uh, not while the man's speaking."

I look round for something else to throw, but there's only

Lizzie, and even someone as morally-bankrupt as I am hasn't quite reached the point of using cats as projectiles.

AA continues, "If you never see Snarkly again, that'll be suspicious. You can count on it that they suspect that you're a journalist, that you only went with him to get a story." He pauses dramatically. "And Brian will come after you. You can count on Snarkly wanting to tie up any loose ends, preserve his clean family image. Nothing like a kiss-and-tell to derail a campaign for Prime Minister."

"But if I—"

"Shh!" AA says. "But, if you keep on seeing Snarkly you can be sure that they'll be following you, probably just the bodyguard. And you'll know to be careful, to make sure you're never followed home."

"Yeah, and what's in it for you?"

AA grins, flashing me rows of white teeth. "You'll be on the inside track, getting information for me."

I sit forward on the sofa. "Why are you so interested in all this?"

He lays his hand over his heart. "What can I say? I'm a patriot. I believe in fighting for free speech and accountability among our political elite."

"Yeah, right."

AA's straight face gives way to a boyish smile. "Wherever there's yin, there's yang."

"Meaning that you've got a better offer from somewhere else to stop whatever it is that's happening?"

"You really are a perceptive girlie at times."

"I don't know about the perceptive part."

AA stretches his legs out before him, reaches to touch his toes. Although he really doesn't look like the most muscular of guys, I know that he keeps himself in relentless shape. You don't want to be too big in our line of work—makes the skulking round all the more difficult.

He straightens up and says, "What I've put together so far is that Snarkly is involved with some guys from the Middle East. They've got some money behind them and it involves getting Snarkly into the driver's seat, politically-speaking."

"And what do my hits have to do with it?"

"That girl, Elizabeth, she was involved in the negotiations. I think she believed she might be able to keep herself onside in the deal by getting romantically-involved with Snarkly. But Snarkly's not as stupid as he looks. He realised that he couldn't trust her, that, in fact, her relationship to him might well jeopardise the whole plan—getting him to be Prime Minister—by tarnishing his image. That's why he brought Brian on board, to help with that aspect of the plan. It's all very well setting Snarkly up within the Party, giving him a direct route to become leader, but it's another matter altogether to convince the media."

"And the other target?" I say.

"Backbencher. Had to be got out of the way. Initially part of the setup. Not only did he know about Snarkly's relationship with Elizabeth, he also had a knowledge of the inner workings of the plan. He was about to blow the whistle on Snarkly, go national." A smile crosses his lips. "He hadn't reckoned on Brian's stranglehold on the nation's media, though, and that Brian would be the first to receive a call from any editor planning on doing a story featuring one of his clients."

"You seem to have this all well-worked out. I don't understand why you need me at all. Who're you working for, really?"

Another grin. "Brian, of course."

"Yes, but there's someone else too. Who's paying you to untangle this whole Snarkly thing, this 'world domination?'"

"I couldn't possibly say. Client confidentiality."

"What if Brian finds out that you're working for someone else on the side, let alone that you're working against Snarkly, one of his clients?"

"With the sums of money floating about this, landing in my bank account every month, I'm willing to run that risk. If Snarkly's operation is large, then the opposition is just so—like I said, yin and yang."

I get up and go over to the window. The afternoon sky's grey and large raindrops splat against the windowpane. The street is quiet, that period just before everyone gets home from work.

"Sooner or later, Anna, you've got to decide which side you're on."

Chapter Eighteen

A FEW NIGHTS LATER, just after I've finished loading plates into my new dishwasher, I get a call from Snarkly. He wants to meet me across the city, in some—no doubt—expensive and exclusive club. I pause while I think it over, considering what AA's said. Which side am I on? I know that sense says I stick with Brian, if I want to live to see out the week. I should break it off with Snarkly, tell him I'm married, or moving away, something final. But, yet again, my curiosity gets the better of me and I agree to meet him in a couple of hours. He offers to send a car to fetch me, but I turn it down as politely as possible. He doesn't make a big deal out of it.

I scrutinise my dresses. Over the past few days I've been shopping, spending some of my blood money. It's funny, though, because when I look at the dresses I don't feel the least bit bad. Those two people I killed for the money were out to better themselves, wanting to get themselves a little slice of power. As I go for a strapless purple number I picked up yesterday, I wonder whether I'm any better.

———

I clamber out of the back of the cab hoping that Snarkly's not watching on from somewhere, because he'll realise how much of a debutante I really am—that I'm nothing of the sophisticated city girl he's probably pegged me as. That said, he still hasn't asked me anything about my background, what I do for a living. Long may it continue.

I do my best impression of a swagger as I approach the door to the club.

The doorman with his hands clasped at his waist purses his lips and waits for me to speak.

"I'm here to see Simon Snarkly."

He looks me over, speaks into a walkie-talkie clipped to his lapel, then waits for a burbled response. Apparently satisfied, he waves me inside.

Jazz music swamps the candlelit interior. For a moment I believe that it's coming from speakers, collected round the club but, when I go deeper inside, I notice the jazz band on the stage. The sunglasses-clad saxophone player is in the middle of a solo, stooped forward, back arched, fingers flapping the keys, sending warm notes oozing through the stale, smokeless air.

I look over to the bar, where several men in suits prop themselves up on stools, their hands clawed round bottles of imported lager. One of them glances over to me, raises his bottle.

I keep walking.

I'm about the go into the toilets, thinking that Snarkly hasn't yet arrived, when I'm confronted by his bald bodyguard. He stands before me, examining me from top to bottom, as if he were some kind of human x-ray machine, then he beckons me to follow.

As we're moving along I want to ask him why he was following me the other day, to taunt him a little but, before I get the chance, we've already arrived at the table, where Snarkly and another man, who looks Middle Eastern, sit with their heads turned in.

The bodyguard motions for me to sit, which I do.

Neither Snarkly or the Middle Eastern man turn to look at me, still enraptured in their own personal conversation. They keep their voices low and that, combined with the music, makes it impossible for me to overhear what they're saying.

About five minutes later, Snarkly breaks off the conversation and turns his attention to me. He looks me over. "My dear, you look ravishing tonight." He glances over the table to the Middle Eastern man. "Please excuse our manners. I'd like to have the pleasure of introducing you to Nadir."

Nadir nods his head at me, but his attention has clearly been drawn elsewhere in the room. At first I think that he's watching the jazz band and then I notice a large-breasted blonde seated alone beside the stage and come to the conclusion that she's the more likely object of his attention.

I'm about to say something, to ask where Snarkly and Nadir met, when Nadir excuses himself and leaves us alone.

Snarkly leans into me, conspiratorially. "Sorry about that, just a bit of business that's over spilled into the evening." He lays his hand on my inner thigh. "But we'll leave that for tomorrow, I believe both myself and Nadir shall be occupied with other matters for the remainder of the night."

I look over to see Nadir wearing a smooth smile. I lip read

him asking the blonde whether he can sit down with her. She accepts, motioning for him to take the seat beside her.

I wonder whether Nadir has a connection with the Middle Eastern man who ordered my hit on the target from the other night. AA mentioned the Middle East so it would only follow that both men are involved with Snarkly. I wish I'd arrived just a few minutes earlier, before that blonde had appeared, then I might've had a chance at eavesdropping on something important.

"How have you been, my dear?" Snarkly says, giving my thigh a squeeze.

"Oh, fine, this and that. Just the usual."

I notice the bodyguard, hovering close by. Perhaps Snarkly has got the impression that a would-be assassin is most-likely to strike in a place such as this, subdued by music and dimmed by the night.

I decide I have to up my game, to at least attempt to turn Snarkly onto what's going on with his plan. "I . . . I didn't want to interrupt anything with you and Nadir."

"Nonsense. Like I said, we can talk about it tomorrow. The problem with Nadir is that he likes to be absolutely sure, to have complete assurance before we act on anything."

I wonder what Snarkly and co might possibly have in store.

We both watch on as Nadir gets up from his chair, holds out his hand and guides the blonde from her seat. Together they cross the dance floor, pass the bar and disappear out the door.

Snarkly chuckles. "Those people and their prostitutes, they can never get enough."

"She's a prostitute?" I say, only half-sure over what's just happened.

Snarkly gives me a side-on glance. "You must know what goes on round here, in this place."

"No, not really."

"Never been here before?"

"No."

"Then it follows," he says, taking a swig of his drink.

I swallow back a biting response, knowing that if I want to get more information off him I have to be the bimbo.

We sit there, in the booth, for another hour or so, listening to the jazz band play. Snarkly orders another few drinks while I nurse the same weak vodka and tonic water. By the time he tells me it's time for us to leave, my drink is mostly melted ice.

I'm anticipating our night together with a sense of inevitability, rather than wonder or excitement. I know that if I can just get through it I can maybe get some more information on how I might go about saving my own neck, because I've come to the conclusion that AA is right—if I try and get away from Snarkly now he'll only have me taken care of, just like he took care of Elizabeth. And, once Brian knows what's happened, he'll ensure that he sends a team after me, not just one assassin alone. I'll be a dead girl twenty-four hours after the order's given.

Instead of going off out the way we came in, Snarkly directs me down another corridor. I suppose he's got some kind of secret exit, down a side-alley, his car waiting, engine running, so that there's simply no possibility of anyone recognising him outside. I have to admit I always thought gangsters lived this way, but I'm beginning to see that my perception of them isn't a thousand miles off what a modern politician is.

However, instead of heading through an emergency exit and into a side-alley, Snarkly releases me and a hand whips round from behind me and clasps over my mouth. I manage to twist enough to see the bodyguard bearing down on me, his eyes dull and expressionless, set on mine.

I try to fight back, jabbing my elbows into his body, but he dodges out the way. He's definitely had some kind of professional training—hell, for all I know he might be ex-Army too—why wouldn't Simon Snarkly pay to have the very best muscle?

He pulls me backward, into a side room and shoves me down onto a frumpy sofa with several white stains on it, what I suppose to be paint from the last refurbishment of the club.

I rock back on the sofa, feeling a little light-headed from what's just happened, having believed that I was just about to end up in the back of Snarkly's car, and be on my way back for some more 'basic' sex.

The bodyguard stands before me, hands clenched into fists.

Snarkly slides out of the shadows and rounds him.

The whole scene tickles me, like the evil genius flanked by his brainless hulk, and, with the tang of vodka in my mouth, sizzling my brain, I can't help but giggle.

Snarkly gives me a seedy smile. "Now, Hannah, or should I say, Anna? Want to tell me who you really are?"

Chapter Nineteen

MY GIGGLE DIES in my throat and I look back at him with something approximating fear. I wonder what's at stake here with my answer. Perhaps his bodyguard will just take care of me, right here and now, not even bother to get in touch with Brian—do it clean.

Snarkly's smile fades from his lips. "I had David here go through your handbag while we were in my city flat. All he found was your phone, unfortunately. But he did find out your full name: Anna Harris."

My heart squeezes and I anticipate an attack, for him to lash out at me, spittle to form on his lips as he screams at me, demanding to know the answers. But, instead, he rocks back on his heels, and considers me. I guess he hasn't got as far as he has in politics by being a hot-head. Looking at David, I'm sure that he's got other people who'll gladly get hot-headed for him.

"So, Anna, why did you lie to me?" Snarkly says.

I need to think quickly, come up with some satisfactory answer. "I . . . I don't know."

Snarkly shakes his head. "That's not good enough." He takes a step forward. "What is it? Are you a journalist?"

No, I'm an assassin, I want to tell him. I murdered your last lover. I came here because I wanted to find out what kind of dangers I was getting myself involved with, but now I'd be more than happy to butt out, to take the contracts on their face value.

"Speak to me, Anna. David here isn't just window-dressing, you know. He can pack a punch when he must."

Looking over the biceps almost bursting from the sleeves of David's suit, I don't doubt it.

"I'm no one," I say. "That day, when I met you at Yawley's, I stole a voucher from one of my friends, she works for a company in the city. I registered my name as Hannah when I arrived, I didn't want her to find out."

If Snarkly decides to do the research he'll find me in the system as Anna Harris, see that actually my name's cross-referenced with Mathewson Media. I have to trust in my scared-little-girl act to see me through here.

With an effort I squeeze out a tear.

Already, Snarkly's features are softening. But he's not completely convinced. "Why did you tell me your name was Hannah, then?"

"I wanted to be consistent. I know it sounds silly but I didn't want you to mention my name to someone and have them ask me questions, tell me I wasn't supposed to be there." I manage a sob. "I felt so out of place, worried that someone might throw me out at any second if they found out who I really was."

Snarkly nods to David, who retreats from the room. Snarkly stoops over me, rests a hand on my cheek and wipes my tears clean. When he speaks next the harshness is gone from his voice. "There, there, dear, I'm sorry. You know I have to be careful. It's all about image, really. I have to be careful."

As he combs his fingers through my hair I almost disregard the slight stickiness. I can hardly believe that he's actually falling for this routine, that I've managed to manipulate him. It sends a thrill through my body to think that I can influence someone so powerful, supposedly so 'careful' as he puts it. Then I recall Elizabeth and inject a dose of wariness into my thinking.

We remain there, me on the sofa, him with his arms round me, bringing me to his chest, mumbling that everything's okay. I wonder whether he does the same thing with his son and daughter when they've woken up after a thunderstorm—like the target would have done if I hadn't killed him.

Time passes and then Snarkly returns to an upright position. He brushes himself down, as if I'm dusty or something, then he says, "I'm sorry we can't be alone tonight. I have to get back home. I've a meeting early in the morning then more business later." He rolls back his sleeve to inspect his watch. "We'll have to make more plans this week." He grins. "I'm really quite smitten with you."

I force myself to take that as a compliment.

"Let me drive you back home."

I think over the situation, try to get to grips with what's just gone on here. The way he was treating me, touching me, I'm certain that he was being sincere. But can I really be sure? He's a politician first and foremost after all—a professional liar.

However, for my routine to have been a success I need to keep playing the innocent card, to accept his kindness and allow him to put his arm round my shoulder. And if I've truly done my job right, then he'll have no further suspicions. In fact, if I have him drive me home then he'll have seen where I live, that I'm no threat to him, and I'll no longer have to fear his bodyguard, David, following me through crowds.

Managing to let loose a fresh burst of tears, I nod, adding a lip quiver for good measure.

"Come on, then," he says, helping me to my feet.

———

I'm already regretting my decision as I ride back in his car. But I've given him my address now. There's no turning back, short of opening the door and leaping out of a moving car. There's a red light which shines through the backseat gloom, indicating that the back doors are locked behind the driver's partition. That makes me wonder whether they're taking me home at all.

My fears are eased as we draw into my neighbourhood. I watch Snarkly's expression turn from one of calm indifference to smug observance. He literally looks down his nose at the multi-cultural shop fronts: the Chinese takeaways, Middle Eastern supermarkets, the South American salsa clubs. When he turns in his seat, his suit groans against the leather. "You live here?"

I turn my attention to my own window, watching a group of black teenagers, with their hoods drawn up over their faces, swaggering their way along the pavement. "I told you I was nobody."

He reaches over, actually pinches my cheek. "Don't worry, we all started somewhere."

If we were anywhere else, under any other context, then I would slap him and smash the window for good measure. As it is, though, I smoulder inside, while giving him a hapless smile. "I won't ask you in for a cup of coffee, then."

He seems to miss my vague recoil, still absorbed in looking out at the street.

I wonder if he's thinking to himself that someday all this will be his, warts and all.

The car purrs down my cul-de-sac, rolling slowly as the unseen driver counts down the house numbers. Finally, we arrive outside my house and the car stops.

Snarkly casts his eye over my home, devouring it. He taps on his door, which I take to mean, judging by David rounding the car, that he wants it to open.

David lets Snarkly out before arriving outside my door and letting me out.

I step out into the night air, onto the quiet street. Only the sound of televisions and a few shouts in the distance break the silence.

Snarkly swivels, does a full three sixty, taking in the whole street.

David continues to stare at my house, perhaps burning the number into his mind for future reference.

For a horrible moment I think that Snarkly *is* going to ask to come into my house, and I'm not sure how I would react to such a request. It feels like it would be a step too far to allow him to invade my own personal space—the last refuge I have against the wide world.

Instead, though, he leans forward and pecks me on the lips. "We'll speak soon, Anna," he says, then ducks back into his car.

David stands in the road a moment longer, looks over at me —perhaps considering that he could've killed me by now, taken me out of the equation—then he gets back into the passenger seat, beside the driver.

Snarkly rolls down the window and waves goodbye. As the

car proceeds to the end of my cul-de-sac, I watch the window wind back up in record time. The engine roars as it speeds off round the corner and away.

I bet Snarkly could just feel the figures rolling off his net worth as he spent time in this place. He'll get back home, pour himself a large drink and think about how he's earned it after having to venture into this slum.

The engine fades into the night, mingling with all the other noises.

———

I roll over in the middle of the night, not having slept, and check the clock beside my bed. It's just gone three in the morning. I can't sleep. No matter how much I try, I can't shake the feeling that, right now, Snarkly is sending someone out to kill me, that he's decided he can have me put down quickly and easily—cut his losses.

I rummage through my wardrobe and withdraw my knife from the box. I unsheathe it and bring it over to the bed. Then I pick up Lizzie, tucking her under the duvet with me, purring her head off. Still holding the knife tight beneath my pillow, I close my eyes and hope for daylight to come soon.

Chapter Twenty

BRIAN'S ALREADY HAD SEVERAL WHISKIES by the time I get to his office. I can tell because he's slurring his words, and I've almost never heard him slur his words, only once at a Christmas party he demanded I attend almost a year ago—and even then it was around three or four in the morning before he started to show the signs.

I'm not quite sure why he's asked me here. To be honest I'm quite glad that he's half-cut, because I'd rather not have to come up with some reason for being drowsy, the dark bags that I'm sure I haven't completely plastered with concealer.

He stands over at the window, gazing downward, considering his empire. He brings the half-full glass to his lips and drinks it down in a single gulp. Then, all of a sudden, he lashes he arm forward and tosses the glass toward me.

I duck just in time, to hear it whistle over my head.

It smashes into the wall into a thousand fragments which tinkle dully as they fall to the wooden floor.

He stands there, staring at me, his shoulders rising and falling rapidly with his hard-drawn breaths.

When my heart regains something like a normal rhythm, I say, "What's wrong?"

He shakes his head, massages his temples with his fingers. "Oh, it's not you, Anna. It's this whole . . . thing. Sometimes I just wonder whether it's all worth it, if there's any point in me carrying on with this farce."

Although I've never experienced a temper tantrum of this proportion from Brian before, I know from instinct that right now isn't the best time to throw in my two cents. So I just expend my efforts on catching my breath and trying to ignore the tiny pieces of glass about my feet.

Brian picks up the phone on his desk. "Send in a cleaner, would you, Candy?"

The way he delivers the words is frosty, rough and direct. I wonder whether he's had some kind of knockback in his approaches toward Candy, if she's somehow managed to miss the whole reason lying behind her appointment.

Brian replaces the phone, clears his throat then looks at me. "You need a new gun, don't you?"

I'm a little taken aback because usually he scolds me for being too explicit about the nature of my job in his office.

"Well, do you?" he says, his look and tone hardening.

"Yes."

He nods to himself, licks his lips. "I'll get AA to sort one out for you."

The mention of AA, and the confidences which have passed between us—unaware to Brian—make me feel itchy and sly. I don't like having to hide things. But sometimes it's the only choice.

There's a knock at the door. Brian grunts for them to enter. A cleaner steps inside. She's in her sixties, dressed in a light blue apron and carries a dirty white bucket—that must be the first dirty thing I've ever seen in the offices of Mathewson Media.

While the cleaner brushes up the mess, Brian summons me over to him, indicates for me to sit on the sofa. Once I've sat down, he joins me. The cleaner works on in the background as he draws a deep breath and says, "I've decided you need to know more about what's going on."

My nerves tingle a little.

"The client," he says, eyes wandering over the cleaner before snapping back to me, "it's Simon Snarkly."

I try to hide the tweak in my gut. "Erm, who?"

Brian flaps his hand. "He's a politician. Education Secretary."

"Ah."

"He's absolutely loaded, I'm charging him through the nose by the hour to keep the facts out of the papers. He's planning on running for Prime Minister, that is, his foot's already in the door. The only thing standing in his way is his taste for women." He wipes a stray fleck of whisky from his chin. "Women other than his wife."

Although I feel like I'm already three steps ahead of Brian, thanks to AA, I don't want to give any indication. I need to run the same act that's served me so well with Snarkly thus far. "But what about the Middle Eastern gentleman, on the phone?"

"Yes," he says, with a fleeting smile, "the less said about that the better."

If only I can drew a little more out of Brian, get him to spill the deep details of Snarkly's plans then it would negate the need to pump Snarkly for information. "Are they . . . are they business partners, or something?"

Brian frowns. "Whatever gives you that idea?"

Too direct. "I mean, what's his connection to Snarkly?"

"I really couldn't say."

A flash of anger passes through me. "What do you mean you can't say? You drag me into the office, then you tell me you're going to let me in on what's really going on. And now, after telling me that Snarkly plans to run for Prime Minister, you clam up about the shadier side of things, just when my interest's piqued."

I notice the cleaning woman watching us from the other side of the room. When she catches my eye, she returns to her work, finishing up, brushing the pieces of glass into her bucket then leaving.

Brian looks stern, and I'm worried that he's going to snatch up the closest blunt object and beat me to death with it. But, just at the last moment, his whole face cracks. He lets loose a chuckle which becomes a thundering, drunken roar. He slaps me on the knee.

The slap stings a little, but I play along, smiling with him.

"You're perfectly right, Anna. I'm not acting at all rationally, am I?"

I continue watching him, knowing that the tension of our meeting hasn't quite broken. I wonder whether something's gone wrong with Snarkly's plan. It must be something enormous, nothing less would ruffle Brian's feathers.

Brian shakes his head, crying with laughter, as he crosses the room, going back over to his drinks cabinet, where he withdraws the decanter of whisky and pours himself another drink.

"Brian?"

He glances up me, laughter lines still wrinkling the skin round his eyes.

"I think you've had enough."

He replaces the decanter in the cabinet, then picks up his glass. I see that his hands are shaking, and he's filled the glass so full that whisky spills down the sides, splatters in puddles on the floor. He arrives back at my side, cheeks flushed and pupils dilated. He places the glass down on the table between us, looks me firm between the eyes and says, "Don't you ever tell me that I've had enough.

———

Following my baffling meeting with Brian, I take the Tube to Arnold and the kids' house. Remembering that I'm supposed to call ahead, I whip out my phone and ring Arnold's mobile. There's no answer. Although I know, technically, I should go back home, I feel a little on edge, not having totally shaken the fear that Snarkly is really onto me—that there might be someone there waiting to kill me.

If there's one thing I've garnered from my meeting with Brian it's that he has no idea that anything's going on between me and Snarkly. He seems to have his head full of other preoccupations, trying to keep Snarkly's profile on track.

When I knock on the door Kate answers.

Chapter Twenty-One

MY BREATH FLUTTERS IN MY THROAT. Somehow, with everything else going on, I'd forgotten all about her.

Kate smiles at me. As before her hair is a beautifully-sleek ebony. Her eyes a pair of supernovas. I'm a little surprised—and a touch proud—that Arnold's managed to get his hands on someone like her. "You're Annie, aren't you?" she says.

"Anna," I say.

"Yes, I think we just missed on another the other day. You were on your way out."

A hint of embarrassment strikes me. Why did I act like such a little girl, running away that day? I manage to smile back at her. "Sorry about that, I was in a hurry." I look beyond here, into the house. "Are Josie and Ben around?"

"They've just gone to the shop with Arnold." She steps back into the house. "Please, come in, we can have a cup of tea."

It's strange following Kate through Arnold and the kids'

house, as if she were an imposter pretending that she lived there. All the familiar photos stare at me from the walls. The smells are the same, that unmistakable mingled odour of my ex-husband and two kids.

We get to the kitchen and I sit down, feeling equally awkward.

As Kate puts on the kettle and removes some cups from the cupboards, she says, "You know your kids talk about you all the time."

Not believing her, I say, "Really?"

"To be honest, I find it quite intimidating. Ben's always telling me that you were a soldier, in the Army. Before I met you I kind of built up this image of a big, butch woman." She laughs nervously. "I thought you might come round one day, all guns blazing, demanding to know who I was."

I smile weakly. "Yeah."

She brings over the tea and sits down in the chair opposite. "So what do you do, exactly? Arnold told me you left the Army."

"Oh, I've been out a while now."

She continues to beam at me, wanting me to follow up on my current situation.

"I've been a little stuck between jobs recently. But I just landed an opportunity working security."

"Security?" she says with a pout. "What does that involve?"

I have the urge to ask her what she believes her role is in Arnold and the kids' lives, but I hold back, telling myself to be a good girl—to play nice. "It's not as interesting as it sounds. No action and adventure. Just lots of standing round, watching over warehouses at night, you know, that sort of thing." And then I realise, to be polite, I should be asking reciprocal questions. "And what do you do?"

She clasps her mug in her hands, savouring the warmth, then says, "I'm a solicitor."

I manage to make agreeable noises, but, I've built up something of a hatred for the occupation following the divorce proceedings. It seemed that at every step, no matter how helpful me and Arnold were to them, they wanted to turn the knife, to get to the bottom of everything—rake up our personal history and poke through it, like technicians examining faecal samples in a laboratory.

"The family business," she says, still smiling, bringing the mug up to her lips.

"How did you and Arnold meet?"

"Speed dating, that old romantic avenue."

Again, Arnold surprises me. I have to give him credit, when he sets his mind on something—a new and improved mother for his children—he takes no prisoners.

"Yes, it was so refreshing to find someone else out there who wasn't a lawyer—that's all the speed dating circle seems to comprise of these days. So, when Arnold mentioned he was a plumber, owned his own business, I snapped him up."

I bet you did, I think, scowling over the rim of my mug.

There's a raking of a key at the door, then a *squeak* of hinges. I hear the footsteps stamp on the hall carpet. Kate tilts her head back, exposing her milky-white throat. It would take no effort at all to slice through it, to draw blood.

"Dear?" Kate says.

Arnold murmurs something in the hall.

I hear feet stomping up the staircase: Josie and Ben going off to their rooms.

Arnold enters the kitchen, meets Kate's eye, then, slowly, absorbs the fact that I'm there too. A look of confusion crosses his face and then a smile forms at the corner of his mouth. "You're not ripping each other apart."

Kate hops up from her seat. She's a good half a foot smaller than me, that perfect, dainty size that men love—think they can manipulate. She has to stand on tiptoes to give Arnold a peck on the lips. When she draws back, she says, "We've been getting to know one another."

"That's"—Arnold searches for the word—"wonderful."

I get up, thinking that I can sneak off upstairs, say hi to the kids then beat a hasty retreat. It's funny, the idea that someone might be waiting for me back home—wanting to kill me—pales in comparison with the awkwardness of sharing the same room as my ex-husband and his new lover.

"Actually, Annie," he says, "there's something I wanted to speak to you about."

I linger in the doorway, not bothering to correct the name this time. "What is it?"

"It's Josie."

My blood curdles in my veins.

"Nothing really drastic, it's just that there's been some bother at school with her and another girl, calling each other names."

I recall my conversation with Josie, her telling me about Francesca.

"They called us into school to talk about it with the head teacher. It seems like it's got a little out of hand, hair-pulling, pinching, that sort of thing."

I try to stay calm but this is my girl involved. When I speak, my icy tone turns both Arnold and Kate's expressions to discomfort. "*Us?*"

"Yes," Arnold says, putting his arm round Kate's shoulder. "We both went in to talk with the teacher."

"Why didn't you call me?"

"I thought you might be busy, with the new job and everything."

Kate's eyes sparkle. I have no idea how she manages to do that on demand. "Didn't want to bother you."

I snap onto Kate. "It wouldn't have been any bother. Josie is my daughter!"

"Annie," Arnold says, "you're shouting."

Overhead I can hear the sound of feet on the landing, Josie and Ben coming to look round the banister. Through my fury I can see that I'm the unreasonable one. But it's like I'm swept up by a tide that I have no control over. It washes over me, stealing all rational thought.

Before I can get a hold of myself, I lurch forward and snatch hold of Kate's blouse, my fingers clawing through the button-holes, getting a hefty grip. I throw her against the wall.

She bounces off, limbs sprawling like a ragdoll, and lands in a heap, clutching her wrist.

Arnold gapes at me.

I shoot Kate a final look then turn on my heel and rush from the house, not even looking back over my shoulder to my kids at the top of the stairs, terrified at what's unfolding. Only when I reach the Tube station, trot down the stairs does the seriousness of what I've done dawn on me.

———

As I leave the Underground station, emerge back into the daylight of my own neighbourhood, I see that I've got two missed calls from Brian. A text message comes through and I read it: CALL AA.

Chapter Twenty-Two

A A CLUCKS HIS TONGUE on the other end of the line. "Can you stop that?" I say. "It's giving me a headache."

"What's the matter? Time of the month?"

I fume in silence.

"Brian wants us to work together on the next one. Says it's a two-person job."

"You mean he wants you to hold my hand so I don't go and screw everything up again?"

AA laughs. "Like I told you, he planned that all along. He wanted a mess. He set you up for a mess. Really, believe me, it had nothing to do with you."

"Why don't you keep your little conspiracy theories to yourself from now on?"

"Christ, you really are spiky today."

"Just tell me where and when."

He tells me he's going to come over to mine. Since we're not meeting till evening, I shovel up Lizzie and we go off upstairs for a well-deserved nap. I've only been sleeping for about half an hour before my phone buzzes again. Brain feeling like putty, I answer it. "Hello?"

"Annie?"

It's Arnold. My stomach sinks.

"I want to speak about what happened today."

Since I really have nothing to say, no rational defence, I just let him speak.

"We've decided not to contact the police, nothing like that. We know that it was an emotionally-charged moment and we have no conception of how you must feel right now, about the new relationship, the new situation."

My minds spinning with all those we's. Anyone might think they'd melded themselves together into an amorphous hunk of human skin.

"But," Arnold says, giving the word space to ring itself out, "we do believe that it would be better for you to call ahead in future, tell us in advance if you're coming. You know, like we agreed?"

I rub the pits of my eyes.

"Annie?"

"Yeah, yes, sorry that's no problem. I promise to call from now on."

"Great, that's great, Annie."

Why does he have to be so reasonable all the time? If this had been me, I'd been the one with the kids, and me the one with the affronted new partner, I would've wasted no time in calling the police. Then again, I guess Arnold's just an all-round better person than I am. "How's Kate's wrist?"

"It should be okay, she's got ice on it. Be a nasty bruise in the morning."

I ponder whether I should send her some flowers in the morning, to apologise. What does she think about the butch Army mother now?

———

AA gets to my house just after dark. I've cooked up a lasagne for him, not having had anything else to do during the day. Today he's wearing a long grey coat with a waistcoat underneath, an actual bowtie sprouting from his collar. And it looks like some-one's combed extra grease through his hair.

"What's all this fuss for?" I say.

"Don't know why you're laughing. You're going to have to get as dressed up as me."

"Why? Where are we going?"

"Party fundraiser."

"In honour of who?"

AA breaks out into a smile. He rests his hand on my shoulder. "Just Simon Snarkly."

Upstairs AA gives me some fashion advice. He nods or shakes his head depending. I can't believe it's taking me so long to pick out an outfit, but I'm completely panicked that Snarkly will recognise me there. It would make for something of an uncom-fortable showdown with his wife, that's for sure. And I still really don't know where I stand with him, if he's aiming to have me taken out of the picture as soon as possible, or if he's realised that I'm just not worth the hassle. Either way, I'm offended.

Finally, I pick out a purple-blue dress with a white sash. He hasn't seen me in this one before. Under AA's guidance, I slap on some makeup, finding his winces and sucking of teeth distracting. Nothing like a backseat makeup artist.

We descend to the kitchen, fully-dressed, looking like an economically-mobile couple, as per the requirements of the hit. AA is Dwayne Hilsbury for the evening, while I'm his wife, Esmeralda. Whoever picked out the names certainly had a broad sense of humour.

In around an hour, a posh car swoops up to the curb outside the house, honks its horn.

I say goodbye to Lizzie, leaving her an extra-large portion of cat food, before heading out the door, arm-in-arm with AA, who insists we have to keep up the front from now on.

In the back of the car, AA produces a brown envelope from the inside pocket of his jacket. He shows me the details: a map and a photograph of the venue, a Victorian mansion. On the map an area marked 'ballroom' is where the event's taking place, while a red circle indicates the target's bedroom.

Since security in and out of the mansion is going to be tight, the idea is to get inside and stay there. When we arrive, we have to blend into the crowd and wait out the evening, before sneaking up through to the bedrooms to take out the target.

We have no weapons on us, as AA points out that there'll be a full suite of security to go through before we can enter the mansion. One of AA's associates is already inside the mansion, working undercover as one of the kitchen staff, and he's taped a silenced pistol to the inside of a cistern in the ladies' toilets. At least Brian's still trusts me to handle weapons, is willing to give me another chance at not messing something up.

AA tells me a few jokes, and I laugh. I know that he's trying to get me to lighten up, to blow away any nerves I might have—

baggage I might be dragging along behind me following my last, disastrous hit. Those sleeping children still haunt my dreams.

However, when he hands over the last part of the brief, the photograph of the target, my heart lodges in my throat and a creeping nausea overwhelms me.

It's Nadir, the Middle Eastern man I met in the jazz club with Snarkly.

Chapter Twenty-Three

"WHAT'S WRONG?" AA says, looking at me sidelong.

Trying to erase the image of Nadir's face from my mind, to tell myself that I should have had no connection to the target, let alone have had a drink with him, have seen him go off with a prostitute.

I tell AA what the problem is.

He looks at me seriously. "Are you going to be able to get past it?"

I search my mind, looking for an honest answer. I have no emotional reaction to the target, he's no more than a fleeting acquaintance. "It'll be fine," I say.

AA grins. "So it looks like Snarkly's taking care of all the rough edges now, taking out all the middlemen."

"What do you mean 'middlemen?'"

"This guy," AA says, "he's part of Snarkly's group, the business looking to take advantage once Snarkly gets himself into the Prime Minister's seat."

I think back to the elderly Middle Eastern gentleman I spoke to on the video call, in Brian's office. When I saw Nadir in the club I didn't think twice about it, but, sitting here, the photograph in my hand, with time to think, I observe the similarity. It's striking. "This is the son of the man who ordered my last hit."

AA squints at the photograph. "Really? You're sure?"

"Positive."

————

The signpost outside the mansion reads, 'Everly Estate: Golf Club and Countryside Retreat.' It's all done up in a curly font, as if it adds an element of style. The way they've refurbished the Victorian mansion, washed large sections of it in white, reminds me of a seventy-old woman with a facelift.

Just as the brief details, security is tight. The minute we roll up into the drive, just outside a set of steps which leads up to the reception hall, a pair of burly men—whose muscles are almost bursting from their suits—lead us off to the side where they check through everything: our pockets, my handbag, our shoes.

When I think the search is over, a female member of the security team emerges. She's about a foot shorter than me, wearing sunglasses, and doesn't smile as she gestures for me to turn round as she pats my body for any concealed items. She barely grunts after she's finished, and I take it as my cue to move on, head up the stairs, my arm through AA's once again.

Inside the mansion a string quartet plays the reception hall. The air is ripe with cologne and perfume. There's a queue of people: women in frocks, men in tuxedoes. We join them, shuffling our way forward to where a bespectacled event organiser relieves the arrivals of their invitations and takes their names down on a written register.

When we arrive at the front of the queue, we give our false names. The event organiser doesn't bat an eyelash as he takes our invitations—which I suppose are genuine, in that Snarkly will have had to have given them over to Brian for the purpose of us getting in. Snarkly wouldn't have had any knowledge of who the assassins were, though.

We move with the crowd. On our way toward the ballroom we're offered hors d'oeuvres by waiters bearing silver trays. I accept a little salmon pastry, although I'm still full from the lasagne I cooked earlier. Another waiter, further along, offers us a glass of champagne each. I consider turning it down, but, believing it might look suspicious seeing as everyone else takes one, I accept.

The ballroom's already filling up as we follow the crowd inside. It's a high-ceilinged room with a platform erected over by the windows, which look out on the gardens. Oil paintings hang from every wall—Renaissance men, lords or dukes, or whatever, either wearing ridiculous wigs and standing with canes or mounted on horses, galloping along to slaughter foxes. I suppose I never really got the upper class.

There are several circles of people, most of them with grey hair. I consider myself and AA to be amongst the youngest in the building. Then again, this is a Conventionals meeting. I try to look over the heads to pick out Snarkly, but I can't seem to find him anywhere. Giving up for the time being, I lean into AA. "When shall I pick up the gun?"

AA takes a sip of champagne, feigns a throaty laugh, then drops his voice, becoming serious once more. "Better to get it now, before the champagne kicks in on all these old bladders."

He knocks back the rest of his champagne, flicks his glass in the direction of a waiter. "I'll wait for you here."

I nod in reply and make my way through the crowd, excusing myself and smiling as I go. I notice quite a few looks from the older boys among them, taking their chance while their wives are looking the other way.

The toilets are empty. There's none of that clinical stench of bleach which accompanies all normal toilets, instead this one smells of lavender and, most likely, sugar and spice. I count the stalls, picking out the third from the left, then I enter.

I shut the door and lock it. I close the lid of the toilet bowl and clasp my fingers round the edge of the cistern lid. I pull it off gently, not wanting to risk it dropping from my grip, clattering onto the tiles or, worse, smashing into pieces. That would raise questions, and I'm certain security has eyes and ears all over the place, at the very least a microphone in the ladies' toilets.

I feel inside the cistern and my fingers brush the hard grip of the pistol. I reach round it, feeling for the tape. It takes me a moment or two to peel it back then, feeling the gun loosen from its holding, I take the grip in my hand and tug. The gun leaves its binding behind and I hold it in front of me, gaze at it as if this is the first time I've ever held one.

I check the magazine. It's fully-loaded, all ready to go. I notice that the safety's been left off. I emit a small sigh, worried about AA's choice of confidants. I suppose it's some kid he's taken under his wing, doesn't really know what he's doing—no doubt blond and bony, just as AA likes them.

On the other side of the cistern my hands come across the silencer. I peel that off too.

The door to the ladies' toilets swings open. I hear the clack of heels on the tiles as the woman approaches the mirror, sets her makeup bag down beside the sink.

I flush the toilet then replace the cistern as it's refilling itself. I slip the pistol and silencer into my handbag. They both just about fit inside and I unlatch the door and step outside.

The woman catches my eye, gives me a smile as she applies her lipstick. "You weren't fiddling around with the toilet in there, were you, dear? You'll chip your nail varnish. Should've shouted and I would've got a member of the maintenance staff to see to it."

My heart raps against my ribcage and for a few moments I'm rendered mute, because this woman, standing at the mirror, is Victoria Snarkly.

Chapter Twenty-Four

"YOU LOOK LIKE YOU'VE seen a ghost, dear," Victoria Snarkly, Simon Snarkly's wife, says. "Are you feeling quite well?"

"Uh, yes, thank you, I'm fine."

Victoria Snarkly must be in her early forties. She has strawberry blond hair and wears heavy green eye shadow with thick mascara. Her cheeks are thoroughly rouged and she's in the process of applying a second or third coat of bright red lipstick.

She clicks her lipstick shut and replaces it in her makeup bag. She smacks her lips together and then bites down on a tissue to remove the excess.

I move toward the door.

"Not going to wash your hands?"

I freeze, turn back, realise that she's joking with me, that she wants to talk. I try to create an excuse, but nothing will come. All I can envision is her husband on top of me, puffing and panting away. I manage a nervous smile. I return to the sink, run the hot tap and squirt some soap onto my hands. "Almost forgot."

"Bit nervous, are you?"

"Just a little."

Victoria levers her eye wide, searching for any rogue clumps of mascara. "Nothing to worry about. Best plan is to keep your husband close." She eyes me steadily. "You do have a husband?"

"Oh, yes, of course."

"Much better that way, gives you a sturdy physical line of defence against the subtler offenders. You'll have to keep an eye out for the more spirited ones, though."

I step over to the dryer and hold my hands beneath it. "I'll bear that in mind."

Over the noise of the hot air blowing, she still manages to make herself heard. "And for my husband in particular, especially after a few drinks."

I linger at the door, not sure whether or not she's testing the water, trying to see how I react. Of course she knows that Snarkly goes round with other women behind her back—how could she not, considering his arriving home late or, in some cases, not at all.

I glance back over my shoulder, but she's already busying herself with concealer, dabbing at her nose. Without another word, I slip out of the toilets, feeling the hard form of the gun through the flimsy fabric of my handbag.

———

When I pick AA out of the crowd, he's not where he was before —typical—he's speaking with an older man who I guess to be in his sixties or seventies. AA has assumed an expression with his nose hitched up and eyes wide, most likely an approximation of how he believes posh people act. In any case, the old man seems to be buying the routine, judging by his heaving laughter and, every so often, the stamp of his foot.

I sidle up to where they stand talking and try not to break the flow of their conversation. Inevitably, however, the old man cuts off whatever story he's telling AA and peers over at me. "Well, hello there, my dear." He glances at AA. "So this must be your darling wife."

"My better half, yes," AA says, reaching for my hand.

I take it and draw myself into their circle.

The old man says, "Dwayne here was just telling me that the golf course here is simply spectacular." He jabs AA in the ribs. "We must play one of these days, you know. You'd be surprised, I'm sure I can teach you a few new tricks."

"We must," AA says, taking another swig of his champagne.

I wonder how many he's had now. I notice that my glass is no longer around, so I presume he's drunk that too. Does he really think he's just here for a laugh? To keep an eye on me, make me feel better about myself? I can't afford for him to get drunk.

Through the crowd of heads I pick out Brian's face.

My pulse hammers in my wrists and it feels like my handbag, the gun inside, is throbbing. Of course he's here. He is Snarkly's publicist after all. I look away, not wanting to draw attention to ourselves, but he's already approaching us, moving through the crowd.

Brian gives me a wink. "Hello, there, Esmeralda, fancy seeing you here!"

"Yes," I say, eyeing the older man and AA, who look on expectantly. "I never miss a good booze up in a country mansion."

"Hear, hear," the older man says, belly jiggling beneath his cummerbund.

I judge Brian, trying to work out how he is now. He looks much better than he did this afternoon. His face seems slimmer, his gestures more controlled—no, calculated. He holds forth, tells a few jokes, setting AA and the older man off laughing, then he makes his excuses to leave. Before he goes back, to join the rest of the crowd, he turns his back on AA and the older man—who've both continued their golfing conversation—and says, "Good luck, Anna. I know I can count on you."

I blush a touch.

A waiter with a tray full of champagne passes me by and I pluck one of the glasses off and take a sip. The bubbles burst in my mouth and the sour taste seeps into my tongue. Tonight I'm determined that everything's going to plan.

————

I suppress the urge to yawn at least a hundred times before the event organiser calls attention to everyone in the hall. Up on the stage, standing at the microphone, he seems much weedier, more unsubstantial than he was welcoming guests. His voice too is stuck in a nasal whine. I wonder whether this is some ploy of Brian's—to have an awful public speaker on just before Snarkly, to make the main act look even better. I wouldn't put it past him.

And then the crowd parts and Snarkly makes his way through the crowd. Like everyone else, he's wearing a tuxedo, but he's also got the addition of a violet cummerbund and a violet flower pinned to his lapel. Whoever outfitted him for tonight's event is really pasting the Party colours to the mast.

I duck closer to AA, not wanting Snarkly to pick out my face.

I turn side on so that my face is only in profile, only allowing myself little side glances as Snarkly rises to his place at the microphone.

There are a pair of electronic *thuds* and then Snarkly's voice pipes clean and smooth around the ballroom. "Friends, ladies and gentlemen. Thank you for coming here tonight, for being here with us tonight. First and foremost I must thank the caters for the spectacular job they've done."

A round of polite applause.

Snarkly continues, "And of course thanks to my wonderful wife who has overseen the planning for this event." He whips the microphone off its stand and holds it to his chest, like an embarrassing uncle's impression of Elvis Presley, and crouches down, eyes locked on Victoria Snarkly. He gestures toward her. "My wife, everybody!"

Victoria waves shyly.

Snarkly straightens up and replaces the microphone on its stand. "And I must thank you for all being here at such an historic event. 'An historic event,' I hear you all ask. That's correct. Because tonight is the night that I announce my intention to run for leader of the Party!"

Cheers burst from the crowd.

I hear the older man shouting out, "Hear, hear!" his arms waving, splashing champagne all over a woman standing behind him, who looks on disapprovingly.

Snarkly goes on to elaborate on the plans he's got for the country, how he's going to change it all, top-to-bottom. I reckon he makes just about all the same promises that any pretender to the Prime Minister's job is obliged to make and, equally, obliged to break once they arrive there. I wonder if anyone else here, at this fundraiser, realises that Snarkly is more than just an overgrown schoolboy, that he really does have some elaborate plans.

He wraps up and then the entire ballroom goes ballistic, as ballistic as a roomful of Conventionals can go, that is, and he finds himself stuck amidst a forest of arms, all stretched out wanting to shake his hand.

———————

From then on, rather than breaking out into a carnival atmosphere, the evening simmers down. Drabs of guests shuffle toward the exits, to their rides home. Meanwhile I do my best to keep myself awake as AA entertains old boy after old boy, humouring himself as he occupies the identity of Dwayne Hilsbury, telling ridiculously inconsistent stories to each and every person who dares make conversation with him.

I catch Brian's eye as he leaves with his wife on his arm. He raises his glass of champagne to me, before knocking it back and handing it to a nearby waiter. He slips off into the night.

Before long me and AA are just about the only ones left in the ballroom. AA reels through yet another tall tale, this time about some fictional cabin he's got up in Scotland which he uses during the salmon season. He invites the beleaguered man and his wife to come up and visit sometime, although, in his drunken haze, neglects to give them any way of getting in touch.

Across the room I notice Nadir, standing over by the stage, speaking with a pair of young women. I posture whether they're prostitutes too. Just taking into account their ages, well south of thirty, and their necklines, well south of their nipples, I would be willing to wager.

With no one else in range for us to speak to, I bring my lips to AA's ear. "What now?"

But, before AA can respond, there's a familiar voice. The voice of the soon-to-be Prime Minister.

"Anna? Is that you?"

Chapter Twenty-Five

MY BLOOD FREEZES and I feel all the hairs rise on the back of my neck.

I turn.

Snarkly stands there, a glass of champagne locked in his fist. He eyes me hungrily before looking to AA. He holds out his hand. "Simon Snarkly, pleasure to meet you."

AA's eyes crease with a smile. He's going to enjoy this. "Oh no, the pleasure's all mine. Dwayne Hilsbury."

Snarkly eyes us both. "It is wonderful to see some young blood around here." He slurps a mouthful of champagne. "Sometimes it does feel like we're getting greyer by the year."

"We have been members of the Party for a few years now," AA says. "This is our first fundraiser, for myself and my wife."

Snarkly's gaze quivers over me, scanning for any kind of reaction. I can tell he's adding it all up in his mind. Never had he considered that I might be married, especially after having visited my home.

When he meets AA's eye again, his well-worn, politician's smile reappears. "Anyway, I should leave you two to your evening. It's getting late. Be chucking out time, sooner or later." He reaches for my hand, takes it in his and plants a kiss on the back of it. "Lovely to have seen you, Anna. I do hope you're well."

As we stand there, watching Snarkly wander off, swaying side-to-side slightly, I stamp on AA's toe.

"Ow!" AA says. "Just having a little fun."

"Yeah, I can see that. You've been having fun all night. Have you forgotten we're here to do a job?"

"Who says you can't have fun at work?"

———

For all the commotion of getting into the mansion, the checking of bags and body searches, it's really a cinch avoiding the security sweep after the party. Me and AA get ourselves up to the first floor where we sneak into an empty bedroom.

For all AA's frolicking throughout the evening, he's got his game face on now. Any sense of joviality is lost from his expression. He unbuttons his cuffs and rolls his sleeves up to his elbows. "Got to be careful about why you touch. No gloves, remember."

"Fine," I say, fitting the silencer to the pistol. "So, how are we going to do this?"

"Well, you're going to pop him one in the temple."

Maybe AA hasn't lost all sense of humour just get. I give him a punch in the arm.

He rubs it, mock scowling at me, just like the older brother I never had.

"I saw the target with a couple of girls earlier on," I say.

"No one told me he was a Casanova."

"I think they're prostitutes."

AA shakes his head. "Poor lost boy." He brightens. "I could've shown him a good time if he'd given me a chance."

I thump him again.

"Do you mind?"

"Cut out the jokes, okay? I just want to get this over with and go home."

"My goodness, you really are turning into one of those crazy cat ladies, aren't you?"

One final punch for AA.

————

The lights in the hallway dim just after midnight. We sneak out of our room and along the carpeted landing. I hold the pistol down by my thigh, pointed at the floor. My fingers are restless. I keep tensing then relaxing my grip. I tell myself just to be cool, but somehow my mind's getting the better of me—I keep turning my mind back to Elizabeth, and that guy with the kids, almost praying for this hit to go off without a hitch: for me to come out of this as the golden girl.

When we arrive outside Nadir's room, AA reaches out and holds me back. We stand there, listening. From inside the room there are female giggles. A male voice, speaking in broken English, with a heavy accent. Every so often there's a moan, creaking, then more giggles.

"Okay," AA says, in a whisper, "here's the plan: I get in there, get the girls out the way, then I'll stand guard by the door, while you're plugging him."

I pull away, to get into position.

He tugs me back. "I want you to try and bleed him for information, get anything you can out of him. All right?"

Although not feeling entirely confident about even being able to hold the gun straight, to even kill Nadir, I nod in reply. I'm a bag of nerves and I just want to get through with this. I have no time for AA's little investigations.

Without asking me whether or not I'm ready, AA bursts through the door. I hear his voice drift out, back to me, where I still stand in the corridor. "Time to leave, girls."

Nadir speaks up. "What this about, eh?"

"I'm with security," AA says. "I'm afraid it's against policy to allow illegal activities on our premises. We could lose our licence."

I still don't hear much movement within the room.

One of the girls says, "What're you talking about?"

"Yeah," the other one says. "We're not doing nothing illegal."

"I'll tell you what. You girls can either leave right this second or I can bring the police out here and you can clear this all up with them."

"Hey, where you go?" Nadir says.

"Sorry, hun," the first girl says. "Better if we clear out."

"What about my money?"

The other girl says, "Don't understand, sorry. We just met here."

There's more scrabbling round as the girls collect up their clothes.

I press the back of my head against the wall and stare at the ceiling. When I hear the girls making for the door, I dash to the other side of the hall and stand to one side of the door so they won't see me.

The two girls tumble out of the room, dresses crumpled and

hair sticking up all over. They chatter between themselves dizzily as they make their way down the spiral stairs, back down to the reception and out of the mansion.

This just isn't Nadir's lucky night.

Inside the room, Nadir's still remonstrating with AA, desperately trying to absolve himself from whatever situation he believes to have got himself into. "Who tell you, eh?"

AA says, "Sorry, sir, I'm not at liberty to say. We've been given a tip off."

"A 'tip' what?"

"I'll leave you to the remainder of your evening, sir."

I take a deep breath, check the pistol over once again. All sorts of situations are flowing through my mind now: that when I fire the gun jams or I try to shoot only to find that the cartridge is empty, or, when I enter the room, Nadir is there waiting for me, jumps me from behind and turns the gun on me.

AA leaves the room, steps out into the hall. He wears a stern, business-like expression which breaks into an efficient grin. "Your turn."

"Hey!" Nadir says, from within the room. "You gonna shut the door or what?"

I count to three and then round the doorframe, pistol outstretched, pointing right at Nadir's forehead.

The door clicks shut behind me, as AA seals us inside.

Somehow, my hands remain steady and my nerve stays solid and cold, unmoving. "Move over to the window," I say.

Nadir stays just where he is. He's naked apart from a bed sheet which he holds up to cover his waist. His brow furrows and he bares his teeth. "I know you."

Chapter Twenty-Six

"GET OVER BY THE WINDOW," I say.

"Or what?" Nadir says. "You shoot me? But that is what you will do anyway."

A shudder passes through me. "I can make it more painful for you."

He steps toward me. "How?"

I aim at his left kneecap then squeeze the trigger.

The bullet rips through his bare skin and he keels over in agony. "You bitch!"

I consider what sort of noise threshold security really keep to. I'm sure that all sorts of odd-sounding activities take place here, and their customers pay a hefty premium for them to keep their noses out.

"You want me to hit the other one?" I say.

Hands clapped over his bloody kneecap, he grits his teeth and shakes his head.

"Good, then just sit there and listen."

His shoulders rise and fall with his rapid breathing.

"I want to know about the operation. What's going on with Snarkly and your father?"

He winces. I'm not sure whether it's from pain or revelation. "How do you know about my father? Is he the one that set you up to do this?"

"I'm not at liberty to say."

"Huh?"

I shift my weight, flex my trigger finger, while keeping the sight lined up for a headshot. "Tell me what Snarkly's got planned."

"Do you not know? Are you not his whore?"

"Actually, a whore is technically someone you pay, Snarkly has me on merit."

I can see that that comment stickles for him, really stokes a fire inside. "I can have any girl I want."

"I don't doubt that, just as long as you can pay."

He glowers at me.

This has gone on long enough. It's time to see the hit through. AA will just have to be disappointed. I bring the gun up to my eye and line up the shot.

"No!" Nadir says, holding up a hand. "Please, wait!"

I keep the gun on him.

"I suppose if you are going to kill me there is no reason to keep secrets."

"Go on," I say.

"Simon Snarkly and my father. They . . . they want to create a company here, in the United Kingdom."

"What's so devastating about that?"

Nadir's eyes widen and an almost boyish look enters his expression. "My father, you do not know who my father is?"

"No, should I?"

"My father is a prince, well he was a prince. He lost his throne to my uncle, leader of my country's army. My uncle killed my grandfather and took control. He expelled myself and my father." Nadir sneers. "But not before my father had drained the treasury."

"And what happened to the money?"

A quiver runs through Nadir's body. Blood wells out from between his fingers. His complexion pales. "That . . . is . . . the problem."

I get an itch at the base of my spine and my hand shakes. "Where's the money?"

Nadir sucks in air, grimacing in pain.

"Is that why your father wants to put Snarkly into power? So that he can get at the money you've stolen from your country? To bend the rules and take a healthy cut for himself?"

"Exactly."

"And those two people your father had killed, they were part of the operation too? Who else is involved?"

"Other than my father and Simon Snarkly?"

"Yes."

"Just me."

"Okay."

He doubles over, grasping his kneecap. "What happens now?"

I step forward, gun still trained on him. "I have to kill you."

Without looking up, he says, "Please, make it quick."

———

As I trudge back through the empty mansion, into the reception, with AA at my side, I think over what I've learnt from Nadir. I wonder what else Simon Snarkly has at stake in this whole deal. It can't just be for money, can it? From my evening of adventure with him he wasted no time in showing me a building he owned, and the way he presented it to me—what I've read of his background history—suggests that he's got plenty of other properties. No, either Nadir was lying to me or he hasn't been party to the whole story. Taking into consideration that to reach his position, son of a tyrant, he needed no qualifications, I'm willing the bet he bought into whatever lies his father told him.

Once I've got through explaining what happened to AA, on the car ride home, he turns to me and expresses the same ideas—that Snarkly can't just be in this for the money, it's not enough for him.

"Then what's it about?" I say.

AA shakes his head as he gazes out the window. "Search me."

When we reach my house, AA gives me a kiss on the cheek and I get out, hop up my garden path, in the early morning light, and get inside. I get upstairs to find Lizzie sleeping on my pillow. I wrestle myself out of my dress and cleanse the makeup from my face. Feeling a little hungry, I go down to the kitchen and pour myself out a bowl of cereal, splash in some milk, and flick on the morning news.

As yet there's no report of a body having been found in Everly Estate. I'm sure that, as I sit here munching on my breakfast, Brian's on his phone, jabbering away at his various contacts at the national papers, getting this all quietened down—maybe working with a pot provided by Snarky, paying them not to publish.

Apart from what Snarkly's got at stake in bringing Abdul-Hakam's pilfered money into the country, I wonder about Brian.

For him it's much clearer. Brian's a self-made man and he'll never turn down a deal with money involved. I understand that he's arrived where he has, the top of his own media agency empire, by being ruthless, keeping his eye fixed on the bottom line. I wish it were so simple to work out Snarkly.

I scrape up the remaining few flakes of cereal then deposit the bowl in my kitchen sink.

Outside, in my back garden, I hear the unmistakable *thunk* of someone landing onto the grass, having vaulted over the fence.

My chest fizzes and I snatch the pistol out from the kitchen drawer, where I stowed it, and go to investigate.

Chapter Twenty-Seven

MY WHOLE BODY'S SHAKING as I cross the sitting room. The TV continues to chatter away, set to a low volume. No more sounds come from the back garden, but I know that whoever's there is still waiting, lurking in the shadows. It could be anyone. A burglar, perhaps. One thing's for sure, they won't have bargained with having to face up to a handgun. And, even less so, a ready-made barrelful of excuses which I have in Brian, if I have to shoot whoever's there.

I flip off the small lamp so that flickering TV light is all that illuminates the sitting room. I rest my hand on the door handle, unclip the lock, and then slide the French door open. It's pitch black out in my garden. I stand inside the house, not wanting to fall victim of the standard horror film trope—venturing out to have my throat slit by the killer.

My heart judders in my chest. I still my hands, relax my grip and wait.

A bush rustles.

My attention flies to the location and I point my gun toward it. "I'm armed, you'd be better off coming out of there right this second. If you come out now maybe I won't call the police."

Another stirring, footsteps scraping against the paving slabs. "I know you're the one who killed Nadir tonight."

My throat tightens. That voice is familiar but I just can't place it. "I've got no idea what you're talking about."

The figure moves out of the shadows, hands raised. He's bald and wearing a black jumpsuit. It's David, Snarkly's bodyguard.

"Don't come any closer," I say.

"It's okay," he says. "I just want to talk." He looks round. "Can we go inside? I don't want us to be overheard."

"How do I know Snarkly didn't send you here to kill me?"

"Because I'm working against him too."

I consider for a moment, wondering whether this might all be a bluff, that Snarkly's sent David here just to talk me out of my shell. After all, Snarkly saw me at his fundraiser, he knows I was there—amongst the last to leave. He's not a stupid man, perhaps he's put two and two together, realised that I was the assassin that Brian sent. And what now? Will he inform Brian?

I ask David inside, closing the French doors behind him.

He takes a seat on the sofa.

"How did you get here?" I say.

"A car dropped me off."

I sneer. "And what's with the jumpsuit?"

He pinches the jumpsuit material between finger and thumb, as if testing its elasticity. "I'm on duty tonight, keeping a watch on Snarkly's surroundings, making sure no one gets inside."

"What happens if someone gets in while you're here?"

"You mean if someone gets inside and kills Snarkly?" He grins. "Then all the better."

That piques my interest, makes me reconsider where David's loyalties really lie. This could all be an act, of course, but his manner, his delivery of the words is so perfect that it gives me pause for thought.

"How do you know I'm not working for Snarkly?" I say. "You might be incriminating yourself right at this moment. As soon as you're gone I could call him up, tell him about your visit here, what you've revealed to me."

"I don't think you are working for him, at least not directly. I saw the surprise on his face when he met with you at the fundraiser. He clearly had no idea what you were doing there. In fact"—he scratches his nose—"he asked me himself, asked whether I had expected to see you there, if I had known that you were married. For a politician, he's surprisingly candid in private."

Now I need to ask the question that's been bothering me throughout. "Why do you want Snarkly dead?"

David shrugs. "I've been around for all their conversations, the meetings between him and Abdul-Hakam. To be honest, their dealings sicken me to the stomach."

"Why would he let you be around for those meetings?"

"He trusts me, I've saved his life more than once."

"So there are others who want him dead?"

"I've counted at least three occasions where I've actively neutralised assassins. Who's to know how many others have ditched their attempts because of my presence?"

"Why didn't you let them go through with it?"

A sliver of a smile creeps across his lips. "Let's just say I've had a crisis of judgement since those occasions, a moral dilemma. Hence my slackening of protection for Snarkly."

"You mean someone's offered you more money?"

"There is that, but I also mean what I said about the whole idea sickening me. I don't want to be party to this robbing of a third-world country. Unlike Snarkly I come from working class stock, I served in the Forces—just like you—and I have a concept of what it means to steal from a nation. For me it's the most disgusting thing you can do, to rob people of what they've paid for."

With every word I'm beginning to like David even more.

"It was only when Adam Alderknot got in touch that I actually realised I could do something about it, that I wouldn't just get chewed up by Snarkly's publicists, have my family threatened."

"You know AA?"

"Of course, who else?"

"So AA's highly involved in the opposition, in wanting to stop Snarkly from going through with the plan?"

"More than that, I would say the buck stops with him."

The more I think about things it seems like I am going to have to make a choice soon, pick sides. It seems like a storm's brewing between Brian and AA. Deep down I know that AA's on the moral side of things, that he's doing what's right from a moral perspective—saving all those people's tax money—but, like David says, there's a real dilemma in stepping away from Brian's operations, indeed doing anything to piss him off. Because Brian, simply put, controls everything. I'm better off sitting on the fence for the time being, not showing too much of my hand.

"So how do we proceed?" I say.

"You are on board, then?"

I need to stay enigmatic, make no promises. "I'm like you, I've worked for a living my whole life."

He nods, apparently that's good enough for him. "I'm going

to work on Snarkly, make sure that he still trusts you, I'll work to eliminate any doubts from his mind." He gets up from the sofa, ventures over to the French doors. "Expect a call."

I get up too. "Really, don't you want to leave through the front door?"

He smiles at me, then makes to cross the sitting room. "Sorry, didn't want to impose."

Chapter Twenty-Eight

S NARKLY'S MESSAGE COMES IN about a week later, just as I'm about to leave for my appointment with Julie. He wants to meet up that night, at his penthouse. I'm not sure, in my role of mistress, whether I should be offended that he doesn't feel the need to invite me out anywhere posh, or, in my role as Brian's assassin, relieved that I won't be seen in public with him. David's correct in one thing, that he has a strong hold over Snarkly in that he's managed to convince him of my outstanding character. I make a note to myself that owing someone your life carries a certain weight, even with a politician.

I arrive in Julie's office feeling somewhat calmer than usual. She has me lie down on the sofa, like usual, and before I know it I'm sprouting whatever's coming into my head while Julie makes sympathetic noises. And then, just as I prepare myself to reel through my most recent family trauma, the whole pushing Kate over deal, my mind does a U-turn and I decide now's the time.

Julie has an old-style carriage clock sitting on the mantelpiece.

I guess she's inherited it from one of her grandparents, back when companies actually gave a damn about people. It ticks away, its interior spinning round within its glass case, as if hypnotising me, telling me that this is the right time.

I straighten up on the sofa, wait for Julie to stop writing and to look up at me, to meet my eye. "Everything we talk about here stays confidential, right?" I say.

"Yes."

"I mean, I know that whole rule about harming someone else. But"—I pause, searching for the right expression, not wanting her to totally flip out on me—"if you don't know who the person is that's going to come to harm, would you still be obliged to investigate, to find out who they were?"

She smiles. "You're making me out to be some kind of Nancy Drew." She slaps a tower of folders beside her, making it rock. "I have to get through all this at the end of every day." She pops her glasses back up the ridge of her nose. "To answer your question, if I suspect you or someone else might be in any immediate danger from your actions then I'm obliged to do what I can."

I suppose that's as good of an answer as I'm going to get. I feel like if I can't spill my soul to Julie then I'll never have the chance with anyone else. Of course I could tell Brian or AA, but Brian's my employer and AA—well, he'll probably just say I'm a dizzy little girl, or words to that effect. I need to confide in someone who doesn't have the same blood on their hands, who may well be suffering the same issues.

"Anna? Are you okay?" she says. "Would you like a glass of water?"

"That'd be good, thanks."

Julie nods, then gets up and goes over to the sink, where she fills a tumbler then brings it over to me.

When I take it from her, my hands are shaking.

"You're sure you're okay?" she says.

I take a sip of water then place the glass down on the table. "There's a sensitive subject I want to bring up with you, something which I think will probably mean that you'll reassess me. In fact it'll probably mean that everything makes a lot more sense."

"Anna, you know you can tell me anything. You shouldn't feel that you have to hide anything from me. Please, tell me what's the matter."

Another sip of water, to get some moisture into my tongue, then I say, "I kill people for money."

Those words hang in the word for the longest time, mingling with the *tick, tick, tick* of the carriage clock. They swell between us, pushing us both back in our seats.

Julie purses her lips. "Are you speaking in a metaphor?"

"No."

"You mean what you said literally?"

"Yes."

Another long silence, then Julie says, "Anna, I really . . . I really had no idea."

This is all a huge mistake. I was so wrong to tell her what was on my mind. I should've listened to my common sense. I lift myself off the sofa. "I'm sorry, I know what kind of position this puts you in, Julie, but I couldn't suffer being dishonest any longer. I had to give you the truth, had to tell someone."

Julie crushes her lips together, fiddles with a button on her cardigan. "There are things I can help you with Anna, but, well, I don't think that I can take on such a burden."

"Okay," I say. "I understand completely."

"Anna?"

What an exit this is. Whatever possessed me to tell her the

truth? I reach the door, settle my hand on the knob, getting ready to leave this place for good. I turn back to her.

"Do take care, won't you?" she says.

"I will."

———————

Bob informs me that I have seven new messages on the phone. Five of them are from advertising companies, wanting to sell me double glazing, new plumbing, and other stuff I don't take the effort to pay attention to. At the end of the marketing pitches is a message from Arnold. He's asking me whether I want to come over that evening, and then, when I see the calendar, I realise that it's Ben's twelfth birthday. It had completely slipped my mind, what with the hit yesterday. When I look at my mobile I see the reminder blinking at me, telling me to buy him something.

It takes me four or five goes before I have the nerve to call up Arnold, after what happened with Kate I feel awkward about the whole situation. But I do it, I do it for Ben, not wanting him to think that his mother doesn't care about him on his birthday—even if he is glued to his games console throughout the entirety of proceedings.

Ten minutes later and I'm on the Tube, heading toward their house. I pick up a DVD from a corner shop. The front cover features guns and muscular men so it should appeal to a twelve year old, or that's my line of logic anyway. Before I know it I'm standing on the doorstep, ringing the bell, feeling that this is the worst idea since telling Julie that I'm an assassin this morning.

Thankfully, Arnold answers the door. He smiles at me but I can see that there's a veil over his eyes, a foreground worry that I'm going to explode at any given moment.

I want to give him some sort of assurance, but it's not the kind of thing you can just make better with words, is it?

He invites me inside, where I can already hear boys laughing, the sound of feet stepping all over the place. I keep in file, behind Arnold, and skirt by several boys shooting along the hall. When I reach the kitchen I see Kate standing over at the counter, putting the finishing touches to a large chocolate birthday cake—twelve candles all ready to be lit. However, my attention is drawn to her wrist, which is in plaster.

I put the DVD down on the table and approach her, shrugging off any sense of foreboding I had about being around her again. "Kate," I say, my throat feeling sore, "I'm so sorry. I had no idea."

She turns round, apparently startled to see me there. "Oh, Annie." She glances down at her plastered wrist and runs her good hand over it. "Really, it's no issue. I know that it was hard for you, that day, and that you've been feeling pressured, what with your new job and everything."

I never thought I could be as much of a monster as this—such a bully. To think that afterward I kind of felt good about it. All that's disappeared now, though.

I take a step closer.

She flinches.

"I just thought I'd pop by," I say, "be in and out quickly."

She brightens a touch. "Oh, no, Annie. Please stay as long as you like."

I can read the contrast between her words and actions. She wants me out of the house as quickly as my legs can carry me. I'm sure that she's keeping her mobile close, ready to dial up the police at a moment's notice.

I hold back, trying to keep my arms at my sides, to act as neutrally as possible. "Where's Ben?"

"Up in his room, I think," she says, injecting a false sing-song into her voice.

I know that all this positivity is just an act. Even Arnold would struggle to live with someone who was up like that twenty-four hours a day. I give her a calm smile and then slink off, Arnold still at my side, like a faithful old dog.

Ben's in his room, sitting on his bed, surrounded by his friends. There are about half a dozen on them, all staring at the screen. From what I can work out only four of them actually have controllers while the other two just watch on.

"Ben?" I say.

He's wrapped up in killing zombies or whatever those grey humanoids on the screen are. One of them splatters into a million bloody pieces, and I wonder whether he's got his mother's high threshold for gore.

"Ben?" I say, again, a little louder.

One of the boys nudges him and Ben looks round, his face dopey, controller dangling from his hand. The screen freezes as one of the kids presses pause.

I hand over the DVD. "Happy Birthday."

He takes it from me, looks at the cover, manages a fleeting smile, to make eye contact with me for precisely quarter of a second, then says, "Thanks," before turning round and continuing the game.

His friends look away from me too. All eyes on the screen.

I feel Arnold's hand on my shoulder. "Just at that age, I think," he says.

"Yeah," I say, feeling empty inside.

"Do you want to see Josie?"

From Josie's room along the corridor, I can hear her speaking with her friend. I don't want to intrude on that.

"No, it's okay," I say.

"Do you want to help us with the cake, then?" Arnold says.

Together we get down to the bottom of the stairs, then I turn to him. "I think I'm going to head off."

Arnold wrinkles his forehead. "We haven't even sung Happy Birthday yet."

"It's all right, I don't think he'll miss me."

"Of course he will." Arnold lowers his voice, presumably so that Kate, still in the kitchen, won't hear. "You're his mother."

A sob emanates in my throat and I have to be gone before I break down completely. Nothing could be more embarrassing. I mumble something and then slip out of the door, back up the garden path, feeling Arnold's stare burn into my back.

Chapter Twenty-Nine

I NEED SOME KIND OF CONSOLATION after losing my therapist and running out on my son's birthday party in one day, so in a way I'm glad that I've got Snarkly's affections to look forward to—whether or not they be lecherous and degrading.

Still, once I've had a shower, put on a nice dress and done my makeup, I feel about a hundred times better. Now I feel like another person, kind of like a secret agent getting stuck into this assignment on Snarkly. Tonight I'm determined to make a breakthrough of some sort. With David on my side I know that I can play this harder, be a little more direct. David will sweep up any misconceptions I manage to transmit.

I give Lizzie a twenty-minute cuddle, hugging her to my chest until she wriggles free, yowling her head off. Sometimes I get to feel so alone in this house. It hurts all the more to see Arnold doing so well, raising our kids in such a normal way without me. I wonder if I'm really required at all.

When I get to the penthouse it's much as I remember it from

the last time—the stunning views have almost lost their effect after my first visit. Now I'm starting to come round to imagining how Snarkly sees the world, how it must've lost its sheen for him a long time ago. I've had first-hand experience at what happens when women lose their sheen for him.

David meets me in the sitting room, informs me in a stuffy tone, obviously reserved for being in proximity of his boss, that Snarkly is taking a shower and will be with me momentarily. Then he gives me a half smile, from the corners of his lips, and goes off somewhere else in the penthouse. Maybe Snarkly's given his bodyguard his own bedroom. There are perks to being a corporate leech—although if he's a leech, what does that make me?

I sit on a squishy, chair-high orange cushion. It looks like it would be more at home in an art gallery, or a rubbish tip—depending on your perspective. I pick up the remote and scan through the channels, looking for something interesting. Not having seen the news all day, I decide to go there first.

A perky blond reporter wearing a smart trouser suit beams at the camera and tells the viewers all about how Simon Snarkly has announced his intention to run for Party leader, that he's believed to be at the head of the race, the vote is thought to be something of a formality.

Snarkly's face fills the screen. He's looking up slightly, a light gloss to his forehead. He looks much younger in the photo-graph, plumper somehow, yet the image conveyed gives me a warm impression of him—despite knowing what he's really like.

Once again the reporter sums up the situation surrounding the resignation of the previous Prime Minister, before diving into the same barrel of crap about this being an opportunity for the citizens of the United Kingdom to learn to trust again, to give a new man a chance.

Yeah right, I think as I kill the TV.

Snarkly emerges from his bedroom, wrapped in a cream towel. He leans up against the doorframe. "Did someone say my name?"

"You were on the news."

He puckers his lips. "Did they capture my good side?"

I actually summon a titter at that remark, pretty sure that's the closest he's come to cracking a joke since I've known him.

Then he gives me the eye. "Is that any way to say hello?"

———

The whole time we're in his bed, his soap-scented, warm skin all over me, I've got my mind on David—that he must be hearing this whole thing. If he really does intend to kill Snarkly then this might be his best opportunity. He can act now, while he's occupied. But, I recall what he said about his family, that he didn't want to get himself wrapped up in anything complicated—he'll be complicit in murder but won't actually pull the trigger himself. The world needs more people like him.

It's over pretty much as soon as it's begun and Snarkly's lighting a cigarette, scratching at his groin beneath the bed sheet, as if I couldn't see what he's doing. He turns on his side, cigarette dangling from his lips, ash landing on the sheet. "You never told me you were married."

"You never asked."

He blows out a cloud of smoke. "True that. I've never really asked you anything much, have I?"

And that's how I'd like it to stay, I think. "Not really much to tell. You've seen where I live. I have nothing to hide."

He shoots me a wry smile. "Nothing except a husband tucked away here and there."

"No."

"That's all right, I'm no saint either. We've all got our secrets. I think it's what keeps life interesting, keeps us on our toes—gives us a sense of danger."

"Maybe."

He goes on to speculate about the nature of secrets for several minutes more, before he's talked himself into a circle and confused himself. He sounds like he's been at the drinks cabinet. I really hope, for his sake, he gets someone to write his speeches. He has a good, strong voice, but his thoughts seem hopelessly muddled. In fact, I hope that when he does become Prime Minister, providing no one manages to kill him first, they don't trust him with any shiny, red buttons that launch nukes—if they even exist.

"Been a bloody hectic day," he says. "Media here, media there, photographers everywhere."

Yes, he's definitely been at the booze.

He chuckles away to himself for about five minutes, then swings himself out of bed and dresses himself in a smoking jacket, an actual smoking jacket, and shoves his feet into a pair of, what look like, velvet slippers.

With the cover draped over me, obscuring what little dignity I have left, I watch him cross the room.

He pauses when he stands within the doorframe. "Dinner should be ready in about an hour. Feel free to freshen up in the bathroom in the meantime." A knot appears in his throat and he looks round the room, apparently distracted. "I've got some important information I'd like to share with you, sensitive information. I . . . I wouldn't trust just anyone with it. You must understand that I'm telling you because . . . because I think I love you, and you deserve to know."

I watch him walk out of the bedroom, into the sitting room, hands dipped in his pockets and a fresh cigarette in his lips.

Chapter Thirty

ALTHOUGH I'M ANXIOUS to get into the sitting room, to hear whatever this 'sensitive information' pertains to be, I wonder whether this is another advent of David's, if he's managed to convince his boss to let me into more of what's really going on—if that is the case then I've surely made a powerful ally in him.

I dry myself off, reapply makeup and then pick my dress up from where it lies crumpled on the floor. As I examine it I notice that, in his passion, Snarkly's snapped one of the straps. It'll be okay for this evening, since we're not going out anywhere, but I'll need to get it repaired sometime this week. I catch myself thinking about my sewing machine, which I keep in a dusty box beneath my bed, and then I remember the kind of money I've got in the bank, and know that, for the foreseeable future, I won't have to do any more sewing.

The sitting room table's set for two, silver cutlery, tangerine-coloured placemats and silk napkins. A three-pronged candlestick provides illumination. Just as I think the room's empty, Snarkly speaks from his place in the corner of the room where he reads a large tome beneath an electric lamp. "You took your time," he says.

"You know women."

He closes the book and replaces it on the shelf. He removes his reading glasses from his face, folds them up and tucks them into the breast pocket of his smoking jacket. "Shall I tell the chef we're ready to dine?"

"Okay."

Like the gentleman he is, Snarkly pulls back my chair and then plants a kiss on my cheek, before sitting in the chair opposite. He unfolds his napkin and tucks it into his shirt collar, as if we were in the fifties.

A waiter appears out of nowhere. He's wearing a tuxedo, which I guess is standard costume for a servant in Snarkly's employment, and he brings our dishes on covered trays which he dramatically uncovers first for me, then for Snarkly.

It's fish, what kind I'm not completely sure. It's accompanied by some sort of yellow rice and a miniscule side salad. One fact remains the same with men, rich or poor, they don't do greens.

I'm itching to pick up my fork and eat, but, before I can, Snarkly raises his glass and says, "To you, my dear."

I eye my glass of white wine, pick it up—thinking that it'd be rude not to accept his toast—and I take a small sip before replacing it beside my plate. Then we eat, without speaking at all.

As I get toward cleaning my plate, I notice David slink into the sitting room. The way he moves seems so sleek, like he's had infinite opportunity to practise getting in and out of rooms without any fuss. I suppose, in a way, that's his job description. Unseen, but deadly when needed.

After we finish, Snarkly helps me out of my chair and leads me, by the hand, to the sofa, as if I were too stupid to find it for myself. I perch on a corner, not trusting its surface not to suck me down inside of it, leave me on my back, legs sprawling in the air, knickers on show.

Snarkly looks me in the eye. "I've told perhaps four or five other people outside this room what I'm about to tell you. So I hope you'll appreciate the weight of it."

I think of the other people, knowing that at least three of them are now dead. The others he's referencing must be Brian and Abdul-Hakam. If only they knew that their partner was giving away the inner-workings of their scheme to some girl he's met, let alone the assassin working the contracts who they intentionally left out of the loop.

Snarkly rests his hand on my knee, but doesn't try his usual trick of continuing up to the inner thigh. This is important. "As you know, dear, I'm running to become Prime Minister, and as things stand there's really nothing at all standing in my way." He breathes in deeply. "However, there is one certain aspect which could potentially undo my entire campaign."

"What?" I say, kind of already knowing the answer.

"You, my dear."

I put on my best doe eyes.

Now his hand does ride up my leg, heading for his favourite spot. "It's been quite a ride, hasn't it?"

He gives me no chance to comment.

"I've really become quite taken with you, and it's really all I can do not to think of you for every moment of the day." He runs his fingers in circles on my inner thigh then withdraws his hand. "But, I'm afraid, in my line of work, it's really not on. A messy divorce never does a prime minister any good while he's in office. So we'll have to keep things secret for the time being. Perhaps until I have had my fun."

I catch David's eye, he's watching me from across the room. I snap back to Snarkly, telling myself I have to pay attention to him. "I see." I smooth down my dress. "Is that all?"

He looks a little taken aback by my question, then he composes himself. This time he keeps his hands to himself, rubbing his thumbs together. "No, not quite."

Again I look to David, who remains stern, apparently not listening.

Snarkly continues, "With you being somewhat inside my circle, it's inevitable that you shall be privy to certain conversations. That said, it'd be better that you get the full story, from the horse's mouth, so to speak, so as not to baffle yourself putting all the pieces of the puzzle together."

I wonder whether he wooed Elizabeth in the same way. Then again, I suppose she had a few more skills out on the table, was more involved in the operation. The whole lover aspect would've been nothing more than an afterthought—as Snarkly saw it, a means to get her claws into his power.

Then I realise that I've reached the point where Snarkly truly believes me to be a bimbo. He thinks that by telling me what's really going on now might implicate me in the whole thing and I can only speculate what he has in store. Maybe he wants to leave me with the blame, use me as a scapegoat if everything goes pear-shaped. He's in for a nasty shock.

Snarkly twirls his hand. "This whole business has become awfully complicated, I want you to understand that. My only real interest is to be Prime Minister, that's where my ambition begins and ends. I have all the money, all the property, I could wish for.

However, I'm a little embarrassed to admit that I'm being blackmailed."

My ears perk up at that remark.

"Yes," he says, with a sigh. "I'm afraid that a client of my publicist has been making rather rotund demands of me, and they've both turned on me."

I shoot another look over to David, who looks on with indifference, then say to Snarkly, "What do you mean?"

"Ah, my dear, the problem is that with the Prime Minister's job comes great responsibility. I'm sure you've heard of Brian Mathewson, Mathewson Media?"

I nod my head.

"Well, I went to Brian a while back, probably eighteen months ago, and announced my designs on the Prime Minister's job to him. Of course, nowadays, a publicist is a necessity, we all have skeletons in our closets, don't we, dear?"

"Some more than most."

Snarkly chuckles. "Yes, quite right." His joyful expression slowly disintegrates. "You see, what happened was I managed to back myself into a bit of a hole."

"How's that?"

"It seems that Brian had other clients, just as interested in my run on the Prime Minister's job. One chap, a Middle Eastern gentleman, seemed to rise above the rest of them, take precedent. And then one day Brian approached me telling me something about a pot of money this man was looking to bring into the country, stolen treasury funds, something like that. Anyway, of course my first reaction was to tell them where to hike, but . . . but then everything got out of hand. Brian . . . Brian threatened me."

When I look over to his I see that there are genuine tears in his eyes, and that overgrown boy is back with us, waiting for his mother to step in and make everything right—to tell the bigger boys to play nice.

"How did he threaten you?" I say.

"He . . . he said he would go public about everything, my affairs, destroy my profile. Said that I would never make it to be Prime Minister. And . . . and"—he splutters on his tears—"he's started to kill others involved in this. My . . . my old girlfriend, Elizabeth Newman. He said that she knew too much. She had to go."

He reaches for my hand, wraps his fingers round it and digs his nails into my palm.

Spurts of pain shoot up my arm but I'm not really in any position to complain with this bawling middle-aged man beside me. When I look up I see that David's pulled off his silent vanishing trick. Typical, just as things take an emotional turn, the *real* men make themselves scarce.

Snarkly releases my hand, straightens up and wipes the tears out of his eyes. "He had another of my close acquaintances killed." He pauses, swallows. "He had his own son killed. This man, this Middle Eastern man, will stop at nothing to get what he wants, to bring his money into the country, where he believes it will be safe. Both him and Brian, they are in this together. They're only interested in money, obsessed with it."

I have to say that although this news has come as unexpected, the motivations behind it—Brian's motivations—fit quite well with everything I've built up around him. Now I can see that Snarkly's no more than a pawn, just a convenient player who arrived at just the right time for Brian to manipulate, mould to his own whim.

And then, as I'm taking stock of these developments, trying

to make sense of where I'm fitting into all this, how I've been played worse than anyone else—at least they've known where they've fit inside the system—I feel Snarkly's fingers travelling up my inner thigh and his damp face nestling in my breast.

I shut my eyes and wonder if there's any way out of this for me anymore.

Chapter Thirty-One

AS I MAKE MY way back home, in the back of Snarkly's car, I watch the buildings rising out of the early morning fog. I see a homeless man awaking from where he's been sleeping, lying on spare pieces of cardboard. He stretches his limbs, reaches up, and, against all odds, gives a toothy grin.

I turn my attention back to the shiny buildings slipping past on the other side of the road and realise I'm no longer worried about Snarkly attempting to kill me—he's more afraid of Brian than of me telling my story to the papers. He's well past the point of acting rationally, I can see that this whole situation has turned into a nightmare for him. He just wants to get his buttocks into the Prime Minister's seat, do whatever Abdul-Hakam and Brian demand of him, then get on with his life—he might be disappointed when I don't hang around to console him afterward.

One doubt does remain, however. Snarkly had all my details, at least David had possession of them. He had the opportunity to run my information past whatever channels he wished. It would've made sense that he didn't pass them through Brian, so I can put that worry to rest, Brian must have no knowledge of my association with Snarkly. I just have to be careful and maybe I can get out of this mess with my head still fixed to my neck.

I tell the car to stop off at the corner shop and I go inside, aware that I must look fairly odd going inside to buy an extra-large tin of tuna in an evening gown. The shop assistant just gives me a look up and down without making a comment. Lizzie is delighted when I get back, peel the large tin open then deposit the contents in her bowl.

———

Later in the afternoon I get a phone call from AA. I think about leaving it to ring out, but, in the end, my curiosity gets the better of me.

"Meet me at The Arch Café at four," he says.

Who am I to argue? It's not like I have anything else to do.

I get to the café at about quarter to four and I take a table by the window. I ask for some fancy coffee that I forget the name of as soon as I've ordered. To me all these coffees are just a bunch of varying quantities and shapes of foam. My selected coffee has a heart lovingly-painted in cream on top. I stab it with my spoon, mashing it into a light-brown mulch. I'm desecrating my second coffee by the time AA arrives.

Today he's wearing a smart, waist-length blue-grey jacket with a scarf wrapped round his throat—even though it's at least fifteen degrees outside: suffer for fashion, or so the saying goes. He orders then takes his seat across from me, he's wearing a smug grin that tells me he knows something I don't know, that he's about to drop another bombshell into my life.

"You ready to meet who we're working for?" he says.

"You mean who you're working for."

AA waves his hand. "Whatever, you're just as caught up in this as I am. Don't think you can wheedle your way out now."

Now it's time to drop my own bombshell, show AA that he's not all that. I stir up the remnants of foam in my coffee cup with my spoon, then deposit its contents in my mouth, licking it clean. "Snarkly's being blackmailed by Brian and Abdul-Hakam."

"Yeah, I know."

Damn.

AA stiffens his shoulders then relaxes them. He loosens the scarf round his neck, but doesn't move to take it off. I begin to wonder whether he's hiding a love bite of some kind. He looks me in the eye. "We know that Snarkly's really just caught up in all this. The real guy behind this all is Brian."

"So you want me to sleep with Brian now?"

AA grins. "Not such a bad idea. Might loosen the old boy's tongue." His attention's drawn from me to a man who walks in through the door.

The man's fairly weedy, wearing an untucked, checked shirt and jeans. His hair has that combination of near-shoulder length and oiliness, like a canteen cleaner's mop after a hard shift. He flinches when he turns his eyes over us, then approaches, taking the spare chair and sitting on the very edge. "Hello," he says, then sticks his hand at me. "Name's Finch."

I observe the fingernails, the grubby, yellow-brown gleam and the black dirt stuck beneath them. I accept his handshake, keeping my grip limp, as if it might prevent me from catching whatever diseases he might be carrying. "Anna," I say.

Finch glances over our faces, then out the window, his eyes constantly shifting along people moving through the crowd, as if the assassins might be outside rather than sat right in front of him. He looks back at me briefly, before taking hold of a napkin and worrying it. "I suppose AA's let you in on what's going on?"

"I'm beginning to get an idea."

"Good, good," he says, with almost Tourette's-style delivery. "Better not to explain too much here, to go into too much detail."

I look over the table at AA, wondering what in hell's name he's got us involved with here. This man, Finch, reminds me of just about every stereotyped neo-hippy in the known-universe. No doubt he's still coming down off whatever it was he was taking last night. I'm sure he's passionate about whatever good he believes he's fighting for—saving these Middle Eastern people's taxes—but that doesn't necessarily translate into professionalism. Finch could get all of us killed.

Finch lowers his voice, his pupils bob around the base of his eye sockets. "AA tells me you have an in, with Snarkly, that you're close to him."

"Maybe."

Finch bobs his head up, stares at AA. "Maybe? Maybe?"

AA moves to reassure him. "It's okay, she's cool. Yeah, she's got herself on the inner track with Snarkly, getting into his confidence. All being well she should be able to get herself a fresh perspective that our other contact wouldn't be privy too."

I'm guessing that AA's talking about David.

"That true?" Finch says, flaring his nostrils in my direction.

"If you mean that I get him in that period just after he's ejaculated when he's baring his innermost psychological turmoil, then yes."

"Good, good," Finch says. "That will help us a great deal, now that he trusts you."

I decide that I'm going to cut through all this pretence,

demand to get down to the basics of this situation. "What's your stake in all this?"

"Stake?"

"Yeah, what have you got to lose if this money gets into the country?"

Finch puffs himself up. "My stake is liberty and freedom for all. I do what is right, protecting the values in this country and those in far-flung places no one seems to care about. My mission is to force politicians to keep their promises. To—"

"Yeah, yeah," I say. "That all sounds really noble and everything, but you didn't answer my question. What makes you want to get involved with this money?"

Finch cracks a smile. It's not a pretty thing to observe, lots of crooked, green-coloured teeth, several black spots where some dentist has tried to paper over the cracks. "Ah, well, if you want to go way deep then I'll tell you." He leans over the table so that a stench of body odour washes over me, almost makes me gag. "You see, back when we were at school, me and Simon Snarkly were rivals." He clears his throat. "That is to say that he was my bully. This is my chance to take care of him while saving the world."

Chapter Thirty-Two

THANKFULLY, ME AND AA manage to get away a few minutes later. As AA walks me to the Underground station he tells me more about Finch, how he's a self-made millionaire—something about computers. It appears that I've just been introduced to the yang of Snarkly's ying.

As I reach the stairs, readying to leave AA behind, I turn to him and say, "Do you think this is all getting a bit schoolyard?"

AA tucks his scarf into itself. "Schoolboys have got to grow up sometime."

"But that doesn't mean we need to have anything to do with it."

"We're just here to make a few quid."

"And there I was thinking you were all noble about this, wanting to do something for the greater good."

AA flashes me a grin. "Can't I do both at the same time?"

I thump him on the arm then descend the stairs, down into the Underground station.

———

Bob informs me of several messages on my phone when I get back. I'm surprised to hear that Julie's called. Hers is the first message on the machine:

"Anna? I'm sorry about how our last session went. I'm just calling to apologise. What you did was very open and honest and I acted in a non-professional manner. While it's . . . difficult for me to comprehend your occupation, I believe that I can offer to help you. Please give my secretary a call to arrange our next session. Hope to speak soon. Bye."

When I last left Julie's office I had been convinced it would be for the final time, so it's strange to hear her telling me that I'd be welcomed back. Should I go back, though? She's right about it being a burden for herself, something that she could do without. From her message I can ascertain that she wants to do the right thing, but that's not to say I wouldn't be dragging her into my world. But then, I imagine the situation whereby I have absolutely no one to speak to, outside of my business, and I decide that it's not a choice. I have to continue my sessions with her.

As usual, the other messages are from Arnold. The first, predictably, a 'check-up' call following Ben's party and a lingering, unasked question as to my increasingly odd behaviour. I don't bother to listen his the other messages, knowing they'll only make me angry or sad, or both.

Later on I get a call from Snarkly, asking me to join him at Tulips again. Since I'm not doing anyone any good sitting around at home, I decide to go out and meet with him. This getting dressed up fancy is becoming easier each time I do it.

———

Snarkly's dressed in a dark emerald suit with matching tie. It looks like some creation from the deepest, darkest eighties. I might imagine that he's taken it out of his father's wardrobe if I didn't know for a fact that no Snarkly ever wears the same outfit twice.

I catch David, sitting at a table in the corner. He holds a menu in front of his face. When he notices me, he momentarily dips the menu and nods. I show no acknowledgement, not wanting to bring any kind of relationship between me and him to Snarkly's attention.

Like a good lady, I pause as the waiter pulls back my chair for me to sit, then I look across the table into Snarkly's eyes, doing my best impression of adoration. I've certainly got a few questions for him tonight, mostly connected with his time at school—I want to see if I can subtly drag up any information on Finch.

Although the waiter gives us two menus to peruse, I let Snarkly do the choosing, not wanting him to think I'm getting too many ideas in my pretty head. He orders us wine and insists we have another toast, again to him becoming Prime Minister.

As we wait for our food, he informs me that the Party vote, to elect a new leader, shall take place the following week. He tells me that this might well be our last meeting till then, so we have to make the most of it. He then gives me a repulsive, twitching wink, as if he's got a fly stuck in his eye. I can tell by the way his hands tremble on the stem of his wine glass that he's apprehensive. I suppose he's worried about something coming out in the papers, sullying his good name—even his own party might take against him considering the kind of dirt Brian's holding on him.

Once he's through with feeding me the minutiae of his day, believing a day in the life of a politician to be just about the most fascinating thing ever, I manage to get him talking about his childhood.

Snarkly titters. His cheeks are already flushed from the wine. "My, it does seem a long time ago now, thinking about it, being a boy." He shakes his head and stares at the shallow puddle of wine at the base of his glass. "My goodness, can hardly remember anything, and yet, sometimes I get these individual recollections, a scent, an image, and they're so strong."

This isn't the kind of wistful remembrance I was angling for, so I decide to feed him another hint. "What about back at school? I read somewhere that you went to Fryson's."

He brings his hand to his forehead and grins. "Oh yes, Fryson's. Funny how, at the time, school seems the most dreary of all activities, and then once one is an adult we think about how happy we were."

I think back to my own school experience. I can't say I was happy at all. I spent most of my time pulverising the other girls at sport, while getting thrown out of just about every classroom. When an Army recruitment officer visited us in our last year, I was the first name on the list.

"Yes," Snarkly says, sipping more wine, "school is probably what I remember most of my childhood. I can still picture certain teachers, Mr Horsham, my maths teacher, I recall that he would wear a wig, and one day . . . one day"—he sobs with laughter—"one of the chaps stole it from the staff room, dunked it in baby powder."

I smirk.

Snarkly's laughter grows louder, his shoulders shake with the effort.

A woman from a nearby table turns in her seat and scowls at him.

"Then . . . then," Snarkly continues, "when he got back into the classroom, one of the boys asked him what shampoo he used, and Mr Horsham asked him what he meant, then the boy say, 'Well, if it's anti-dandruff it can't be doing you any good!'"

I wonder whether they get up to similar tricks in Parliament —if it's one great big boys' club. When Snarkly's composed himself, replaced his napkin in the collar of his shirt and drained the remainder of his wine glass, I go more direct. "What about any weak kids, did you have those? You know, the nerdy ones?"

Snarkly runs his tongue lightly over his upper lip and looks toward the ceiling, as if it were an autocue. He squints then says, "There was this one boy, a real sad case. Remember that he was there on a scholarship, think he made do with the same uniform for all five years. What was his name . . . ah, yes, Raymond Finch!"

Now we're getting somewhere.

"I . . . I remember running into him, at the last school reunion. We're all different now, grownups, of course, he told me that he has a computer company, or something like that. From the way he was conducting himself it seemed like it was going rather well."

"What did you do to him at school?"

Snarkly waves his hand. "Oh, nothing that bad, just pranks, harmless fun."

It's funny that what for Snarkly is innocuous can be the source of another person's lifelong resentment. Would he be surprised to find out that Finch has spent his whole life trying to get back at him, that right now, as he's about to reach the height of his life achievement, Finch is working to destroy him?

Snarkly barks for a waiter to bring us another bottle of wine.

"What did you do to him, though?" I say.

Snarkly examines the tablecloth, his eyes scanning the blank surface. Out of nowhere, still among his own thoughts, he snorts then looks up at me. "I can remember one of our pranks. It was a cold day, end of January, if I remember rightly. We were all getting changed for rugger when Dean Roper pulled me aside, just as the others were heading out to the school field, and told me that we should do something to Raymond's uniform."

The waiter arrives with the fresh bottle and pours out a healthy glass for Snarkly. When he approaches me I cover my glass with my hand.

Snarkly continues, "Anyway, we got hold of Raymond's socks and shoes. I waited for Dean to tell me what to do, and he said we should hide them outside. I had a better idea, though, I said that first we should piss in them, then put them outside. That way, even after he'd hobbled around looking for his shoes and socks he would find them piss-soaked and frozen." He chuckles. "It really was just a lot of childish high jinks."

"And what happened after? Did Raymond find his socks and shoes?"

Snarkly brings the wine glass to his lips. "Oh yes, poor devil."

With further prompting, Snarkly gushes out several more stories involving the increasingly unfortunate Raymond Finch, and I'm starting to build up a picture of not just why Finch resents Snarkly now, but what's pushed him on to be the success that he clearly is. That said, Finch clearly wants to be the one to deliver the punch line. To me, this all just seems so petty and cruel. But, everything considered, I find myself siding with Finch.

As a waiter helps me into my coat, I notice a familiar car arrive. It's sleek and purple, with tinted windows. It takes me another second to register that it's one of Brian's.

I mutter something about needing the toilet and slip away

from Snarkly. I exchange glances with David on the way, who's also clearly noticed Brian's arrival, appreciates my need to disappear. He takes over, keeping Snarkly occupied.

As I walk toward the toilets I keep my eye out for an emergency exit, but I can't see a single sign. Feeling a touch giddy, I consider myself lucky that there's no fire, I might be burning to death instead of filing myself for one in the near future.

When I get inside the toilets, it smells of lavender. I wonder who thought up the idea of putting lavender in toilets, it always reminds me of Army training in the Highlands, trekking through chest-high mud to reach the higher ground to pitch a tent. I take up residence in one of the cubicles, giving the lid a wipe and then sitting on it, waiting out the meeting between Brian and Snarkly.

I'm sure they really don't have that much to talk about. Brian is an expert in breaking away from unwanted social situations and surely he has better things to do with his evening than have his ear talked off by an over-anxious client. Then again, Snarkly isn't just any client. All going well, next week he will be Prime Minister.

The more I think about it, the more I believe that the only possibility is Brian inviting Snarkly to dine with him, to drink another bottle of wine. What does Snarkly value more, a sure thing going back to his penthouse, or a bit of back rubbing from his publicist. I really couldn't say.

I count out the seconds in my mind, when I reach three hundred, five minutes, I decide that I can't wait any longer. They might send someone to look for me, and that would create a fuss —exactly not what I need right now.

I flush the toilet for good measure, check my makeup in the mirror—it's still in place—and then I scoot out into the main dining hall once more. At first I can't locate Snarkly. And then, when I do pick him out, on the other side of the room, bending over Brian's table, making conversation, my heart dips.

Before I've processed what might be about to happen, I trot across the restaurant, meandering between tables till I've reached the other side of the room. Without pausing, I step out into the night where David's leaning up against the car, looking at me with a wry smile. "That was a bit close, eh?" he says.

"You're telling me."

As he opens the back door of the car for me, Snarkly bursts out into the street. "Anna? You missed meeting my publicist, I wanted to introduce the two of you. Would you mind coming in and saying a word?"

This is novel, I think, who on Earth goes round town introducing their mistress? I duck my head down and get into the car, keeping my lips firm and eyes down. "I'm tired, I want to go home."

The twinkle disappears from Snarkly's eye and he resembles something of a scolded cherub with his puffy cheeks and unkempt curly hair. He lingers at the entrance of the restaurant, caught between his publicist and his lover. "Right you are, dear, I'll be back in a second."

As I slide along the back seat, I look back into the restaurant, through the front window. I see Brian easily, looking out at the car, and—I'm almost certain—he's looking right at me.

Chapter Thirty-Three

WE ROLL ON THROUGH THE NIGHT, Snarkly working his way up my arm with fish-lip kisses. But there's nothing I can do. I can hardly shrug him off or he might throw me out into the street, decide to keep me at an arm's length from his business affairs after all. So I just sit there and let him.

Everything goes off as before. I keep my performance consistent, pretending to be a touch cross about him preferring to speak to his publicist, over going home with me, and then I let him seduce me.

When he's finished, with his customary cigarette in his hand, he looks to the door and says, in a quiet voice, "What do you think about David?"

The question catches me off guard. "I . . . I really don't know what to say."

"Just give me your impression of him."

"He seems professional, always well-dressed, like he knows what he's doing."

"Hmm, yes," Snarkly says, tapping ash over the side of the bed. "My thoughts precisely."

A draught blows in through the window and sends a shiver across my skin. I draw the bed sheet up to my throat.

Snarkly snorts. "It's just you can never know quite who to trust in this world. For all I know my most loyal employee might just be waiting to stab me in the back at any moment."

Worried that Snarkly's getting somewhere close to the truth, but also that since David was the one who reassured Snarkly about me, it puts me in a precarious position by taking it to the next logical step. With all that buzzing round my mind I can't be seen to be pushing the issue so strongly. "I think you're just concerned about next week. You're inventing things, being paranoid."

Snarkly brings the cigarette back to his lips and sucks on it. The end glows red and he blows out the smoke in a long, impossibly long, stream. "I think you might be right." He shakes his head, presses his finger, holding the cigarette to his temple. "God, what was I thinking? David's saved my life more times than I'd like to admit. Without him I wouldn't be in this position in the first place."

Glad I've got the opportunity to relax, I lay my head back on the pillow and stare at the ceiling, wondering how long I have to wait before making an excuse and disappearing off back home.

———

After calling up to schedule an appointment, and being told that she's available, I arrive at Julie's office feeling a little sheepish, not quite knowing what to expect from her. But now she's told me that she'll at least hear me out, so I'm hoping she'll stick to her word. I really hope she does because I can't imagine opening up to anyone else in the way I do with her.

Everything seems so normal when I step into her office. The carriage clock continues to tick away and the flowers are in their place. Julie sits on her chair, legs crossed. Today she's wearing an aquamarine jumper with the collar of a cream-coloured blouse sticking up through the neck.

We don't talk about the developments in terms of my career at first, just probing at the old familiar family problems. Like always there's some recent tragedy—Ben's birthday party, not to mention actually having broken Kate's wrist. Probably because there's an elephant in the room we gloss over the family issues somewhat before Julie lets out a long breath of hot air and says, "All right, Anna, I think we'd better talk about your career."

My heart does a dance in my throat. "Okay."

"You said that it affects everything in your life, do you think that's an accurate assessment?"

"I wouldn't have said it if I hadn't meant it."

Julie scribbles something on her notepad, propped up on her knee. "Right." She taps her pen against the pad. "Why don't you take me back to when it started, when you got into this . . . this line of work."

It seems so long ago now, like it doesn't really matter at all. I don't want to sound heartless, but those hits seemed so much easier than they do now—like I had no real idea about what I was doing, the meaning of taking someone's life away. I suppose it was something of a hangover from the mentality I developed in the Army. If I'd thought twice about snuffing out another human being, it would've meant my own neck. The difference now is that they haunt me afterward. While I go through the motions, neutralise the target, it's the period following which drags me through the mire.

I haul myself upward and sit with my back pressed up against the sofa, meeting Julie's eye. "I'd rather talk about what's been going on recently, if that's okay."

"That's fine, whatever suits you."

I analyse Julie's delivery of those words, sure that I find a little ice there—some kind of judgement. Sometimes I detect it, usually when I reel through some crisis or other with my family, not often, but occasionally Julie's professional veneer cracks. I tell myself how lucky I am to have her to confide in, that she would've been well within her rights—within the law—to turn me away.

I look round the room, trying to find those images from that night with Elizabeth, to bring back the thoughts and feelings I had. Already they're dulled. What was the most intense experience of Elizabeth's life is already fading from my memory. "I had to kill a girl. A politician's lover."

Julie scratches away at her pad. I know that most likely she's just trying to do something with her hands, so she doesn't have to stare at me. Once when I got a glimpse of her pad I saw that it was just covered in doodles.

"When I cornered her," I say, "I pressed her down against the floor. I couldn't kill her right away. I . . . I don't know why. I think that's when this problem started, when I started to have second thoughts about what I do for a living. That was my mistake. I should've killed her without thinking."

Julie glances up from her pad. "And what happened instead?"

"I talked to her. That's strictly prohibited. During the hit we're supposed not to have any connection with the victim, not even know their name. But I had to speak to her. I wanted to know what I was involved with. Where I fit into proceedings."

"That's understandable. You wanted to have a more tangible grasp of your worth to your employer, to feel more appreciated."

I'm about to deny it, to tell her that this really has nothing to do with some sense of job satisfaction, but I stop myself, knowing that she's right. Because despite all the faith Brian's consistently shown in me—the way he's bent over backward to accommodate my mistakes—I admit I want to know how important I really am. And so, now I know, I'm really up to my neck in it, and, for all I know, Brian might be ordering a hit on me right now—wanting to take care of me after seeing me with Snarkly last night in Tulips.

As I get ready to reel through some more of the hits, wanting to get onto the target, and that girl jumping at me through the gloom more than anything, my phone rings. I apologise to Julie then slip it out of my pocket.

When I get off the phone, Julie says, "Is that your employer?"

"Yes," I say, getting up. "Sorry, I have to go."

Chapter Thirty-Four

BRIAN WANTS ME in his office right away. I have no
doubt in my mind as to what it's about. Now I know that
he saw me at the restaurant last night, with Snarkly. I stop dead
on the pavement, really thinking through what I'm doing. Is it
really a good idea for me to go to him? If he did see me last night
then I might just be walking in there to sign my own death
warrant. But then I give it some more thought. Surely Brian
could have me killed without mentioning a word to me, let alone
inviting me into his office to do it. Maybe, maybe he's giving me
a chance to explain before setting an assassin on me.

For another few moments I linger on the curb, flushing
various situations round my mind, trying to get a handle on one
of them, whichever seems most likely to me. In the end I decide
to go. Perhaps I can explain it all away, play the innocent as I've
been doing so well with Snarkly. Brian doesn't know so much
about my private life. He doesn't know whether or not I'm the
type of girl who gets her kicks from going out with millionaires.

Candy's knelt down at her computer tower, picking through the wires, when I arrive outside Brian's office. She gives me a smile. "Hi, Anna."

"Still here?"

"Huh?"

"I mean, Brian hasn't fired you yet?"

"Oh no," she says. "He's very happy with my work so far, he's always telling me so."

A sparkle flickers in her eye, something which suggests something secret's going on—some arrangement between her and Brain. I knew he would get his nuts away with her eventually. Thinking about it makes me cringe, so I stop, change the subject. "Is he in a mood today?"

Before Candy gets the chance to answer, Brian boulders out through the large wooden doors, a smile on his lips, and he strolls up to me, crooking his arm round my shoulder. "Anna! How delightful it is to see you."

This is exactly the opposite reaction I was expecting. I wonder whether it's some well-worked charm, designed to catch me off guard and let down my defences. I suppose when you've decided to have a hit taken out on an assassin, it's best not to give them too much warning.

"Let's go get some lunch, shall we?"

I have approximately half a second to think this through, that he might want to take me out of his office to have me taken care of, before he's sweeping me along the hall, back down the stairs and out the building. He hails a cab and, my head spinning, we hop inside and power off down the road.

Everything about this reads just wrong to me. Leaving Brian's office, travelling in a taxi—I don't think I've ever seen Brian go with a taxi over his chauffeured car. I decide to stop panicking, that he's not going to drive me out to the docks, set my feet in cement then chuck me into the Thames. Not in broad daylight, in any case, that could only lead to bad press.

In fact, when we do arrive at our destination, I'm even more taken aback to observe that it's Tulips, the restaurant from the previous night, where I was with Snarkly. I look over Brian's features, trying to pick out some clue there, but, as always, there's no emotion, no give away, just his blazing smile and unbreakable enthusiasm.

Brian pays double the fare the cab driver asks, telling him the rest is a tip, then he shepherds me out onto the pavement. He arches his eyebrow in my direction. "Ever been here before?"

A tremble runs through my nerves. "Uh, no."

He studies me, shrugs, then says, "It'll be a real experience then."

With the realisation that I've just lied straight to Brian's face, I follow him inside the restaurant. It's not like I'm going to straight out admit I was here with Simon Snarkly. If he's already got it into his mind to have me killed, I don't think a little lying is going to make things any worse.

The waiter from last night leads us to our seat. He gives me a familiar smile but says nothing. I could get down on my knees, kiss his gleamingly-polished shoes and thank him, but that might give me away.

Brian whistles quietly to himself as he scans the menu. I can't remember ever having seen him this happy—and I can't help shake the feeling that it must be a front, like I thought before, he just wants me to be completely unsuspecting, give me a false sense of assurance so I sleep sound tonight, while someone dribbles poison in my ear.

I decide to cut to the chase. "What're you so happy about?"

"Oh, just life, I suppose," he says, with a grin.

"Which aspect in particular?"

He smirks. "I don't want to overanalyse it, let me enjoy my happiness while it lasts, won't you?"

I know that Brian's up to something. If it's my impending death then I take it as a gross insult, but I'm almost certain it's not—it must be something else, something important has gone well for him. Perhaps Snarkly's agreed to give him a job in his impending government.

When the food comes we eat in silence. All through the meal, Brian keeps up his carefree expression. It even seems like his hands are dancing his cutlery over his plate, launching his food into his mouth. He hums while he chews.

After the main course, he insists we order dessert, despite my protests, and I eat about a quarter of a chocolate cake before, at his request, sliding it across the table for him to devour.

I'm speculating what this whole dinner is about when he produces a familiar brown envelope from his inside pocket and slides it across the table. For the first time during our lunch, his grin lapses. "Tonight's target."

I take the envelope, slip it into my handbag for later.

Brian dabs at his mouth with his napkin then tucks a fifty pound note into the waiter's pocket once he's paid by credit card. He shakes all the waiters by the hand on our way out of the restaurant, before stopping at the maître d' and giving him a few words, another fifty pound note in his pocket. The maître d' rocks back in laughter—if he's faking then he's doing a very good job. Maybe he's an out-of-work actor, as so many waiters seem to be these days.

I'm wary when I see Brian's chauffeur-driven car appear at the top of the road, roll to a stop on the pavement. I can't remember Brian ever calling up to tell the driver where he was. Perhaps they have Brian on GPS, or something.

Brian sets one foot inside the back seat and looks up at me, over the opened door. "Where're you off to, then?"

"Back home, I think."

He nods to me. "I'd offer you a lift, but I'm really in a hurry, got a meeting on the other side of town."

"That's okay, I don't mind."

He lurches forward, gives me a kiss on each cheek then, still glowing, shaking his head, tittering to himself, he closes the door.

The car pulls out, accelerates off down the street.

I watch it disappear round the corner and consider what's driven Brian so crazy. One minute he's throwing whisky glasses at my head, the next he's laughing his head off, skipping all over the place as if we lived in Wonderland.

I spot an Underground station close by and work my way along the pavement, not going too quickly with my lunch still digesting in my belly. As I approach the steps I recall my assignment and remove it from my handbag. I keep it beneath my arm as I push through the turnstiles and then elbow my way in through train doors. By some miracle I manage to get a spare seat. After getting settled, clasping my handbag between my thighs, I tear the envelope open with my index finger and remove the stapled sheets of paper from within.

I turn through the many typed pages and reach the photograph of the target at the back. It's a crystal clear picture, printed in high-definition colour. But, even if it were in grainy black and white I'm sure I would recognise the person.

It's David. Snarkly's bodyguard.

Chapter Thirty-Five

O N THE TUBE RIDE back to my station, a thousand
hypotheses cross my mind. The first of which is that
Brian's set me up for this hit convinced that David will take care
of me, kill me before I have a chance to kill him. But Brian's
unaware that David's working against his boss, that, in fact, we're
supposedly working together.

And then, as my station approaches, another more likely situation appears from the depths of my brain, that Snarkly suspects
David and wants him done with. If Brian did see me with
Snarkly the other night then he's decided to keep me around
anyway—decided that I might still be of some use. Perhaps he's
unsure whether I saw him seeing me, which would mean he's
using me. But, if he's decided to spare me another few days, then
all I can do is what he orders.

And that would mean killing David.

I think about calling up AA, telling him what's going on. But I feel like I've been kept so far away from all this, what's really going on, that it just seems like he might laugh at me, tell me that I can't see the wood for the trees. Anyway, I never really said that I was on his side, only insinuated it. What has the opposition, Finch, offered me? Nothing, just a bunch of loose 'moral' reasoning. That's fine for them, but I've got bills to pay. First and foremost I am an assassin, and Brian pays my salary. I have to do what needs to be done, without letting sentiment get in the way.

I go about my preparations. I've still got the silenced pistol from the night at the fundraiser. It's still got five bullets left. I decide to take it with me, strapping it to my thigh. Then, as a secondary measure, I hook the knife onto my belt too. I'll have the element of surprise, as always, but it's always a good idea to have a backup, especially when facing someone as unpredictable and well-trained as David.

Before I head out the door, I pull Lizzie up to my chest, feeling her warmth seep into my bloodstream. As I listen to her endless purring, I take a moment to get my thoughts together, to try and forget all my interactions with David—to somehow dehumanise him. It's more difficult that it seems. But I tell myself that whatever his goals and motivations are, they are in direct conflict with those of my employer, and that it's my duty to take him out. I can do nothing about it. I purge all that he said to me, about having saved Snarkly countless times, that's immaterial now, because the order's been given that he's to die. Something or other has triggered Snarkly into thinking he's not to be trusted.

———

The details within the envelope specify that David will be located in Snarkly's penthouse that night. So that's where I go. The details give me the address of the penthouse, but I don't need it, already having visited twice I'm quite familiar with where it's located.

What puzzles me most is getting into the building. The front reception area is well-lit and the exterior has floodlights shining all over. The porter stands at the desk inside, flipping through a magazine.

This is where my information does help out. The map highlights a door round the back, an unguarded service entrance. I round the building, slipping past several plastic skips on wheels, brushing past them to the door I can see up ahead.

However, just as I'm about to step out of the shadows, I notice the camera, just above the door, juddering in an arch, swooping its lens over the area. Again, I find myself thinking that perhaps Brian wants me to get caught, that he purposefully told me this entrance was clean in the hope that I would just rush in without checking properly. I check myself, reasoning that the map is only a guide, not to be relied upon. As always I have to use my senses to protect myself out here. On a job I can't rely on anyone else.

I pull on my balaclava and keep myself low, holding my body against the wall, hoping that I won't show up on the security screens. As I go, I unclip the pistol from its thigh strap and screw in the silencer.

When I reach the steps leading up to the back door, I crouch down and wait for the camera to swing to the far side of its arc. When it does, I shift up the steps quickly and shoulder barge the door. Nothing. It's locked. I note the keyhole halfway up the door. I leap back down to my hiding position before the camera rotates toward me.

As I wait there, breathing heavily, I consider how I'm going to get inside the building. There's no way I can go back round the front, it's just too light. I'd have to remove the balaclava, so that I don't completely scream 'robber' at them, and then the porter would see my face, recognise me.

My best bet is to entice the porter outside, through the back door, then somehow sneak in before he has a chance to realise what's going on. I reach the conclusion that the best way to achieve this is to damage the camera in some way. I look round, notice a rock and pick it up. Just as the camera swings the other way, I toss it right at the camera. It cracks against the casing but the camera rolls on, apparently unharmed.

I examine the camera, trying to come up with something a little more savvy, and that's when I notice the wires snaking their way up the wall, before disappearing into a hole. I unsheathe my knife and creep up to the steps where I work at sawing the wires. It takes me about half a minute to crack through the outer shell —I guess that they've been designed with serious wear and tear in mind. With the frailer wires on show I jab the knife in.

Sparks fly and smoke curls out.

I give it another swipe, just for good measure, and then I return to my hiding place to wait and see what's going to happen.

There's a rustle inside, the clanking of the handle being opened, and then the porter steps out into the night air, a scowl firmly fixed on his face.

Chapter Thirty-Six

THE DOOR SLAMS SHUT BEHIND THE PORTER. It's on a spring of some sort. I'm going to have to wait until the porter goes back inside or get my hands on the keys somehow.

The porter strides up to the wires, still spurting sparks. He scratches his scalp, then his arse, and peers closer.

I feel the weight of my jumper against my chest as I breathe. I order myself to be patient, to wait there, let the porter step away from the staircase. As time goes by, though, I realise that I'm going to have to do something. The porter's making no motion to step away from the door and, to my horror, I watch him pull out a mobile phone, no doubt to call up an electrician. The last thing I need here is more people on the scene.

As the porter crooks the mobile between his ear and shoulder, nattering away to someone on the other end, I sneak up behind him, and lock my arm round his throat. He gags and drops the phone. It clatters onto the concrete beneath our feet, the voice on the other end still blabbering on. I strengthen my grip, feeling the muscles in his neck tauten, the air strain to trickle through his lips.

We stand there, frozen, for several minutes. I know that, very slowly, I'm killing him. I frantically try to think of another option, some other way I can deal with the porter. There might be somewhere I can stow him inside.

Keeping the porter within my clutches, I bring my mouth to his ear. "Where're your keys?"

He shudders within my grasp, on the point of fainting. With the last strength remaining in his arm, he indicates his back pocket.

I rifle through it and produce a key ring. "Which one is it?"

He mumbles something.

I relax my grip on his throat a little.

He lets out a gasp. "Small . . . the smallest one."

I pick it out, slip it into the keyhole and turn it. The mechanism clicks and I kick the door open. Grasping the porter tight I drag him through the door with me. We emerge in a bright room, lit by a bare bulb dangling from the ceiling. The floors are covered in a sticky slime, caked in dust and dirt, while a stench of disinfectant and sweet rubbish juice tickles my nostrils. I notice a cupboard with a slide lock on the outside. It's marked 'Supplies.' I yank it open and shove the porter inside.

Before he can cry out for help, I've already shut the door and locked it. He's clearly still recovering from my choke hold before he doesn't immediately rock up to the door and bash his fists against it. Perhaps he's got the sense to realise that I'm a mite stronger than him, that if I'd wanted I could've killed him just now. He'll wait a while before calling for anyone. His phone's still outside, on the ground, so he's not going to get anyone running to his aid quickly.

I readjust my balaclava before moving on through the supply area, and then getting into the reception. It seems bare without its porter and I hope that no one returns home, notices his absence and takes any kind of action. Time is on my side. It must be around two o'clock in the morning now, and since it's the middle of the week normally most people will be tucked up in bed. Then again, 'most people' don't live here.

I trudge up the stairs, keeping my back flat against the wall, to give me maximum vision round the corners. I suppose most people who live in this building take the lift, but I don't want to take any chances. When I get up to the floor with Snarkly's penthouse I'm out of breath, feeling sweat dampen the back of my neck. I get my gun ready, hold it out before me. I keep my footsteps as silent as I can, sneaking up to the door. With my gloved hand, I turn the doorknob and it opens.

I stand inside the silent penthouse sitting room. The flat screen TV situated up against the far wall reflects the moonlight streaming in through the blinds. I look off to Snarkly's bedroom and see the door's open. No harm done in checking in on him. I slink over to the doorway and peer inside. The bed's empty, the sheets tucked into the mattress. It all looks untouched. I suppose that tonight Snarkly's spending the night with his wife—it only makes sense for him to have an alibi the night his bodyguard is murdered.

I return to the sitting room, eyeing up the door to David's room.

Several panicked imaginings pass through my mind, that perhaps he's sitting upright in bed, hands gripping his gun or, worse, that he's pressed up against the wall, beside the door, just waiting for me to open it up so he can deal the killing blow.

With each step my feet seem to drag more, lead weights of expectation and anxiety pulling me back. Finally I reach the door and reach out for the handle. I take what might well be my final breath then jerk it open, gun pointing into the room, right at the bed.

The room before me is empty, bed made.

I spin round, gun held straight in my arm, but there's no one to be seen. I step further inside. My brain goes wild, speculating, everything from this being a setup to someone having tipped off David—that even now he might be headed for me, with backup, ready to teach me a lesson. Maybe I've underestimated Finch and his opposition to Snarkly. Perhaps they're even more influential than Brian, might they have spies within his organisation?

I back out of the room and go on to check out the rest of the penthouse. Everything is pristine, it reminds me of an anonymous hotel room. It's as if no one has ever been inside this place.

I think back to the report, sure that I must've missed some detail. I know that it was planned for tonight, I'm certain. The target was supposed to be in his room, sleeping. It should've been an easy job, an easy kill.

As I complete the post-mortem on yet another botched contract, I notice the sound of the lift doors sliding open and then feet scuffing against the doormat, outside the penthouse. I hardly have time to duck behind the sofa before the doorknob turns and two men enter.

"You never lock the door, then?"

The voice is all too familiar. I don't even need to look round the sofa to confirm it. It's AA.

Chapter Thirty-Seven

MY CALF AND THIGH muscles burn from crouching. I tell myself that I have to stay here, that any movement will alert the men to my presence.

The door whispers shut.

"Nah," David says. "Never any point locking doors in this place. Security's so tight. It's kind of like a small town village in the middle of the countryside, where everyone knows everyone else. Difference here is that everyone's got so much money that they don't have to worry about anyone stealing anything."

"That's nice," AA says.

Their voices are slightly woozy, a touch too loud. I'm guessing they've spent the past few hours in a club with deafening bass, knocking back a bottle of vodka, or two—if I know AA at all.

My mind does a double-take, trying to piece together why AA and David are together in the penthouse. A late night meeting to discuss the intricacies of Mathewson Media?

"Want a drink?" David says.

"As long as it's on the house, I'm game."

David's feet shuffle over the thick carpet and I hear the distinctive *squeak* of the hinges of the drinks cabinet. This is followed by the *slosh* of spirit hitting crystal and then the *clink* of glasses and the "Cheers" exchanged between the two.

I can't wait here much longer, listening in on this encounter. I need to act sooner rather than later or I'll lose my nerve. I can't think of these two as any connection to me. As far as the contract is concerned, AA is just another lump of flesh, if he gets in the way I need to take him out too.

"You usually have to break in?" AA says.

Cramp sets into my legs, prickling needles all over.

David's now standing only a matter of feet away, apparently looking out the window at the city lights. "Nah. Don't know what happened to the porter. Sometimes he scarpers off to the back room to have a nap." I hear him inhale, savouring whatever it is he's drinking. "Poor sod, can't blame him, having to stay up all night. No way to live, that."

"You've worked night shifts before, then?"

"Yeah, a long time ago, when I first got out of the Army."

AA's footsteps approach David's position and there's a long pause.

I have the urge to pop up from my hiding place, whip off the balaclava and announce that I'm there. But, with them being able to deduce what I've been sent to do, their reaction would be entirely unpredictable. If I were in their situation I know I would strike out at me, neutralise the intruder.

The silence goes on until I hear the unmistakable slopping, mashing sound of tongues lolling over each other. Kissing. And then it strikes me. The penny drops. David and AA are lovers.

My mind does a somersault. How? When? I suppose, considering that they're both inclined that way, it makes sense—all that danger, the collusion as part of the opposition to Snarkly's plans, working in close proximity. But, still, I would've thought AA would think to tell me. Or maybe we don't have quite the close friendship that he likes to make out.

I press the snout of the pistol to my temple and force myself to think. If I back out now, somehow manage to escape the penthouse without either David or AA noticing, then I'll have to face Brian, give him some explanation for not having gone through with the job. And, I'm sure, that'd be the final straw, that he would send someone after me—maybe even AA.

In the very best scenario, Brian would send me back, let me have another go at taking out David, and even if he did give me that opportunity, my nerves would be shot. I know that I've humanised David too far, have got it into my head that I will never ever be able to kill him. No, it needs to be tonight. I must kill him tonight.

I listen into the kissing, trying to pick my moment, improvise some sort of plan. If I were to rush out now, I might hit both of them. With only five bullets, I don't want to take on two targets. That would be too much of a risk, at least one of them is likely to survive. And, however terrible a person I am, I really don't believe I can finish either of them off with the knife—not now that I've hesitated, now that my hands are shaking.

They're murmuring words to each other, too low for me to hear. I have a horrible second where I panic, believing that they've spotted me, seen where I'm hiding, and they're only planning how to attack. But, seconds later, AA raises his tone. "Bathroom's through here, then?"

"Yeah, second door on your right."

AA's footfall sounds dampened on the carpet, before

becoming hollow and echoing when he reaches the wooden floor.

This is my opportunity. I have to do it now. Quickly. Reflex. No thinking.

David breathes loudly now that he's alone, sucking up air through his nostrils before exhaling through his mouth. I hear the *tinkle* of ice as he brings the tumbler down from his lips.

I grip the pistol tight then leap up, out of my hiding place. I train the gun on David's head and then freeze.

David flinches. He drops the tumbler and it smashes on the floor.

I don't know whether it's David's flinch or the sound of breaking glass that sends a pulse through my trigger finger, shoots the bullet into his brain, leaves him falling backward, arms clawing at the window.

I stand over David, hearing the flush of the toilet, somewhere in the back of the penthouse. His eyes loll in their sockets, I swear that he's looking right at me, that he still has life—if he had control of his limbs he would reach out and throttle me. And then the motion is gone and I'm staring into jellied eggs. They're not eyes anymore.

I shoot him another two times in the head, to make absolutely sure, before marching toward the exit. As I bring the door shut behind me, I hover for a couple of moments, to hear AA leaving the bathroom. With my ear pressed to the sturdy door, I make out AA's words.

"What was that sound?" AA chuckles. "Did you drop a glass or something?" There's a pregnant pause, then, "Oh, Christ!"

I trot down the stairs and then out across the reception area. There's a button beside the door which releases the lock and I rush out into the night air, anticipating my lonely walk home, with plenty of time to think about what I've done.

Chapter Thirty-Eight

I'M WOKEN by a thumping at my front door. My clock reads just after five in the morning. When I get up, Lizzie stirs at my feet, tilts her head up at me. I stroke her ears, pull a dressing gown round me then, as an afterthought, snatch hold of the knife lying on my beside table before heading downstairs to see who this nutter is.

I look through the spyhole and, in the dim morning light, see AA standing there, eyes drooping with dark circles and thick five o'clock shadow clinging to his cheeks.

He pounds his fist against the door again.

I toy with the idea of going back to bed, not opening up, but if I do that he might come round the back, smash his way in, and there's no way I'm going to get the police involved, not after I've just killed someone.

So, I slide the door chain over and open up a crack.

AA shoves his face right up to the opening. His eyes are wild and his hair unkempt. "David . . . they've got to David!"

I blink away the sleep in my eyes then slip the chain off and open the door fully. "Come in, then, you're going to get the neighbours round with torches at this rate." I close the door behind him and lead him into the kitchen. "I'll make you a hot drink, you look like hell."

AA lands himself on a chair and holds his head in his hands, staring at the table. "It . . . it happened so fast. I don't know how they got in, how they managed to . . ."

I don't ask AA to complete the sentence, knowing that he's still steeped in shock. Although in our line of work we're accustomed to killing, the feelings afterward, we're also used to locking those feelings away. Before any hit we've already psyched ourselves up, given ourselves some kind of code to justify what we must do. But, when death comes out of nowhere, in our ordinary lives, it's a different matter entirely. We're just like any other normal person, caught off guard by tragedy.

I slide a cup of hot chocolate beneath AA's nose.

He doesn't notice it, keeping up his thousand yard stare.

I take up the seat opposite, with my own cup of hot chocolate. "What were you and David doing together?"

AA shakes his head. "Does it matter?"

I decide to let it settle. I make a pledge with myself, that if AA really tells me about their relationship, I'll tell him who killed him. Trust has to work both ways.

I clasped the hot mug between my hands, soaking up the warmth. "What does this mean for the opposition, for working against Snarkly?"

"I don't know."

"Did someone work out that David was working against Snarkly?"

"Maybe . . . yes, I really don't know." He releases a long, staccato sigh. "The fact is that Simon Snarkly, as you probably know, is unpredictable, dangerous. He swings from loyalty to suspicion just like that." He snaps his fingers. "But David was careful. There's nothing to suggest that Snarkly didn't trust him. At least nothing that David noticed and told me about."

I recall the questions Snarkly had asked me, last time I met with him. He asked whether there was anything odd about David. I think I answered well, giving him everything he wanted to hear. Might I have said something then to save David? It hurts to consider it. The more I think about it, the more I believe that I planted something in Snarkly's head, some doubt in his mind. Did I have any role in this other than simply pulling the trigger?

AA turns his attention to his hot chocolate at last, sniffs at it and then takes a sip. He winces as he scalds his tongue, then looks at me with a weak smile, watery eyes. "Guess it just leaves you in Snarkly's camp, now. You're the only one with the inside info."

"He's going to become Prime Minister next week. Is there really anything any of us can do to stop him?"

"There's always something that can be done."

———

I plan an emergency appointment with Julie for the next day. It's not enough that we just about got round to raising my job in the last session—only touched on the issues that have been eating away at me all this time.

When I'm lying down on the sofa, staring up at the ceiling, I say, "I want to talk about the time that I nearly died."

Julie twitches her nose and taps her pencil against her notepad.

"It was one of my first jobs, just after I got out of the Army. I met my . . . my employer and he told me that he would give me an easy assignment, since I was just starting out. This person I had to kill, she was a model, not famous really, though, I think she'd done a few discount underwear catalogues, maybe topless modelling for some of the lower-end men's magazines—I really don't know much about that world. Anyway, I got my hands on a gun and was told simply all I had to do was get inside her house and shoot her, then walk away, as if nothing at all had happened."

I note that Julie's now holding the pencil between her fingers, quivering it. I know nervous tension when I see it. But I have to plough on with my story, get it out in the open, just so that I can tell myself that I've told it to someone.

"So, I got inside, it was fairly easy, she left one of the conservatory doors open, round the back of the house. There was a motion-sensitive light but when it went off I kept to the shadows. I was sure that no one had seen me. Once I was inside, among the dead silence, I remember the tingling sensation ebbing its way across my skin, squeezing my stomach. I thought that the ground might open at any second and that I might drop through, right to the Earth's core." I laugh nervously. "And that was when she leapt at me, out of the darkness."

I observe Julie's eyes dart away from mine, down to her notepad. She stops quivering the pencil in her grasp and, instead, begins to wriggle her toes, visible through the ends of her sandals.

"If this is making you uncomfortable we can stop," I say, "forget that you ever agreed to hear me out."

Julie stays quiet a moment or two, as if she's giving the idea serious consideration, and when she breaks out of her daze her voice is croaky, almost a whisper. "No, please, go on."

And so I do. "The girl just appeared out of nowhere and before I can react she's bringing this blunt object—I guess it was a fire poker, or something—down on my head over and over again. The first hit dazed me, sent me stumbling over backward, and then the second one seemed to dent my skull, stick cloth in my ears and make the world go dim.

"As she stood over me, panting, her hair sticking up all over, I thought that it was the end, that she would finish me off there and then. I . . . I remember thinking about my children, reading about what had happened in the newspapers, finding out who their mum really was, what she'd been doing when she died. A deep, empty darkness opened up within my chest and seemed to drag me into it, as if turning me inside out." I pause, getting a bit tearful. "I'm sorry, am I making any sense?"

Julie just nods.

"Just before she struck me for what I was sure would've been the final time, my last breathing moment, I managed to speak and I said to her, 'Please don't kill me. I don't want to die.'"

I screw up my eyes thinking about the corniness of those words, pretty much verbatim from every terrible film I'd ever seen. So similar to Elizabeth's shock when I was at the point of killing her.

"That made her pause, just for a second. I remember the poker, or whatever it was, shake in her grasp. And that was my moment. I cast off my dizziness, the blows she stuck to my skull, and I launched myself at her, knocked her back. I can still hear the reverberations as that poker clanged against the floor. Then . . . then all I remember is reaching for my gun, pulling the trigger and there just being blood everywhere."

Julie's staring at her toes, her lips puckered together as if glued.

"And ever since then it's all just seemed automatic. Like none of it ever matters. Maybe it had something to do with her hitting my head, perhaps she reprogrammed something deep inside my brain and I just lost that moralising capacity. I call it my Kill Switch. Now I just turn it on and everything else goes away." I run my tongue along the ridges of the roof of my mouth. "That is, until recently. Until the girl I told you about yesterday. And everything else afterward. Now I can't seem to refind the Kill Switch. It seems like it's gone forever."

Julie takes me off guard slightly when she breaks her silence. "And how does that make you feel?"

I smirk a touch at the therapist-speak. "Weird. Kind of like waking up after a dream. Like, until that last contract, I was living on some other plane of reality. Now it feels like I'm amongst the living again."

Julie nods to herself, scrawls a few notes then stops mid-flow, as if an urgent thought has caught her. She opens her mouth, closes, then opens it again. But no sound comes out.

"This isn't right, is it?" I say. "I've asked too much of you."

"No," Julie says. "It's . . . it's just. Your world, it's completely different to everything I've ever imagined. I never thought that such cruelness existed, such mindlessness. I suppose I always think the best of human nature, that everyone can be cured."

"You're saying you don't think I can be cured?"

Julie shakes her head. "I genuinely think there's hope for everybody. We all need a chance. There's no such thing as a hopeless case." She swallows, looks me in the eye for the first time in our session. "Anna, you've got to find your own peace, decide what's normal for you. Otherwise you'll be lost forever."

Chapter Thirty-Nine

LATER IN THE EVENING I get a call from Arnold. He wants me to look after the kids for the weekend, because he wants to take Kate away for her birthday. I challenge him, asking whether he really trusts me with the kids, alone. He sounds a little shaky when he responds, but he says that he does. I can hear Kate in the background, whispering something unintelligible to him, but it doesn't affect his answer at all, and there it is, I'm looking after the kids this weekend.

I make a special effort to make myself look presentable, putting on some makeup and picking out a pair of jeans without too many rips in them. I might be doing well financially but my natural thriftiness is preventing me from splashing out on anything as extravagant as clothes. Maybe once all this Snarkly business has blown over the world will stop spinning long enough for me to take some time for myself.

I also decide to take Lizzie and hopefully deflect some of my bad mothering onto her, let the kids occupy herself with a pet while I inevitably do something neglectful.

When I get to Arnold and the kids' house, Kate and Arnold are in relay, running up and down the stairs, clutching various things: jewellery, clothing, fistfuls of cash. The car boot's already crammed full with luggage and I wonder how they're ever going to fit anything else in.

I keep Lizzie clutched to my chest—I still haven't had the presence of mind to go out and buy a cat carrier—as the bustling action passes me by.

Kate stops at my side, clutching what looks like a makeup bag. She sets the bag down then, with her good arm, reaches over and strokes Lizzie on her head.

I try to telepathically order Lizzie to bite, but, being the undiscerning animal she is, she purrs out loud as if Kate were just another human being.

"So cute," Kate says, then stifles a sneeze.

"Got a cold?" I say.

"Oh no," she says, still holding her nose. "I'm . . . I'm—" She sneezes again and again, then has to dash away to the toilet. She returns, tissue pressed to her nose. She speaks through it, making her sound nasal and whiney. "I'm allergic to cats."

"I can see that," I say, rubbing Lizzie's belly.

Arnold and Kate finally get their things together, while I watch on, standing on the porch with Josie and Ben at my side, Lizzie still purring away in my arms.

They betray their frail show of confidence somewhat because they say goodbye about a million times, each time looking to me as if I'm a thermonuclear warhead that they expect to go off at any moment. Then, after a final dual glance at me, they're reversing out of the drive and then motoring away from the house.

I stand on the step with my kids, wondering what happens now.

The kids seem just as uncertain as I am, not really knowing what they're supposed to do with their mum. A few seconds later, Ben excuses himself and heads upstairs, back to immerse himself in video games. Josie, however, hangs round at my heels, playing with Lizzie's tail, twirling it round her finger.

"How long are Dad and Kate gone for?" she says.

"Just a couple of days."

"Oh."

"Is that okay?"

Josie seems to consider this. "We'll help you."

I manage a smile. "That'd be great."

While Ben taps away at his video games in his bedroom, me and Josie watch some TV. I don't know what parents complain about when they talk about being tired all the time. This parenting stuff isn't so difficult.

My mobile vibrates in my pocket. I check the caller ID and see that it's AA, and I hang up on the call. I'm really in no mood to talk about conspiracy, national-level politics or escaped tyrants looking for a new home for their state-stolen funds. But he calls back another nine times. On the tenth I decide to put him out of his misery and I answer.

"Look, AA," I say. "I'm with my kids this weekend. What do you want?"

There's a long silence, then he hangs up.

Josie rests her head on my stomach and looks up at me with her wide eyes. "Who was that, Mummy? Was it your boyfriend?"

I stifle a chuckle. "No, that wasn't my boyfriend."

"Do you have a boyfriend?"

I think about Snarkly. There's not really a suitable term that a nine-year-old girl would understand to describe our relationship. This is one of those moments that demands a simple white lie. "Nope, I don't."

Josie sits up on the sofa, eyeballs me. "Why don't you have a boyfriend?"

"Dunno," I say. "It just doesn't appeal to me."

"But all the other mummies and daddies at school that don't live together have boyfriends or girlfriends."

"Oh, I'm sure that can't be true. There must be a few that are single."

"Nuh-uh, Francesca's mummy has a boyfriend. Her daddy lives in France and he has a girlfriend there, too."

This conversation-slash-psychological assessment is starting to get on my nerves. "Good for Francesca's mummy and daddy."

We watch some more TV then, at about eight thirty, I decide it's time for Josie to go to bed and I tell her so. She does what I say. No resistance whatsoever. Once again, I question all these myths making it out that parenting is hard. This whole evening's been a complete breeze.

Josie takes herself off to the bathroom to clean her teeth, while I go into Ben's room and check on him. He's playing some army game, in some jungle setting, shooting a bunch of vaguely foreign-looking people.

I spot a man up on a ridge. "Up there, on your left."

He points his virtual gun at the man and fires.

The man drops onto his front, then, a little theatrically, tumbles down through the air groaning.

"You'd better turn off soon," I say.

Ben mumbles something at me, but keeps playing.

I leave the room, go to see to Josie who's already tucked herself up in bed, her bedside lamp now providing the only light. I perch on the end of her bed. Her bedroom smells so clean, like someone had washed the whole place with soapsuds. I lean over her and plant a kiss on her forehead, my heart rapping at my throat. "Sleep tight, sweetheart."

She gives me a smile then keels over on her side, to face the wall.

I stay there for a moment, just looking at her, thinking about what a good girl she's turned out to be, and how little influence I've really had over her childhood. That's a sad thought so I ward it away, slip out of her bedroom, closing the door so that it's only open a sliver, and then go back to check on Ben.

Predictably he's still glued to the screen, fingers tapping away at the controller, men dying by the second in the video game, all with their synthesised groans.

"Bedtime. Now," I say.

He plays on, the little bugger pretending that he's not even heard me.

"Oi, cloth ears!"

Still no reaction.

My attention turns to the screen again, I spot another man, creeping up on the periphery. "On the left," I say.

He kills that man too.

The screen fades to black and the word 'Victory' appears in gold lettering. The game sums up Ben's performance on the last level, detailing his firing accuracy, men he's 'neutralised' along with something about hidden items, he's found all fourteen of those.

He turns round and looks at me. "Wanna play?"

I consider the invitation. It's still early, although I really have no idea what time a twelve year old should go to bed. Anyway, I sit beside him, feeling the rigid wooden bedframe beneath my bottom. "Don't you get sore sitting here all day?"

"Nah," he says, thrusting a controller into my chest.

I hold the controller in my hands, baffled by the various coloured buttons, the three sticks. "Uh, what am I supposed to do?"

"You were in the Army," he says. "This should be natural."

"It's a little different. You know in the Army we don't get given these little control pads. It's much simpler there's just one button on a real gun."

He points at a green button on the pad. "That's how you shoot."

"Good to know."

We play a few games. It's just us, shooting at one another. Ben kills me over and over again. I've really got no chance since it's just about all I can do to keep my character moving in the direction I want, let alone shoot. Although we don't talk it's like an unspoken feeling passes between us, that we're closer than we've ever been before.

I'm aware of the clock sitting on the TV screen which has just ticked over to ten and I'm just about to call it a night when my mobile buzzes again. I look at the caller ID. Who else?

This time I duck out of Ben's bedroom and answer while standing on the landing. "What is it, AA? What do you want?"

There's just static again and I think that he's on the point of hanging up—as if he's making a prank call—when he says, "I know that you killed David. How could you?"

Chapter Forty

AA'S WORDS render me speechless for a few moments. Every time I try to form a reply I just can't find the strength to get the words past my lips.

"Nothing to say to me?" AA says. "Just going to keep on going like it was just another hit? When were you going to tell me?"

I break out of my stupor. "You never told me about you and him. How was I supposed to know?"

"This has nothing to do with me and him. It has everything to do with working against Snarkly, making things right. You've put the whole operation in serious danger."

Tears prick my ears and my cheeks flush with anger. "What operation? I have no idea what in the hell is going on with anything! I was doing my job, nothing more."

"I thought you were one of us."

"When did I say that?" I say, then remember the kids, remember to lower my voice. "You know that my first duty is to

Brian, I have to take care of whatever business he wants me to. What would he have said if I'd turned down the hit on David?"

The sound of AA's breathing crackles down the phone line.

"Well?" I say.

"You should've come to me, told me what he wanted you to do."

"Oh right, I see, so you're my boss now, is that it?"

Another long pause. "I can't believe you did it, Anna. What if I'd got in the way, would you have shot me too?"

I don't speak for a few moments, not wanting to answer that question directly. There are some very wrong answers I could dish out right now. Then I settle on what I know is all I can tell him. "If you'd been in my position, doing your job, you would've done exactly what you needed to, to fulfil the contract. Don't tell me you wouldn't have."

AA swears beneath his breath, then says, "God, I can't talk about this right now. This is just all . . . all wrong."

"Tell me about it."

He hangs up.

I stand on the landing, staring at a painting of a yacht in a rough sea. It's from mine and Arnold's old house, the house we had just after I came out of the Army. It's strange seeing it here, out of context, like someone lost at sea turning up in the garden one morning.

I let myself simmer down then go back into Ben's room where I pick up the controller and continue from where we left off. It's after midnight before I realise how late it's got. I observe the lines etching themselves round Ben's eyes. He needs to get rest, and I tell him so.

Once he's turned off the TV, I head to where the bed's made up in the spare room. The bed sheet is crisp, not a wrinkle anywhere. I wonder how long Kate spent getting it just right. Did she do it so I would feel comfortable here, or so that I would see how much of a failure I am, how much better she is than me in every single way?

I strip down to my knickers and remove my bra. Then I yank back the bed sheet and crawl inside, staring upward at the window in the ceiling which offers a view of the clear night sky, stars blinking down on me. I feel like a teenager again, staying over for the night at a friend's house.

Lizzie slips round the doorframe, leaps onto the bed and curls up at my feet.

At least I'll have some company tonight.

———

The rest of the weekend is moderately successful. I manage not to burn down the house or kill either of my kids. On Saturday we visit a zoo nearby. I gawp at the prices before realising that I'm somewhat flush at the moment. Still it seems exorbitant to shell out just to watch some bored animals watching us back—no matter how exotic. The Sunday we go to a park round the corner in the morning, somehow managing to wrench Ben away from his video games, and then watch bad family films on TV in the afternoon.

I've lost track of time when I hear Arnold's car pull up outside, the engine idle then turn off. Both kids, as if radio-controlled, leap up from where they lie on the sofa and rush the door. I try to remember the last time they reacted in that way to one of my visits.

Never, that's when.

Kate and Arnold bound in, both of them grinning as well they might after an entire weekend of shagging.

In amongst all the welcoming, I sneak my way upstairs, locate Lizzie, then shunt her beneath my arm. Her purrs vibrate through my skin and calm me a little in the face of the situation. I get down to the bottom step, about to complete my retreat, when Kate intercepts me.

"Annie?" she says. "You're not going home right now, are you?"

I murmur something about having stuff to do.

"I was just about to put a shepherd's pie in the oven. It'll only be half an hour or so. They're worth the wait, even if I do say so myself."

"No, really, I have to go."

Ben's eyes wander over mine and he gives me a feeble smirk, knowing that once more his mother's going to pull her disappearing act—be gone as quickly as she came.

I give him a wave and think about saying goodbye to Josie too, but I can hear her high-pitched voice tremolo from the kitchen, where she's deep in conversation with Arnold. And I really don't feel like having an awkward farewell with Arnold, not today.

Kate calls to the kitchen, wanting to bring Arnold out, but before he does I've unlatched the front door and I'm halfway down the path, on my way to freedom.

————

When I get to the top of my street, I notice that something's wrong, that the front of my house just looks wrong. As I get closer I realise that the front door's wide open. Getting closer, still, I see that it's been jimmied open, the wooden frame in splinters. I hold back, worried about the danger, and then I tell myself I'm a fearless assassin and manage to take a few steps toward my house.

Lizzie squirms from my grip and, before I can recapture her, she's escaped, trotting her way inside like it's just another normal day.

I wait to hear some response from inside—I don't know what I'm expecting, perhaps for one of the burglars to say, "Hello, puss."

Inside it stinks of alcohol, spirits. Since I have nothing alcoholic in the house I presume that it must be some homeless person who's broken in. I glance up the staircase, thinking about my gun, two bullets nestled inside, the knife stowed away in the box. I hope they haven't dug them up.

Then I hear a sob coming from the kitchen.

It sends a tremor up my spine. I tread closer to the source of the sound, keeping my eyes alert, telling myself that I'll have the advantage over whoever's in there—they'll be off their face on some combination of drugs and liquor.

I round the doorframe and find AA sitting at the kitchen table, a large bottle of gin in front of him and his head in his hands, whimpering away to himself.

Chapter Forty-One

"WHAT THE HELL IS THIS?" I say.

AA flinches. He raises his head, wipes his nose and eyes on his shirt sleeve. "Didn't hear you coming in."

"What've you done to my front door?"

His eyes seem to be pressed back in his skull, considering me from the back of his head.

I notice sprinkles of cocaine on the kitchen table. "Jesus, what're you doing in my house, in this state? Couldn't you see that I wasn't home?"

"Needed to speak to you."

"And you couldn't just call me up? Don't you remember me telling you I was at my kids' house this weekend?"

"Must've slipped my mind."

As I get closer to him I realise there's a puddle of vomit at his feet. I shuffle past it and duck down beneath the sink to get out a bucket and a bottle of floor cleaner.

"I had nowhere else to go, Anna."

"Nonsense," I say, pouring floor cleaner into the bucket, then sticking it beneath the hot tap. "You've got a perfectly serviceable flat. Nice views. Much nicer than this flea pit."

He glances round himself. "You got fleas here?"

"Maybe not now. You probably killed them all with your body odour."

He nods to himself as if this were an unalterable fact.

I pull the bucket out from beneath the tap and lug it over to AA's feet. He doesn't move as I clean round him, diluting the vomit.

"I don't blame you, Anna."

I straighten up. "What did you say?"

"I don't blame you." He sniffles and then continues, slurring his words. "You know, for killing David. You were just doing your job. I know that."

"Glad you've come round to seeing my point of view."

While AA remains slumped in the chair, I finish up my mop work then pour the bucket out into my front garden. It absolutely reeks of stomach acid and booze. I swallow down an urge to puke myself, then return inside.

I approach AA, hold out my hand to help him to his feet. "Come on," I say. "Let's get you dried out and washed up."

————

AA sleeps most of the afternoon in my bed, while I lie on the sofa downstairs, watching TV. I hear his mobile going several times, vibrating its way along the bedroom floor. About the sixth or seventh time it happens it really starts to bug me so I hop up the stairs and retrieve it. The caller ID shows that Finch is ringing. I look over at AA, on another planet, mouth open and eyelids twitching as he sleeps. I step out onto the landing and answer the call.

"Adam?" Finch says.

"This is his female companion."

"Anna? What's happened to Adam?"

"Let's just say he's a little worse for wear."

"He's . . . he's not dead is he?"

I snort. "No, at least not quite. You'd be better off calling back later, then I can give you a more thorough report."

Finch doesn't laugh or deviate from his straight-laced tone. "You heard about David?"

I'm about to make some quip that I was the one to take care of him, but I decide not to. Not yet. "Yes, I did."

"Terrible business. A good man."

A croak enters my voice. "Yes." Then I try to clear my mind of any sense of guilt or regret—what I did was pure business. "Does this have any knock on effect for the plan?"

"No," Finch says. "The wheels are well in motion. There's nothing that can stop us now. I'm sure of it. David will be mourned but he served his purpose. He's done his bit for the greater good."

I've always wondered what's meant by that statement. I can never seem to comprehend how someone who's dead, that is being munched on by worms, can have any sense of honour or gratification for what they've done. All they are is dead.

Finch continues, "I suppose that Adam has told you about the plan, how it's all going to happen this week?"

I think of AA conked out on my bed, possibly a strand of dribble making its way down his chin. "No, not yet."

"Ah," Finch says. "Right then, I'd . . . I'd better let you in on what's going on."

Lizzie arrives at my feet, brushing herself against my shins.

"Yes, you'd better," I say.

"Now, the idea is to cause maximum confusion, to really leave the whole situation up in the air. We don't just want to destroy this one agreement, between Brian and Abdul-Hakam, we want to stop this from ever taking place again. I—"

But I've already got a strong inkling of where this is leading next. "You want me to kill Snarkly?"

"Yes."

I think of his face, the time we've spent together, while it's been something of a wretched ride, I do find that I have some sense of compassion for him, that I pity him in a strange way. He's never had any choice in his life, been shown down the only road available to him—that of fortune and plenty. Sure he had David killed, but that was an action of fear. He was terrified that someone might break his upward arc to taking what he's always believed to be rightfully his.

This is one hit too many, I think.

"Well, Anna?" Finch says.

"I can't do it. I'm sorry. It's too difficult, I know him too well. I . . . I think I might make a mistake."

Finch stammers, then says, "But you're in the best possible position to take him out. You can do a great thing."

"I'd be working for you, and I don't think my employer would like that."

He scoffs. "What are you, married to him?"

It's difficult to describe the relationship I've built up with Brian. Through all the deception associated with me hanging round Snarkly, being too close to one of his clients, I've studied it further and further—become more sure of the mutual trust that exists between the two of us. Up until now I can see him forgiving me, maybe he already has, after seeing me and Snarkly dining together. But if I were to kill Snarkly, one of his clients who Brian admits is 'paying through the nose' for Mathewson Media's services, then that would be an unforgiveable betrayal.

"I'm sorry," I say. "I can't go behind the back of my employer. He would never forgive me. I work for him and him alone."

Finch sighs. "Very well. Then I suppose I shall have to find someone else."

"I think you'd better. Maybe . . . maybe AA would be interested in the job."

"Adam's head's not in the right place ever since David was killed, but I'm sure that you've noticed that yourself."

I purse my lips. "I had picked something up."

"Goodbye, Anna, and good luck."

I replace the phone at AA's side, then consider what's going to happen next. I have hardly any time to think before the phone's ringing again. This time it's my mobile. And it's Brian.

Chapter Forty-Two

I WAIT ON THE CURB. Brian told me he'd be by to pick me up in a matter of minutes, it's now been fifteen. He's always had a keen sense of keeping people waiting. Perhaps he believes it makes him seem more important. To be fair, if I had Brian's money and influence I'm sure I would do whatever I wanted.

A sleek limousine rolls up and the back door clicks open. I take this as my queue to step inside. When I do, pulling the door shut behind me as I land on the leather seat, I note the scent of champagne in the air. Brian perches on the back seat with a glass in his hand, a grin creasing his cheeks.

Drunk again, I think.

"This one's to you, Anna," he says, then knocks back the glass before replacing it in a holder impressed in the side of his door.

I think back to AA, worrying myself about whether or not I left him sleeping on his side. If he pukes while he's on his back he'll choke to death and even someone as black-hearted as me might have a problem getting over that. "What's this about?" I say.

Brian shuts one eye, points his finger at me, like a pistol. "Always direct, cutting right to the bone. That's what I like about you, Annie."

"Don't call me Annie. It makes you sound like my ex-husband."

He winks. "Advice taken." Then he shifts his weight so that he's sitting face on to me. "Have you got something to tell me, *Anna*?"

"Like what?"

"Oh, I don't know. Anything at all. You're sure you have a clean conscience, nothing on your mind that you'd like to relieve on me?"

All this relieving is going to make me want the toilet soon. "No."

He arches an eyebrow. "Come on, there is something you should be telling me." He cackles. "You've been a very naughty girl."

A lump gets caught in my throat. I swallow it back. "No, there's nothing."

Brian's features press together, going all serious, he lurches forward in his seat and raps his fist against the driver's divide.

The car skids to a halt.

Not wearing my seatbelt, I almost plunge right across the limo, only its obtusely-angled seats save me. I press myself back in my seat, still catching my stomach after the sudden jerk forward.

With no trace of his previous cheeriness, he looks me over. "We've always been honest with one another, Anna. It would be a pity to waste our special relationship."

As if triggered by those words, the windows winds down to reveal a river, off to my side of the car.

A sliver of a smile shades Brian's face. "I wouldn't try to run, if I were you. I've got two of my best bodyguards up front. They'll be on you in a second, ready to dispose of you at my whim."

I look out the window at the muddy water. I spot a condom floating amongst the discarded plastic bottles and scum.

"Now," Brian says, "we saw each other in Tulips. All you have to do is admit who you were there with and we can get on with mending our relationship."

My mouth dries up, my tongue feels like a parched sponge. "I . . . I was there with Simon Snarkly."

Brian cracks a grin, claps his hands together then stomps his feet. "Atta girl! I knew you would come good sooner or later." He taps his fist twice against the driver's divide.

The car window rolls back up and the car drives on, away from the river.

———

On the way back in the car, Brian explains how he first found out I was around Snarkly when David scanned my details—the ones he found in my purse the night I went back to the penthouse. He decided not to act then, to wait and see what was going to happen.

As we swoop round a corner, probably doing about ninety miles per hour—although no policeman would dare stop this car —Brian squeezes my knee. "You remember the day when I threw that glass of whisky at your head?"

"Uh, just about."

"One of my minions had just informed me that your name had shown up during a check ordered by Simon Snarkly. I had no idea how to deal with that information. All sorts of things flushed through my mind, that you might've got involved with someone else, started to work for them."

A slight shudder crosses my skin as I think about Finch, my conversations with him. But I have nothing to fear since I told him in no uncertain terms that Brian's my employer. I made myself clear, didn't I?

Brian raises his finger to the air, as if checking which direction the wind's coming from. "But then, then I realised it might be a terrific opportunity, that you might be in the perfect position for what's going to be the endgame in all this Snarkly nonsense."

"What do you have in mind?"

"First of all, now we're back treating one another like regular human beings, as it should be, I think you have earned the chance to know more about the intricacies of my involvement with Snarkly and this Middle Eastern fellow."

I'm all ears now.

"My stake in all this is quite clear. This Abdul-Hakam character has money he wants to bring into the country—he came to me first, before Snarkly, wanting me to flex my publicity muscle, put him in touch with someone who might be able to help out. He agreed to give me a substantial cut of his funds if I was successful." A grin lights up his face. "Which I'm very close to being."

"But . . . but where does that money come from?"

Brian throws up his hands. "Who cares? This guy's got his hands on it now, so all that interests me—as a businessman—is how I'm going to manage to extract it from him. Money has no smell."

I consider all those people, back in Abdul-Hakam's country, waiting for their money to get back to them—possibly already realising that, like so many others, they will never see it again. "And what happened when Snarkly came in, wanting you to make him Prime Minister?"

Brian knits his fingers together. "I simply combined the two, saw an opportunity."

"So you are blackmailing him?"

"If you define blackmail as withholding certain truths. No, I don't believe that's what I'm doing. Snarkly will get his cut just like the rest of us. He's no sacrificial lamb."

I think back to Snarkly's sob-show, trying to work out whether all he told me was genuine, or if he was just trying to get me onto his side. He is a politician, after all, only concerned with saving his own skin—although I suppose in that way he's been more or less honest.

"What's next?" I say.

The car brakes then stops. Through the tinted windows I can make out the shadowy familiar shapes of the houses on my street. This is my stop.

Brian presses his thumbs together. "This is something of a different job. I'm sure you've reached the conclusion that you killed Snarkly's bodyguard on your last contract, so I want you to keep Snarkly alive in the hours leading up to the vote."

"Doesn't Snarkly have a replacement lined up?"

"Oh he's guarded twenty-four hours a day." A slender smile escapes Brian's lips. "This should be an easy job, the easiest one yet. My brief with Snarkly ends on the day of the vote and I promise I'll give you a chance to let down your hair after this is done."

"Yawley's again?"

"No, I think this calls for something a little more special than Yawley's."

Something more special than Yawley's?

The door opens and a large, black man, wearing a suit—one of Brian's aforementioned heavies—stands there.

Brian winks. "I'll be in touch."

Chapter Forty-Three

I GET AA OUT OF THE HOUSE later that evening. He apologises briefly but I know that he doesn't really mean it. He still blames me for the hit on David even though I was just following orders. Maybe we'll find ourselves with our roles reversed in the future, him killing a beau of mine, and he'll get some well-sought justice. Until then, though, he'll just have to make peace with what's happened. No one told him to get into this business—like me—but, goodness, do I know how difficult it is to get out of it.

Everything goes impossibly quiet for the rest of the week. I realise that all the scheming is going on somewhere in secret, that Abdul-Hakam must be working out the various technicalities to get his funds ready for transfer, while Snarkly's preparing his speeches, having midnight meetings to convince any unbelievers on the backbenches that he should become leader of the Conventional Party. Brian, as always, will be in the midst of it all, muckraking.

When I flick on the TV that night I can't get away from it. All the news channels feature coverage of the leadership election. I wonder whether the fact they've put up three candidates—three different overgrown schoolboys—is merely just for show or if there really is a possibility that Snarkly might not win the election. Funnily enough, Snarkly is the youngest of the three, in his mid-forties while the other two look well-set in their sixties, perhaps even early-seventies. In all other walks of life, all other jobs, age is seen as being a disadvantage whereas—in politics—it seems to exude some kind of fatherly elixir.

Or grandfatherly elixir.

That night I lie awake for a long time, considering my unprecedented brief, to keep someone alive. Do I have that capacity within me? Am I more than just a destroyer?

———

The call comes in the afternoon, the day before the election. Brian tells me to get to Snarkly's flat, that he's expecting me, and to make sure I'm properly armed for the evening ahead. He claims that an attempt on Snarkly's life is quite possible. And, despite the security, he doesn't want me to take any chances. I think about the key taped inside the box and decide that now's the time to use it.

I scrabble through my wardrobe, slide the box out of its place and peer inside. The pistol, with its silencer, and knife are safely stowed there. I tear the key from its place and slip it into the pocket of my jeans. I think about the knife, not sure whether or not to bring it with me. In the end I do take it, slipping it onto my belt then concealing it with my jumper.

Lizzie rubs herself up against my arm and leaps up onto the

rim of the box, staring inside. Before I can stop her she's pawing around inside, making a bed for herself.

I reach in and run my fingers over her head, feeling the vibrations of the purr. Then, deciding I need to get going, I leave her to sleep the box. I head downstairs then out the door, catching a bus which leads out of town.

I rest my head against the cold windowpane as the bus rumbles on, glaring out into the street, the people bustling by in the street. Fifteen minutes or so later, the bus leaves most people behind, taking me out to a flat area of land replete with crumbling terraced houses, time long done with their windows and now working to bring down every brick, one-by-one. I hop off the bus when I reach the next stop, thanking the driver as I go.

The street's deserted as I make my way along the cracked pavement, tiptoeing through the pieces of broken plastic and glass. I reach for my knife, resting my hand on the grip, knowing that if I get into trouble I'll be relying on myself to get out of it. I've never been confident with a knife, much preferring a gun. But, as much as Brian could fix any kind of trouble, I know that today of all days he's busy, and doesn't need to be pulling strings to get some dizzy assassin out of prison for possession of a firearm.

I reach the compound without running into anyone. As I pass through the iron rail gates, topped with razor wire, gleaming in the sunlight, I allow myself to relax. I'm in a position of relative safety now.

The compound is filled with shipping containers, stacked one on top of the other. Their paint is peeling and it's clear that none of these have seen a ship in a very long time. Rickety stepladders litter the yard, leading up to precarious metal platforms which give access to the stacked containers. A whiff of rust clings to the whole place, reminding me of blood.

A dilapidated portable building stands to one side of the path, its windows cracked and a large hole in its side, revealing a soggy, stained blue carpet inside. A crooked sign hangs off the side which reads 'reception,' then, to its side, a dirty-white door-bell, wiring exposed.

I step up to the doorbell and ring.

A few seconds later, a man emerges. He has a large gut which flaps over the waistband of his jeans. He's in the process of doing up his belt. He leers at me and says, "How can I help you, love?"

"Just here to pick something up," I say, producing my key and showing it to him.

Over the man's shoulder I can hear moans and groan coming from within the portable building. I suppose he gets bored around here, all by himself. He cocks his head to one side, apparently unabashed that sounds of his pastime spill out into my earshot. "Gotta sign in first."

"Fine," I say.

He licks his lips, revealing his missing two front teeth in his upper gum. "Thing is, seems I've lost the logbook."

Getting impatient, I shift my weight to the other foot. "Then how do I get to my container?"

He shrugs, a little grin at the corner of his mouth.

I suppose problem-solving skills aren't high on the list for someone who oversees a compound of shipping containers for a living. "It's okay, I know where it is. I'll be in and out in a few minutes."

"Oh no you won't," he says. "Not without signing in."

Feeling uneasy about where this situation is leading, I feel for my knife, touch my fingers to its rough grip. "Then maybe you'd better find the logbook."

His grin slackens. "Or maybe you should find an arrangement we'd both be comfortable with."

My fingers wrap round the knife, ready to slip it out at a moment's notice.

The man lurches forward, arms outstretched, eyes wide with lust.

I side-step, let him go by me, then I wrap my arm round his throat, wrestling him from behind. Before he's even worked out what's happened, I'm holding the blade in position, behind his windpipe, ready to slice it open.

His stench, a mixture of semen and putrid body odour, almost overwhelms me.

"Remember where the logbook is now?" I say.

Voice croaking and body shaking, he says, "Now you mention it, I think I've got an idea."

———

I venture through the compound, my knife still in my hand, not trusting that there's no one else inside, no friend of Fatso ready to come at me to get some revenge. The shipping containers are identified by peeling stickers, each a unique number. I check my key, see the number 357 engraved there and check it along the containers.

354, 355, 356.

I stop outside my container and wait. I look from side to side, checking that no one's around. The whole point of leaving things out here is security, but anonymity is a close secondary concern. I stick the key into the hefty lock and turn.

I remove the lock, clasp it in my hand, and heave open the large steel door. It takes all my effort just to peel it back a few inches, but I've got no intention of going back to reception to ask for help. I got everything in on my own last time so there's no reason it should be a problem now. Then again, maybe my physical condition has slipped a little, since I first came here just after I'd left the Army.

I give the door a final, hard tug and it screeches open. I locate a chair with three legs and use it to prop open the door, before fumbling my hand up the wall of the container to locate the light switch. I flick it on and the whole contents of the container lays bare before my eyes.

Chapter Forty-Four

MY HEART RAPS IN MY CHEST at what seems like a thousand beats per minute. I take in the small crate, nestled toward the back of the container and then approach.

There's a crowbar I've left beside it, discarded on the floor. It's beaten up, hardly a lick of paint remaining on it. I stoop down, pick it up and work the lid of the crate loose.

Over my shoulder I'm aware of footsteps approaching, clattering their way along the iron walkway toward me. I can hear the low hum of male voices.

A tingle runs through my veins and I know I have to act quickly, get this crate opened and then get the hell out of the compound. Next time I'll pick a better place to stash my secrets.

With a final effort I crack the lid of the box and I'm staring down into straw, which covers the inside. I shove my hands inside and feel the metal against my fingertips.

The voices get louder still, only a matter of steps away from the entrance of the container.

I heave the semi-automatic rifle out and hold it in my hands. I've only got a desperate few seconds to inspect, lock and load it, to stuff the ammunition in my pockets. Luckily I'm still in good practice, ever since we had to perform the drill on demand at any time, day or night, during Basic Training. With the gun prepped, I stare through the sight at the entrance to the container.

My brain feels like a soppy sponge expanding and contracting. I know I have to be wary of my surroundings, a misplaced shot could come right back at me, finish me off just as well as my opponents.

I still my breathing, steady my grip and wait.

The first to pop his head round the container is old Fatso himself. He turns his attention to me and flinches, seeing the gun.

"Get out," I say.

He raises his hands.

I can hear muffled voices behind him.

Fatso turns round to his friends and that's when I squeeze the trigger.

The warning shot cracks through the stilted air of the container and the bullet zips out through the opening, clearing Fatso's head.

He stands in shock for a moment before stumbling back, falling into the platform railing.

I stand still, waiting for another target to enter my sights. A few moments later, realising that they're hanging back, I stalk my way along the side of the container, drawing closer to the entrance.

They're still mumbling something between them.

I can't get myself into a situation where they can shut that container door, leave me here to die. I have to be proactive, get myself into a position where I've got the advantage. So I keep moving, getting closer and closer.

And then, with a bounce and a clatter an object lands in the container. It rests before me, just giving me time enough to establish what it is—a smoke grenade.

Smoke sprays from within, squirting itself inside the container, stealing my vision away completely.

I dash through the smoke, still making for the bright daylight which penetrates the entrance, just as I hear the sound of the chair being kicked away, the groans of the men attempting to shut the door, I dive out through the gap, still clutching the semi-automatic to my chest.

Outside, I land on my side and quickly roll onto my back so that I'm pointing the gun upward, toward the men.

They stare down on me, mouths agape and eyeballs round. There are three of them, beside Fatso, and they all look like they could be brothers—the same shaven heads, beer guts and gormless expressions. They probably all stink of semen and body odour too, but I've got no intention of getting closer to them.

Still keeping my gun on them, I get to my feet, then I manage a grin. "Bit more than you were expecting, eh?"

None of them speak, eyes locked on the rifle.

As I back away from them, using the railing to guide me down the stairs, I consider that they'll now probably spend the rest of the day searching all the containers they've got keys on, trying to dig up another gun. Maybe there are others here, other people like me taking advantage of this out-of-town compound to keep their secrets. Nonetheless, even if one of these berks manages to get their hands on a serious weapon I doubt they'll have the brain power to work out how to use it—not without destroying themselves or one of their kind in the process.

When I get back down to the dusty ground, I break into a run, sticking my arm through the semi-automatic's strap and hauling it over my shoulder. As I reach the portable building which stands at the entrance to the compound I slow, telling myself that I can't possibly hop onto a bus bearing a gun.

I glance back, unable to see the men, but certain that they're still standing at my empty container, trying to figure out what just happened. I slip into the portable building, catching sight of the pornography playing out on the TV screen before spotting a sports bag beneath a desk littered with several screwed up tissues.

I whip the sports bag out, ditch its contents, which seems to be a change of clothes for Fatso, a pair of shorts and a stained, plaid t-shirt with several holes. The bag stinks of mud and sweat, but I shove the rifle inside all the same, it'll be better than nothing.

With the bag zipped up I step out of the portable building and jog on down the road to catch the bus back home, to prepare for my bodyguard duties tonight.

Chapter Forty-Five

I ARRIVE AT SNARKLY'S PENTHOUSE at around six o'clock in the evening. Although I haven't really considered how things are going to be between us, since he's realised that I'm working for Brian, I find that I get a mini shudder passing up my spine as I step through reception.

The porter greets me with a smile.

It's the same guy who I locked in the maintenance cupboard when I came to kill David. But, of course, he doesn't recognise me because I was wearing the balaclava. I shunt through into the lift and then watch the skyline unfold out the window for what's perhaps going to be the last time.

Outside the penthouse door, I hesitate and then ring the bell.

There's the shuffle of feet inside and then a waiter opens the door—the same on who served me and Snarkly dinner. He gives me a knowing smile and then motions for me to come inside. "Take your bag, madam?"

I grip the strap of the sports bag tighter. "No, it's okay. I'll hang onto it."

The waiter looks disapprovingly at the flecks of mud on the bag, but retreats. "As you wish."

I step into the sitting room and see that Snarkly's bedroom door is sealed shut. I hear the shower going in the background, the splash of water.

"Can I get you a drink while you wait?" the waiter says.

"Just a glass of water."

The waiter nods then slinks out the room.

I make myself comfortable on the sofa, with the sports bag at my feet. I think about taking the semi-automatic out, checking it over, but decide against it—not wanting to frighten Snarkly when he emerges from the bedroom.

As I wait I get to my feet and look out the window. On the street below I can see a pair of policemen, chatting amongst themselves. I know it's standard policy to have them placed on a politician in the hours before an election. When I look over the street I make out three black cars, with tinted windows, and know that that's the real protection for Snarkly—paid out of his own pocket. I wonder whether they know what happened to his last bodyguard.

When the waiter brings my water, he also switches on the TV and hands me the remote. Everything is swept up in the news from the election. Giddy presenters and panellists spitting a thousand words a minute, covering every angle—not leaving anything uncovered. I can't stop myself smirking when they move to a segment on Snarkly's quiet, untarnished private life, and how that might be the main factor in his selection as Prime Minister.

A few minutes later, the man himself emerges from his bedroom, dressed in a velvet dressing gown.

I get to my feet, then instantly scold myself for doing so, it's not like I'm in the presence of royalty or anything. I study his face for his reaction, interested in knowing how he's going to take me being his bodyguard for the evening.

Snarkly lets loose a chuckle in his throat then shakes his head. "You can't imagine my surprise when Brian let me in on the full story, that you've been working for him all along, keeping me safe all this time."

Quickly I snap my mind into focus, get caught up with Brian's latest lies.

Snarkly continues, "Can't say my manly pride hasn't taken something of a kicking to know that I've been protected by a woman all along."

I grit my teeth and tell myself that, after tonight, I'll never have to see him again—other than on news reports, presuming he does get the Prime Minister's job.

"But I must thank you." He flaps his hands at himself. "Still in one piece, aren't I? That's testament to your skills."

I can't help my eyes wandering downward, to the semi-automatic nestled in the sports bag. I know that I'll get a touch more respect if I bring that out, start waving it around. Not yet, though, better not to use all my best moves at once.

He gives me a wincing smile. "So, us, it was just an act, to keep me close? To keep me safe?"

I consider my options here. This is my way out and I'll be damned if I'm going to pass it up. "Yes, that's right. We had to keep things quiet."

"I understand." And that's it, because, still smiling, he wanders over to the window, looks out down on the street then says, "Got me all wrapped up in cotton wool, stashed up in my ivory tower."

"Can never be too careful."

"I suppose not."

I can't believe that Snarkly really believes his own hype. I think back to Brian and wonder whether this isn't his idea of a joke. Just a ruse to make things awkward for me, some slapstick punishment for not having told me about the relationship between myself and Brian. If there really was a threat to Snarkly's life I'm sure he's got a phonebook full of bodyguards, security services, specialists to call—he just wants me to suffer a little, let me know who's boss.

Snarkly points out the window, up into the sky, with a whimsical expression. "Helicopter, too."

I observe the helicopter. This really is overkill. Would the world really change for the worse were Snarkly to die tonight? I suppose not, but he's got the money to pay for all this and so he gets it.

"All right, Anna," he says, holding out his hand for me to shake.

I take his hand in mine, and he holds the shake for longer than necessary. In the end, I have to pry my fingers out of his grip.

"I'm going to go take a nap, call to check in on the wife, that sort of thing. Please make yourself at home here, feel free to order a film on the television, ask Henry if you'd like something from the kitchen."

I just nod in reply, making eye contact briefly.

He gives a dramatic yawn and stretches his arms to the ceiling. "Well, it's been fun, Anna, I've enjoyed myself even if it's just been work for you." He steps over to the threshold of his bedroom. He blows me a kiss before disappearing inside, shutting the door behind him.

I sit back down on the sofa and thank my lucky stars that I can spend the rest of the evening alone, not trying to fend him off at every opportunity. Now I've got an excuse, a job to do.

———

The waiter, Henry, brings me a cold salmon sandwich around ten o'clock in the evening. He leaves it on the table where it remains, uneaten. After getting bored of the continuous speculation poured out on national television, surrounding the election tomorrow I do opt to go with a film, which I order through a service bearing the logo of the building. I just go for the first option on the list and hit play.

As the film washes over me, I take note of the helicopter above, still buzzing round. I wonder whether anyone in the area is wont to complain. Surely the property prices here promise exclusivity and peacefulness. I don't imagine its residents take too kindly to invasions of this kind.

The blades continue to beat against the air and I get up from the sofa and venture over to the window, where I look out. The helicopter is right overhead now, hovering right above the building. As I look up through the half light of the streetlights I'm sure that I can make out a cable snaking down from the helicopter, coming down toward the building.

I open the window to get a better look. The cold night air blows against my cheeks, sending a shudder through me. And then, on the rooftop above, I hear the unmistakable *thud* of boots. Someone has just landed there.

I glance down below, looking for a reaction from the police standing about on the street, but they're just chatting between themselves, hands stuffed into pockets. Equally, there's no move-ment from any of the parked black cars.

And so, I guess it's up to me to investigate.

I stoop back inside the penthouse, unzip my bag and slip the semi-automatic out. I reload, knock off the safety and then sling it over my shoulder as I step out onto the window ledge.

Chapter Forty-Six

THE WIND BLOWS MUCH STRONGER than I anticipated as I hold myself up against the windowpane, desperately searching for somewhere to find my grip. In the end I settle for a drainpipe which sticks out from the wall and cling on. I gaze upward.

The helicopter has moved away now. I can barely hear its blades. I'm certain that it's performed the task that was asked of it, to carry whoever's up there on the roof, clearly come here to murder Snarkly.

I have to move slow, use the element of surprise to my advantage. The assassin anticipates resistance, that Snarkly will be guarded, but as far as they're concerned, they will believe they've passed the defence, left them down below at street level.

I shuffle my hands along the drainpipe. There's a ladder just on the other side which reaches all the way down to the street— an emergency escape route which leads up to the roof. Since it's not designed to reach the window of the penthouse, there's no way of getting across to it without jumping from where I am.

I check on the semi-automatic, make sure that it's secure on my shoulder and then I bound across, swinging myself round using the drainpipe.

I catch the rung with my boot and, after a stomach-churning glance down at the distance below me, a heady fall, I find my balance, wrapping my fingers tight and bringing myself in, closer to the building. With my eyes turned upward, I climb to the roof.

I lurk on the ladder, still hidden below the lip of the roof for a moment or two, just to get my breath back, and then I launch myself upward, and land, knees bent, on the rooftop.

It's pitch black up here. None of the glow of the streetlights below gets up here. The best I can do is wait for my eyes to adjust to the gloom and hope that the assassin isn't watching me, waiting for me to get up here. My question's answered when a bullet streaks past me, catching the tip of my ear.

Pain shrieks through my skull and, on instinct, I drop to my belly, the semi-automatic clattering beside me, but not slipping off my shoulder. I bring my hand to my ear and feel warm blood welling up there. I wipe my hand on my jumper and then crawl forward, already trying to ward off the shock clawing at my system, screaming out for me to run.

I find cover, behind what appears to be a ventilation duct, maybe even leading down to Snarkly's shower. I keep low, composing myself, preparing the semi-automatic. Despite my panic my eyes have got used to the dark and I can now make out motion, large shapes.

When I sneak a peek over the ventilation duct, I can see the form of the assassin. They're crouched on a raised platform, looking down, trying to work out my location.

I bob back down and bring my fingers up to the nick in my ear. It's a small graze really, not that the blood knows any different, still streaming out, pooling into my ear. The assassin is packing a handgun, nothing more substantial than that. They're equipped to sneak in, kill Snarkly then beat a hasty retreat. Again, I've got another advantage.

A bullet clanks against the ventilation duct.

I flinch at the sound, then swing the semi-automatic round in my hands, psyching myself up. I know where the assassin is. It's just a case of breaking my cover and firing at the spot. One of the bullets will catch him, knock him down at least.

Another two bullets fly above my head.

The way he's going I hope, for his sake, he's brought a spare cartridge. He won't have anything left at this rate.

I listen to the air swishing through my nostrils before heaving it out through my mouth. Now's as good a time as any, before he decides to change his position, thinks that I might be injured and that he can get closer to finish me off.

I grip the semi-automatic and rush round the corner of the ventilation duct. Another few bullets shoot past me but I keep my eyes fixed on my target, the shadowy figure just ahead. I move into a crouch, fix him in my sights and squeeze the trigger.

The kickback keeps me fixed to the rooftop, my kneecaps glued down. I rattle off as many shots as I can, my ears stinging with the hammering gunfire. When I let go, I become aware of the excited voices down in the street, the police, Snarkly's bodyguards and some pissed-off neighbours.

I look off into the dark, trying to get a lock on my target. I can see them, lying flat. Dead, I'm pretty sure. Not taking any chances, I keep the rifle held up in my grip ready to deal another shot if it's needed.

To get up to the raised platform, I have to round a steep slope. I wonder what on Earth it was designed for, since I could never imagine a wheelchair getting up this—unless they're an athlete. When I reach the top I see my target up ahead, the handgun resting several feet away. The target lies on their back, groaning. Their eyes flicker onto mine.

My heart near enough leaps out of my chest. I drop the semi-automatic on the ground behind me and rush over. I kneel down. "AA, what're you doing here?"

Face contorted and lips soaked in blood, AA splutters a reply, but I can't understand him.

I cushion his head with my hands. "It's okay, it's okay," I say, between sobs. "We'll get someone to help you. They're coming now. I can hear them."

There's another helicopter in the distance. I know that it's not the same which brought AA here. As it drones closer I make out its shape, buzzing through the gloom. It moves closer to us, seemingly faster and faster, before it sets down on the heliport.

The pair of policemen who were down in the street, pop up over the ladder. They rush toward us, their handguns drawn. Behind them I see four or five suited men—Snarkly's bodyguards—follow them up.

I turn my attention back to AA.

His eyes loll back in their sockets. He takes a shuddering breath, blood bubbling in his throat. "I . . . I'm . . ."

"Don't speak," I say. "Just be quiet, for once!"

I watch as the police skirt their way round my semi-automatic, then glance at the handgun before arriving at our side.

One of them says, "Got anything on him?"

"No," I say. "That gun was all he had."

"All right," he says, then gestures to the paramedics waiting in the wings.

The paramedics nudge me out the way and I stand back, allow them to get on with their jobs, saving human life. I watch on from behind them, feeling useless, knowing that it's up to them to fix all the damage that I've inflicted.

As they stick tubes into him, transfer him onto a trolley, I consider how I could've done this to a friend, how I had that capability in me all along. I know that it was dark that, really, I had no way of knowing who the assassin was. I had my orders to protect Snarkly and that's what I did.

They spring the trolley up and guide it across the roof to the helicopter. Another man aides them to haul it onto the flat compartment and, before I know it, the helicopter's taking to the skies and flies out of view.

The same policeman approaches me. "Who's in possession of these firearms?"

Through the tears streaming down my face, I manage to reach inside my jacket, where I find a business card. I hand it over to him.

"Mathewson Media," he reads.

Chapter Forty-Seven

B RIAN CALLS ME into his office round noon. For the first
time in weeks, I don't feel afraid of going, knowing that—
on the whole—I've been a good girl, done everything he's asked
of me.

I've just been to the hospital, to see AA. He's doing fine. I
shot him five times, but, luckily, the bullets avoided any of his
vital organs. Nonetheless, they'll be keeping him in the hospital
for the next week or so just to check on him. I got a glimpse of an
attractive male nurse who I'm sure AA's trying to swindle into
giving him sponge baths.

Brian welcomes me into his office with a cheek-to-cheek
smile. He embraces me with a steady grip and leads me over to
his sofa. "Get you anything? Water, fizzy drink, champagne?" he
says, with a grin.

I straighten up on the sofa, getting my back rigid. "No,
nothing like that."

Out of nowhere, he reaches out and prods me in the ribcage,

just above my breasts. "You really are my most loyal trooper, staying by my side throughout all this, hardly a question raised." He smirks. "Not like that AA, going off gallivanting to the highest bidder."

"He claimed it was about morals."

"Morals, money, it's all the same to me—motivation—and no matter what's on offer you stay true to those who treat you well, am I wrong?"

Aware of my intentions, I give him a half-hearted, "No."

"Still," Brian says, with a sigh, "I hope the boy's learnt a lesson. Forgiveness is a great gift to give, or so they say, maybe I can still find a place for him here." He glances at me. "Seen the news this morning?"

"Did I miss anything major?"

Brian cocks his head to one side. "You're telling me that after saving Simon Snarkly's life last night you haven't even checked to see if he's elected?"

"Nope."

He plucks a tablet from the table, wakes it and skims his way to a news front page. "My girl, really, you should take an interest in these things."

The page loads and Simon Snarkly's smiling face lights up the leading news story under the red, blinking, breaking news banner: New Prime Minister Elected.

Maybe it should affect me, but it really doesn't. I don't feel depressed about it—I know that I saved his life last night. There's just an overwhelming neutrality flooding over me, like I will never change anything even if I wanted to. That money from that Middle Eastern country will be split between Brian, Snarkly and Abdul-Hakam. Nothing to do.

"Want to have some fun?" Brian says.

I suppress a groan and ready myself to reel through the speech I rehearsed in my head on the way here, sitting on the Tube. "Listen, I think I've—"

But Brian's already got his mobile to his ear, holding up his finger for me to be quiet. When someone picks up on the other end, he says, "All right, Phil? Look, I've got a bit of a story for you if you'd be interested. It concerns our newly-elected Prime Minister." He listens for the response. "Okay, all set, then? I hate bloody repeating myself so make sure you get this down all in one go. Ready? Okay, then. Simon Snarkly had his ex-mistress slash business partner murdered in order to keep his profile clean." He pauses. "Sources? Are you joking? You know me, Phil, would I ever lie to you? Just print the story and the truth will out."

My whole body numbs. It feels like I'm watching Brian commit some kind of professional suicide—like watching a car crash in slow motion. I know I should step in, snap Brian out of whatever craziness he's sunk himself into, but I'm too absorbed in the words falling from his lips.

Brian continues, "You got all that down so far? Yeah? All right, here's another one. Simon Snarkly, in collaboration with a Middle Eastern contact, also had a close business partner murdered in order to keep an arrangement involving bringing money stolen from an unspecified Middle Eastern treasury quiet. The plan now, as it stands, with Snarkly being Prime Minister, is for him to help this aforementioned Middle Eastern contact— more on him in a second—oversee the transfer of said funds."

He pauses, listens to a rapid-fire reply which just falls below my earshot. "Phil, if you don't stop talking I'll call up your mate at the Daily—what's that? You're listening now? Great stuff. Now, this Middle Eastern contact, his name's Abdul-Hakam, that's right: A-B-D-U-L dash H-A-K-A-M. Yeah, you can run whatever you like on him after you get off the phone, get the background info. All right, so our friend Abdul-Hakam had his own son murdered at the fundraising benefit for Snarkly, a month or so ago, from today."

He stares up at the ceiling, rolls his eyes. "Got all that?" He scowls. "No I'm bloody not going to stand round here waiting for you to read it back to me, you're not working for the broadsheets now, boyo. I've just given you the proverbial scoop of the century, now go enjoy it." He hangs up the call, pockets his mobile and grins at me. "You think I've gone mad, don't you?"

That's exactly what I'm thinking, but what can I say? Brian's my boss.

"It's all about the money, I can tell you. It's all about money and manipulating opportunities. You met with Raymond Finch, didn't you?"

No point lying about it now since Brian seems about a hundred steps ahead of me, like always. "Yes. AA introduced me to him."

"That bloody AA, always poking his nose into everything."

"How do you know about Raymond Finch?"

"Oh, he's another client of mine."

"What?"

Brian's grin widens, clearly enjoying my complete and utter confusion. "That's right. He came to me a while back, been on my books for aeons, really. We've been plotting this together all along, trying to work out how we can get the most of it."

He twirls his hand. "Oh, Finchie's got his heart in the right place, all right, always going on about doing the right thing. When I told him that I was going to take on Simon Snarkly—who he's constantly going on about—he threw a bloody hissy fit, thought his head was going to explode. Anyway, once I got him calmed down, told him that this might work out well for the both of us, I let him in on the happenings with Abdul-Hakam, and his money he wants to 'invest' here. It all fell into place for both of us then. I would go along with Snarkly's plans, help him to keep his profile spotless in the lead up to this party leadership campaign, bleed him dry for all he's got, and then cut him off, leave him high and dry on the crest of his wave."

I knit my eyebrows. "But, then who sent AA after Snarkly last night, why did they come to kill him?"

"Ah," Brian says. "It's all about choosing the right moment to perform the coup de grâce. That job, I think AA was onto me, which you thoroughly-botched—I set you up for that. The idea was for things to get messy, be covered up, just so there'd be no doubt as to Snarkly's involvement in them. Once that news breaks, the investigation will be dug up and Snarkly will be swiftly brought to justice."

Blood rushes to my head. "But does that mean I'm going to be implicated in all this?"

"Oh no, my dear, of course not. I've tied all these ends up very neatly indeed, already got someone on the inside who'll take the time for you—guy who doesn't even *want* to come out of prison."

"That's kind of him, you'll have to remind me to send him some chocolates."

"Anyway," Brian says, holding up his hand, "you're making my head spin, sit down or something, will you?"

I do take a seat. To be honest, my head is spinning too.

Brian continues, "So last night, me and Finchie, we reached our endgame. While I wanted to kill Snarkly with publicity, Finchie wanted to kill him with bullets. Enter our knight in shining armour, AA, who Finchie's paid on the side, without my knowledge, and you take him out like I knew you would."

"But you did think it would happen, why else would you put me there to protect Snarkly?"

"I think you've just answered your own question there. Everyone has a personality, if I were a betting man I would've backed AA to do the 'moral' thing, to take care of Snarkly. Unfortunately what he should've done was trust my judgement. He chose to forget that I come from the working classes too, I had no intention of those people losing their money, no matter how far away they are—whatever I may say to cover for it. I took Snarkly's money as long as I possibly could then stabbed him in the back before he did anything *really wrong*."

"You mean aside from having people killed?"

"Collateral damage. As for the Middle Eastern fellow, I'm sure he'll be extradited to face some home-grown justice before you can say 'bingo.'"

"So, you've been earning twice over, the whole time?"

He beams at me. "Told you I was brilliant, didn't I?"

"You've been taking Raymond Finch's money and Snarkly's?"

"Don't forget about Abdul-Hakam's. Since he wanted me to keep his presence in the country out of the public eye. Nothing like a triple payoff, is there?"

"I wouldn't know."

He steps toward me. "Don't act so glum, anyone would think that you're sore about the whole thing."

"Actually, I've been thinking. I don't think I'm cut out for this anymore. It's . . . I don't know . . . I don't feel good about what I do."

Brian gives me a long, piercing stare, then says, "I'll pay you a holiday to anywhere you want to go, just get in touch with my secretary and it'll all be taken care of. Don't come back until you feel prepared. If you do come back and decide you're out of it then fine, I won't hold you to anything."

I'm welling up inside, caught off guard by all this. "Thanks," I say.

Brian's mobile buzzes on the table. He glances down. "Just go and have a holiday, get your mind together. God knows I at least owe you that, the amount of blood you've shed on my behalf." His mobile rings itself out and he meets my gaze. "Killing's a tough business, breaks you apart inside."

The way he watches me, looking right through me, I've got the inkling that he might have personal experience to back up that statement. I'm beginning to see Brian in a different light altogether.

Brian's mobile buzzes again and he looks down at it, sighs, then says, "My goodness, to think that Snarkly's actually calling me." He shakes his head, wearing a wry smile. "Good press won't save him now."

The End

Author's Note

Thank you for taking the time to read one of my books. If you would like to hear about my latest releases you can sign up for my newsletter here: www.aviain.com

Thanks for reading!

AV Iain

Good Press
The First Anna Harris Novel

Copyright © AV Iain, 2015.
Published by DIB Books
All rights reserved.

Cover design and layout copyright © DIB Books, 2015.
Interior design copyright © DIB Books, 2015.
Cover art copyright © Bruce Rolff / Shutterstock, 2014.

This work is fictional. None of the characters or events depicted in this book are based on real life and any resemblance to real events or persons is purely coincidental.
Neither this book, nor any part of it, may be reproduced without express permission from the publisher.

All rights reserved.

www.ingramcontent.com/pod-product-compliance
Lightning Source LLC
Chambersburg PA
CBHW021004260626
47169CB00006B/1928